THE DOLLHOUSE ASYLUM

MARY GRAY

SPENCER
HILL
PRESS

Spencer Hill Press

Contact:
Spencer Hill Press, PO Box 247, Contoocook, NH 03229, USA

Please visit our website at www.spencerhillpress.com

First Edition: October 2013.

Mary Gray
The Dollhouse Asylum : a novel / by Mary Gray – 1st ed.
p. cm.

Summary:
A group of teenagers are granted asylum from the apocalypse—and then assigned new identities as famous, tragic literary couples and forced to reenact their stories or die.

The author acknowledges the copyrighted or trademarked status and trademark owners of the following wordmarks mentioned in this fiction: 7-Eleven, Ajax, BMW, Disney, Doc Martens, Doublemint Gum, Dr. Seuss, Hasbro, Infiniti, Kleenex, Listerine, Mattel, Photoshop, Sea World, Six Flags, Skittles, Slurpees, Star Trek, Target, Tinkerbell, University of Texas

Cover design by Jeremy West

Interior layout by Marie Romero

ISBN 978-1-937053-64-2 (paperback)
ISBN 978-1-937053-65-9 (e-book)

Printed in the United States of America

For Adam. You are the light I am not.

1

Gruff fingers yank a blindfold off my face, light splashes into my eyes, and I blink. Gray walls swim about my head, and the ceiling soars much too high above me. I don't know this place. I was walking to my bathroom when someone grabbed me from behind and forced a sour-smelling cloth over my face and—someone grapples with my hair, and I flinch. Who—who is touching me?

I try turning in the flimsy chair, but someone's grabbing my shoulders, forcing me not to move. Spasms of fear shoot up and down my arms and legs. I try swinging my fists to make them loosen their grip, but my captor's fingers only tighten.

Raising my arm to jab my captor in the gut, I pause. Someone's laughing. How do I know that sound? It's beautiful and low, a laugh I could recognize anywhere. Glancing around the sun-filled room, I find the source almost immediately. It's Teo, *my* Teo, standing across from me on the hardwood floor, beaming at me. His ebony eyes shine forth like two onyx stones, and even his olive-toned skin makes me breathe a bit shallower. Choking back a strangled laugh—*no one's here to hurt me*—I reach out for the love of my life, too tongue-tied to say anything.

His lips spread into a thin smile, reminding me of his mouth melting into my own. Fire raged beneath my skin with that kiss and it felt like I was lifted up into the air and floating. Six days ago we had our first kiss and we still haven't been able to talk about it. I tried repeatedly to go into his classroom, but it was like our school had purposely decided to schedule a more-than-average number of parent-teacher meetings.

Locking his eyes on mine, Teo asks, "Manicure?"

I glance down at my fingernails, trying to see why he would think I needed a manicure, when my shoulders are released and pale, icy fingers grip my hand. Chills run through me.

A flat, tenor voice says, "Yes." And I'm startled to see my fingernails are actually painted. Clear and shiny.

The fingers drop my hand, and my captor walks around to face me. White uniform, white skin, white hair. He's albino. Who is he?

"Makeup is good." Teo taps lightly on a handheld computer screen. "Hair is so-so." He continues to scan the device, and I don't like how he's picking me apart like he's Photoshopping me. Where are the other students? Or maybe it's more than I could ever hope: it's really just the two—three—of us, and he is finally unveiling his feelings. I never expected to fall in love with a teacher, but when I started at Khabela, the Austin math and science school, Teo was the only one who welcomed me. It took me a moment to understand why a math teacher would care that I read *Tristan and Isolde,* but soon we were knee-deep in conversation about *all* our favorite classic stories.

I wish he'd tell me why he brought me here. Maybe he let my mom know, explained what we were actually doing.

"Teo—?"

But I fail for words, the gray walls seeming to snatch at the fear inside me. My palms break out in a sweat and it's calculus all over again, where Teo asked me to stand in front of my class to share the index card I had made to memorize last year's trig functions. While I hate speaking in front of groups, I did it anyway, my heart slamming against the insides of my chest the entire time. When I'd finished, Teo congratulated me, making the fear worth it.

Tapping his computer screen, Teo trains his gaze on me again, softening a little. "I cannot tell you how much seeing you here pleases me."

My heart flip-flops and it's hard to say anything. *He's happy to see me.* It's all I can do to keep myself from smiling stupidly.

He takes one step toward me and I long to fill the gap. And when he speaks, his voice rings out in a baritone melody. "I hope you enjoy our little neighborhood, Miss Laurent. The women are on one side of the street, the men on the other. They each have their own houses. Seven again." His lips perk up into one of those smiles that I love, and I'm reminded of his reverence for the number seven, how he arranges our desks in three rows of seven.

Glancing at the wooden door ahead, I open my mouth to ask if he'll show me this street when he says, "That is right. You should desire to go through that door. Of course, the choice is yours." He gestures behind me. "The back door is always an option."

I turn to find the back door, only to see plastic shadows, slick and dark—body bags—hanging on a rod by the door. Another one of Teo's jokes, maybe. A metaphorical exercise. *Life without love is not living. See, Miss Laurent, you might as well be dead.* But Teo would never hurt me. When we kissed, he held me like a porcelain doll, treasured me.

"Front door, then?" Teo asks when I manage to turn back to him, his tone light, almost happy. He wants to show me this neighborhood that revolves around the number seven. I'm not sure what to make of it, but I want him to show me.

Teo and the albino grab me by the arms and force me up, but there's no reason to be touchy-feely. Wherever he goes is where I want to be. Teo is brilliant and kind. He would never shatter me.

*   *   *

Teo and the albino march me down a street lined with massive, square houses: seven on one side, seven on the other. No cars, no people, nothing. The way the sun sears my skin and the silence screams into my ears, I can understand why people don't come out—it's too hot, too stifling. Or maybe this is a newly built subdivision. No one has moved in at all. No, Teo said there were seven men and seven women, so maybe this is some sort of resort for relationships. I'm not really clear on how the men and women got here, because the street doesn't connect to any roads: the house where I woke up marks one end of the street and a field of weeds stops the other, just ahead. What is this place?

Shielding my eyes from the sun shooting straight at me, I look up to the brick homes, all two stories, and the reds, browns, and grays of the bricks are washed out, like the color's been erased. The windows gleam in the sunlight like they've never experienced any rain, and—something crunches under my shoe. I look down to find dead weeds; I'm planted in the center of a giant, crushed thistle.

"Good." Teo stops next to me in the field of weeds past the final house. He scans the periphery of his development, and I do the same, realizing taller trees hover over the subdivision, closing us in. I try listening for the sounds of Austin, the cars or people, but the only noise is my own tennis shoes shifting and crunching the weeds.

"I cannot tell you how pleased I am that you have joined us here," Teo says again. He gave me little choice when he kidnapped me.

"Your duty is simple," Teo says, taking a step toward me, and I long to hear what he has planned. "You must choose the right house." *Right* house? "But remember, Miss Laurent—try to leave and we carry you out the back door." He nods in dismissal like we've just met, and my fingers tense, desperate for him to take them in his own hand. We are supposed to be together. Why is he acting like this?

Teo turns away to leave, the albino follows, and together they stroll away from me down the street. But where are they going?

"Teo?" I call after him, needing more of an explanation. Maybe he's waiting for me to actually verbalize something. He is always urging me to speak up more in class. So I try a question. "Teo, what is this place?"

Slowing, Teo eventually turns to face me, but what he offers is a look I recognize, one he has taunted me with regularly in class. His brow wrinkles and his jaw locks: *You know I am smarter than you, Cheyenne. Won't you at least* try *to figure this out?*

Smoothing his brow again, he says before abandoning me, "Welcome to Elysian Fields."

Light flickers from the window closest to me on the right side of the street. I look to find a man peering at me through the blinds. At least, I think it's a man. He has short hair and that's all I see before he closes his blinds. Why is he hiding from me?

I glance at the women's side, but their windows are empty, and their complete absence frightens me more— even the girls at school avoided me because I preferred my classics to their activities.

Spinning, I face the man in the window again, but my foot catches on something—a metal survey stake. Bending down, I examine the metal rod, unable to help wondering if Teo's hands once touched it, too.

I don't understand why Teo would kiss me, only to leave me out here like this. He's always been cryptic—maybe this is one of his games. Like in calculus, when we couldn't find him in the room. Most classes would mess around if the teacher wasn't in class, but we dutifully pulled out our math books and copied down our work, because that's what Teo would expect. Unbeknownst to us, he'd been hiding in the closet the entire time. Five minutes after the bell rang, he popped out. "I am pleased with you," he had said, and promised a reward, a lesson involving an "unparalleled" math.

I brush the clods of dirt clinging to the stake as the wind caresses my face; I wish Teo were here to do the same. I'm supposed to know which house to go inside, yet there are fourteen of them—plus his. It could be any of them.

Walking toward the house closest to me on the men's side, I grasp the stake in case I need it. Maybe I can pry a door open if that man doesn't let me in. Teo expects me to do this without explaining exactly what he wants me to do, like he often did in class. But that's what I love about him. He challenges our brains, always pushes us to think.

The blinds are still turned so I can't see into the gray brick house. I hope I can glimpse a face, a movement, even a twitch of the blinds again, but it's impossible to see through them. I feel like I'm on stage—the theater lights shooting straight in my face. It makes me want to do something dramatic, like flash the men. I would actually never do it, but the idea keeps teasing my mind. And when my fingers start to get twitchy like they might do it anyway, I move further down the street.

On the men's doors hang rectangular, palm-sized signs with black, thin letters spelling things I'm too far away to read. Maybe I should read the signs in case Teo quizzes me later. It couldn't hurt.

Striding back to the first house, I squint to read the label on the first door. Cramped handwriting spells a name I don't know: *Ramus.* I pause and wait, the crisp scent of grass clippings rushing over me as I stand inches from his yard. But Ramus doesn't come out. I could knock, but something tells me I should read all the signs first, like a clue that I shouldn't ignore.

The second house has the light gray coloring of the first, but this sign's boxy writing spells another name: *Abe.* I study the blinds on the front windows of his house when one twitches in the window by the front door.

A dark, dreadlocked head peeks back at me through the window, the whites of his eyes shining in shock. *Hello, Abe.* He's as surprised as I am, and his eyes dart downward, like he's ready to run.

I want to talk to him, ask him to let me inside. But just as I've taken a handful of steps toward his porch, Abe flips his blinds completely shut. *Man,* I feel like he's scared of me. I'm not intimidating. Or maybe Abe's house isn't the right one. I don't know. I mean, Teo might want me to try. I wish he'd given me more direction, like what to look for in the residents, or what other things might be helpful clues.

Unsure, I move to the next house to read the third name: *Tristan.* His awkward writing reminds me of my own, but he doesn't appear to be standing at his window, as far as I can see. His blinds aren't moving, and I'm not entirely sure what

I'm looking for—a flashing "you found it" neon sign? But no. I don't know anyone named Ramus, Abe, or Tristan. But I won't get any answers until I try talking to somebody, so I raise my hand and knock once, softly, then loudly two more times.

I wait a few minutes, but Tristan doesn't come to the door. All I can do is study the brick patio beneath my feet and stare at the traces of pink and green dye that smudge one side of the door.

Tristan doesn't seem to be coming out so, against my better judgment, I place my sweaty palm on the doorknob. The metal is scorching hot and doesn't turn. It's locked! Stupid door. So I slump past two more houses, trudging through this scorching heat. My skin's starting to burn and I really need a drink.

By the time I've made it to the middle of the street, I can almost feel Teo watching my every step, my every look. Naturally, his blinds are turned so I can't see in, but picturing him hovering behind a window makes me yearn to go straight for him, find the comfort he so often offered me. *Do not concern yourself with those ninnies,* he would say of the girls who snickered at my choice of books. *You may not have passed the test with flying colors, but you will get it. You shall see.* But today is not a day Teo holds his hands out for me. That's what he does when I'm on the brink of something. I'll show him I can do this, find the "right" house.

Turning to face the women's side of the street, I find that the houses look the same—nothing looks suspicious or obvious. The other houses remain still. All brick, all huge. Even their roofs are the same shade of gray-black. The towering houses make me feel so small, like they're swallowing me.

It takes me a minute to realize the women's homes don't have signs like the men's. They have mailboxes, which is weird. No mailman could come here with both ends of the street halting in grass. Maybe it's a clue. A clue! I race toward a mailbox with a flag pointed up, and am about to yank the door open, when a female voice yells, "Don't!"

Freezing maybe five inches from the mailbox, I glance around the street, trying to find the source of the not-so-helpful voice. What's so wrong with opening a mailbox? And why is she screaming? Or maybe Teo asked her to.

But someone called out to me. I scan the red brick house in front of me, two away from Teo's on the end of the street, when I find the source of the voice on the porch: a black-haired, caramel-skinned girl leering at me. A short, black dress hugs her body so tightly, it's like her curves are about to pop. Two curves in particular—it's obvious she's had those puppies enhanced. Her appearance is so pristine, I'm suddenly very aware of my ragged jeans, now sweat-soaked T-shirt, and messy, flax-colored ponytail. Man, I must look like crap.

"Hot date?" I ask, mostly because she so obviously flaunts everything. Black eyeliner extends past the diva's eyes and ornate beading weaves through her jet-black hair. "Funny," I say, crossing my arms, "I didn't know the Egyptian style was in."

"Move on." The girl's pouty lips jut outward as she leans in her doorway like she's working the corner or something. Maybe this is part of Teo's plan, to test my patience just to throw me off. But she was the one to talk to me, and I'm not about to let this opportunity slip through my fingers, so I throw out the first thing that comes to mind. "Can I have some water?" Because my throat hurts.

But the diva swats at me like I'm a gnat. "Go!" she yells, which is more than a little frustrating. I open my mouth to tell her she looks like a streetwalker in that dress, when a voice cuts me off.

"Let her in, Cleo."

It's coming from right across the street. I move to see who it is but change my mind. I don't want to lose my footing with "Cleo." Still, I turn around to take a peek at this boy's house, but I'm not surprised to see that he isn't showing his face; he's only shouting through his cracked-open front door.

"You let her in," Cleo yells before slamming her door shut.

Breathless, I don't miss a beat. This boy wanted her to let me in. I can work with someone who will help me out. I sprint for his house, knowing he'll help me next. Even the boy's voice sounds nice.

"Hey!" My feet hit the pavement, my ponytail slapping me in the face, but the door starts to close. "Wait. Please. I need a drink."

As I scramble up his porch steps he slams the door closed—*crap*—but maybe I can talk him into helping me. "Hello?" My voice sounds both loud and small in the silence of Teo's mansion-filled subdivision. Scanning his sign for a name, I spot it right away. "Marc?" He wouldn't have called out to Cleo if he didn't want to help me out.

But he doesn't answer me. At least, not outright. Maybe he's shy—just needs a little time. I can be patient, chat through the door, show him I'm a nice person before he lets me inside. But several more seconds pass before a muffled voice answers. "Why are you here? There are already seven."

"I know," I say, pressing my fingertips to the wood-grained door. "Teo—" I wipe the sweat dripping into my eyes, "—gave me a job."

Several awkward seconds languish past and I'm left wondering if I will ever get inside, get a drink. Which sucks. I need to focus on Teo's mission, stop wasting precious brain cells on the minor detail of my parched throat.

Marc sighs like I'm more of a nuisance than anything. "I can't believe this."

Wait. I know that voice. "Marcus?"

Several seconds pass before Teo's younger brother responds. "I go by Marc now, Cheyenne." But the way he says my name isn't right, not like that. He used to sing my name, "Chey-yi-yi-yenne," every time he saw me at the math meets. And before he sang my name, his blue eyes would swim in a barely controlled typhoon so that I could only smile at him before looking away. But now, he sounds beaten down, flat. And it's not hard to imagine that his eyes have also changed.

He said, *I go by Marc now, Cheyenne.* Which is odd, because once he threw a spitball at one of the judges for calling him just "Marc." *It's Marcus*, he had said, and I braced myself because the judge had to pause everything to pick the spitball out of his hair. One of my friends, Josie, had wondered why they let the artsy kids from Griffin compete with our school, and I halfway wondered the same thing. Not because I didn't like them—they just always came in last. And they never focused on the questions like Khabela. We were the math and science school; math meets were our thing.

But I can't believe Marc's here, too. I'm surprised Teo didn't mention that. While I can't wait to talk to Marc more, for some reason he doesn't seem excited to talk. Like Teo, Marcus has always been hard to read. But I need to know what's going on, and if I can keep him talking, maybe he can help me figure out which is the "right" house.

"So, what are you doing here?" I finally ask.

"You need to go." Marc's words are a slap. We always chatted at the math meets, and I swore those blue eyes watched my every move. His order only makes me want to dig in my heels and stay. I lean back against the side of the house, my cotton shirt sticking to the brick. Folding my arms, I plan to dig in, convince him to help me out, when he asks me the last thing I'm expecting:

"Are you vaccinated?"

Apart from my childhood vaccinations, everyone was vaccinated last year. "Are you vaccinated?" became the new "How are you?" Everyone asked it, like a fee for entry, but that was for the outbreak in Beijing two years ago, the Living Rot. The sickness was so horrific, so deadly, that everyone involved with the quarantine made sure it was buried as deeply as the core of the earth. Beijing would never happen again. The cannibalistic disease would *never* be repeated.

Despite my ingrained assurances, I have to ask, my lower lip trembling slightly, "What do you mean?"

The seconds that tick by languish longer than the time during finals week when all I could see was the live footage of the Chinese people turning on their friends. Their sagging skin and blood-dripping teeth. The citywide burning authorized by the United Nations. The military strike units forbidding anyone to enter Beijing.

Eventually, Marcus responds and he does little to answer my question, "You'd better talk to my brother, Cheyenne."

His reaction makes me want to lash out. *His brother* was the one who told me to find someone else to let me inside. So I try once more, desperately hoping Marcus will soften. "Please, Marc? Just a drink?"

Silence answers me. I hold my breath and will him to answer. But there's nothing coming from the other side. He's ignoring me. Waiting for me to move away. But then the floorboards squeak; he's coming closer. I've convinced him to open the door. Metal clicks against metal, and I'm watching the doorknob, preparing for it to turn, when it doesn't. That's because that metal clicking against metal was him turning the deadbolt—*locked.*

He's locking me out. Marcus is Teo's brother, my friend. Or he was. Sometimes he could be a colossal jerk. Especially compared to Teo, who must have gotten all the good genes in the family: manners, intellect, tact.

"Find a girl!" Marc barks, which proves I'm right. "Tell her you're clean." And then all Marc's movements from the other side fade away, and it's just the door and me.

I smack the door with my fist, very nearly scraping it with the stake in my hand. There's something seriously wrong with these people. I've been placed in the heat, in ninety-degree weather, and *no one is helping me*. I'm not a threat to anyone. I need to get inside.

"You need to *go*," Marcus growls, apparently back at the door. He doesn't have to growl at me. He was always so playful and eager to help. Like when I'd managed to tangle a wad of bracelets at a math meet. I'd been so done with them, about to rip them off, when Marcus had reached over and untangled them for me, smiling. I'd thought he was sweet.

Now I don't understand why he won't help me. But, wait a second. "What about the vaccine?"

"You don't—"

A sound I don't recognize comes from nearby. A whoosh, crisp and neat, catching the wind. But quicker. And close. Just beside me in Marcus's front lawn lies a foot-wide hole in the ground, which wasn't there before.

Curious, I step cautiously to peek inside the hole. Maybe Teo is sending me something. A note, or water, maybe. I'm two, three inches off when two eyes and a forked tongue slink out of the hole. A snake, and it's looking directly at me.

I freeze, too terrified to speak. Black and yellow coils glisten in the sun, and I wish I were the sort of person who could find some beauty in the thing. It's horrible. Death, scales, teeth. I've been terrified of snakes since I was a little girl. Ever since one of my mom's boyfriends thought it would be fun to taunt me with one, I've avoided the reptiles more than I avoided the stupid ninnies who laugh at the books I read.

As the snake slinks out, I see it's much larger than I originally thought. Four feet long or so. I can't have it lunge at me.

I repeat the mantra my mom taught me when I was small, in case I ever found one at the park, on a walk, or in the street: *Walk slowly and it will lie flat.* Walk slowly...walk slowly...but it doesn't look like it's going to lie flat. The beast is lifting its head. He's hissing at me, which is worse than nails on a chalkboard, like pterodactyls screeching. My mouth is open before I know what I'm doing, and the noise tearing through my throat causes it to lash out at me.

I'm screaming, flailing across the yard and down the street. Snakes don't need to be near me. Snakes can have their own feast. Just not me. Not me. I shake away the image of dozens crawling over me.

Marcus told me to find a girl, so I will. With things like that around, there's no way in hell I'm going back on his side of the street.

*   *   *

I'm back at the place I started, that small patch of grass where I plucked up that metal survey stake. Tossing the stake to the ground, I glance up at the sun where it sears me from the sky. It's directly over my head, so it must be noon, and my back, neck, chest—everything—drips with sweat from the heat.

I need shade. But those trees on the periphery of the subdivision look like they're the only place that offers it. Or the houses themselves. Or the porches. But I'm not going to linger on any porches any longer—I saw how well that turned out.

So far, this is what I've learned: I'm stuck in a hellhole filled with an unrelenting heat. Seven men stare at me from their houses, and Cleo is the only one of the women to come out. The men's homes bear signs, and the women's sport mailboxes. I'm not supposed to touch the mailboxes, and freakishly large snakes pop out for any girls who venture on the wrong side of the street. For the life of me, I can't see why Teo likes this place.

I need to study the other women's houses, like the one closest to me. It's similar in coloring to Cleo's: dressed in red brick, two stories, and towering. So maybe I'll knock and announce that I'm not leaving until they let me inside. I'll bring the stake again and threaten to use it if I must, because Teo is waiting on me. I need to prove that I can do this.

Teo knew I would take the complicated route, that I wouldn't try the closest home so I could learn what I needed from the outside. I always did that in class, too. *Solve this equation, Miss Laurent,* he would say, taunting me with the jerk of his upper lip. I would scramble for my notes, wrack my brain for the proper method, and then he'd remind me of a simple mnemonic. And instead of feeling like a fool, I'd be awed by his simple trick. So now, Teo knows I won't linger on the men's side of the street after seeing the snake lash out. I have always struggled with bravery, something Teo no doubt has seen.

But today, today I am hot. And thirsty, and sweaty, and cross. Perhaps Teo wants me to do something specific. This game where he plays master and I play puppet is precisely the type of thing Teo does to test us. *Let down your hair, girls,* he once said. *Not for aesthetics, but to relax your brains so you can better think.* We all dutifully listened to him. But this time I will not be his puppet. I'm already tired of this game.

He may have an issue with perfection—my little manicure is evidence of that. The new homes, the perfect lawns, even the trees are minutely placed. I'll never be perfect. I wish I was, but I'll never be able to change that. It's time to get inside, go in the home that makes the most sense: the home closest to me on the women's side of the street. And I'll take my weapon—this little survey stake—in case this woman is anything like Cleo and fights letting me in.

Avoiding the street completely, I cut across the yard. Scanning the precision of the red bricks lining the exterior of the home, I note the two dainty trees held up with pencil-thin ropes; with care, they'll grow to be something great. Maybe that's how Teo sees me: dainty, but having potential, like the trees. I do and do not like the thought. I love him precisely the way he is—no matter how quirky. What if he wants to change me?

Raising my empty fist to the door, I knock once, and the weight of my fist causes the door to creak wide open. It's open. It's open. My pulse quickens as I step through.

2

"Miss Laurent, you pass."

Teo, wearing a black suit, sits on a bench in a living room that doesn't have the interior décor I would have expected. Painted vines and dark arches on the walls give me the impression of Rome or Greece, and a crack painted in the center connotes conflict—something I'm surprised Teo would choose. From what I saw of the first home, the décor made much more sense, with its simple colors and furniture highlighting the aesthetics of the room. Like the wrought-iron staircase I see before me that sweeps over a good portion of the room and dominates everything around it. If I didn't know better, I'd want to slide down the rail. But Teo would find that foolish. And he is right. I'm not a child. I'm a grown woman—the way he kissed me proved that. He wants to be with me; that's why he brought me here. Not quite the reception I would have preferred, but he's here, smiling at me.

Moving to his feet, Teo reaches his hands out for me. "Welcome to Bee's home. You shall meet her shortly."

I have to force myself not to reach out for him. Just because my daydreams consist of embraces and kisses doesn't mean Teo is ready for that affection now, so I keep my arms where they are, force them to remain unmoving by my sides.

"You did well," Teo says, smiling his moonbeam smile. It was the one he reserved for me after the math meets, when I won. Come to think of it, Marcus seemed to notice that smile once. It was several months ago, and I looked at Marcus, surprised he noticed our bond. Nobody else saw it, but for some reason Marcus did, awkwardly ducking his head and scratching the back of his shaggy, dark hair. Maybe because he knew his brother could decipher his facial expressions the way no one else could. I hope Marcus is wrong, that there are no repercussions from Beijing.

"You know now why you needed to enter *this* home," Teo says, smiling at me.

I nod, because it's all become so simple now. "I always take the complicated route."

His eyes light up, the ebony more beautiful in this noonday light. "You do! But that is why you have these tasks. It was your first one—" There are going to be more? "—and I am pleased you accomplished it so fast. I know you." Teo waggles his finger at me. "You have a way of mulling over everything many more times than once."

I swallow, my throat parched from the heat, and spot two filled wine goblets resting on an small table next to the bench. Teo thinks of everything. He plucks the goblets up and holds one out for me.

"And what do you think of the décor?" Teo asks as I take the goblet from him and sit next to him on the bench. I take a sip. It's only water, but water is all I need. Rest and air conditioning and water. And Teo beside me.

I glance at the large cracks in the center of each wall, not sure what to make of them. "It's very…unique."

Teo pauses. My response was clearly not what he had hoped. Teo likes his ego stroked, never questioned. One of my classmates once suggested he grow his hair out, and he'd spitefully shaved his head every day for a week. He even smiled a little when she failed a test, which always kind of bothered me. He didn't have to punish her for liking longer hair.

Heart hammering, I shift on the bench, trying to find something positive to say about the odd décor of the room. But instead of scowling, Teo unleashes my favorite laugh, the loudest one—not boisterous or obnoxious—but the one I expect the gods in mythology sounded like.

"You have questions for me," Teo says, eyes twinkling, and a thrill runs through me to see him so calm. "I would love to answer them if I can."

I take a sip of water as my mind swims. I need him to tell me what this place is exactly and why there's a need for a vaccine. Surely, Teo's happier now that I've passed my test.

Glancing at his hand resting lightly on his lap, I yearn to take it in my own. If I could express to him all that's going on inside my heart and my head, he could see how much I want to be with him. Please him. Because he's the person I think about all day long, even when I sleep.

Teo reaches over and gently grabs my chin. "Perhaps the first question is, 'What is next?'"

I hesitate. That is not the question at the forefront of my mind, but disagreeing with Teo would make him unhappy "You are right." But my nose twitches, snags on the smell of tangerine—an air freshener, I think. I scrunch my nose to push the zingy scent out, because I'm *this* close to a sneeze.

Teo perks an eyebrow.

"The smell," I explain, laughing. "It's *really* sweet."

"That would be Jonas," Teo answers drily. "He tends to get carried away with his duties. It's all for the better, you shall soon see."

"Jonas?" I ask, noting the random plants strewn across the floor. From where we sit on the ottoman they look like miniature forests springing up from the hardwood floor. They might be devil's ivy or some sort of spider plant, but my mom is the one who tends our garden. All I know is the plants look prickly and I may have made up those names.

"You met him before," Teo says, bringing me back to my question—who this Jonas is—and the only nameless person I've encountered is the albino, so that must be him. I tuck away this bit of information so I can call him by his real name when I see him again.

The smell of sheetrock and fresh paint mixes with the scent of the tangerine, the purr of a hot water heater abruptly clicks off, and when I let my eyes wander over to the curved staircase I put together that the same curves echo throughout the room. All of the walls and doorways arch several feet above me. That, combined with the high ceilings and granite counters, makes me realize these homes were built to impress. All this for one person seems pretty excessive.

Teo leans back from where we sit on the ottoman, resting his head on the ivy-painted wall. "I can breathe in a room like this," he says, voice low, nearly carefree.

And I know exactly what he means. He's not talking about the air freshener. He means our time together is no longer contained to those heart-stopping moments I stole after class. It's impossible for me to count the number of times I feared we'd get caught. A teacher coming around the corner would see the way he'd slip his hand around my waist when he thought no one was watching, or a student would point fingers when they saw his fingers graze the back of my neck when he walked past my desk. But I lived for those moments, how they warmed everything inside of me, and I hoped that Teo did, too, despite the danger we'd be caught.

I watch as Teo closes his eyes, seeming to enjoy our moment of peace. And I close mine, too, savoring the fact that our knees are slightly touching, the cool water is cleansing my throat, and Teo's breathing labors like he's in a dream.

Time has slowed down in this room. No brassy school bells ring, and there is no onslaught of curious looks from teachers, students, or the janitorial staff. Right now it's Teo and me and one small bench. The stark opposite of when we'd just met.

Some people can't remember first impressions, or it all comes to them as a blur. But everything regarding Teo has been recorded with precision, like how I first heard his name from one of the other students. *It's Tay-oh, not Tee-oh. Short for Mateo, a Spanish name. He's touchy about it, like he's royalty or something.*

Those first few weeks at Khabela were particularly tough. I was struggling to make friends, trying to make myself invisible in class. One day, though, Teo said something that cheered me a little. "I will be teaching you all next year," he said. "Calculus, which holds a beauty like trigonometry. You shall see."

I was elated, but tried to conceal my feelings, so I let my hair fall forward and scrunched down in my seat. I had decided long ago that scrunching was best, because teachers were much less likely to call on the new girl if she was one they didn't notice. But my vanishing act hadn't worked entirely, because it was only a few minutes before Teo sat by my desk, perched atop one of the empty ones to my right.

Placing something on my desk, he said, "I made this for you."

Startled, I looked down to find a single CD in a slim case. Nobody gives CDs anymore, so I stared at it, confused. A lesson for trigonometry? Or maybe a precursor to calculus. I glanced around to see if the others had them, but their desks were empty except for their textbooks and spiral notebooks.

When I looked over to ask Teo what exactly he meant, he was already on the other side of the room. My gut told me he didn't want the other students knowing about his gift, so I quietly slipped the CD inside my bag, intrigued.

That night, when I played the CD on my computer, I discovered a collection of music, songs all containing my name. With a name like Cheyenne, I was startled whenever I came across a single one, but he'd found three. And when the Cheyenne songs ended, there were songs about my middle name, Clarissa, the name I'd gotten from my mom. At first, I was shocked that he would know my middle name, but it must have been on one of the rolls from school. And once I got past the surprise that he had made me a CD in the first place, along with the fact that he had bothered to seek out songs containing my name, I decided that he was the single most thoughtful person in school. I had thought myself invisible, someone no one cared to know. But he cared. So I treasured the gift, marveled over the fact that he had given it to *me*.

I have since played that music so many times I know each song word for word. I never said much about the gift, but when I began to participate more in class, I knew he understood my thanks.

Teo's eyes are closed beside me now. I listen to his steady breathing and study the black stubble of his beard, happy that together we can enjoy this peace—even if I am seeking answers, because somehow I know with Teo there will *always* be answers to be found. He always has a plan.

After a few minutes pass, Teo breathes in deeply. I expect him to comment on the air freshener, too, when he says, "Aren't you rather dirty? You need a bath."

The blood rushes to my cheeks and I tilt my head down. It's silly—if anyone else had said such a thing, I would tell *them* where to go. But no one is perfect; even my Teo has his faults. He can be coarse, insulting even, but his innate goodness is why we are tied to one another. Plus, only the best of people can understand what it means to savor Milton, Chaucer, or Frost.

Feeling the blood ease away from my cheeks, I lift my head, fix my gaze on the oversized bookcases flanking two of the walls. A couple hundred books might be packed into this room. It makes me wonder if the other rooms have more, and if the other homes in the community are the same way. It impresses me that Teo loves books as much as me.

But I'm ready for answers: why he brought me here, and what he plans to do next. If anything, he could introduce me to the other people and let me know when he plans to take me home.

Teo sighs, moving to his feet. "While your transparency becomes you, my dear, answers will come very soon. Shower, and when I return I'll offer more answers in conjunction with your second task."

Second task. I look down, crushed that he found the need for another one. I wish he'd let these tasks go, see how worn-out I am. That I want to be *with* him, that I want things to be the way they were—where we could discuss literature. And kiss.

Teo cups the side of my face and my cheek twitches hungrily beneath his hand.

"Have no fear, my dear," he says. "You shall feel much better once you are clean." And it's true. I want him to find me beautiful, let me again feel those soft lips. I can't expect him to want me looking like this. Especially in a neighborhood with someone like Cleo.

I nod and move across the room toward the hall, and blindly follow the painted cracks on the walls that seem to lead me right to the bathroom. I spy the large mirrors, the marbled floors, and the ivory porcelain sink when Teo calls, "You should curl your hair. That is how I like it best."

* * *

Thirty minutes later, I'm shined up like Mom's collection of antique glass figurines. A black, silken robe hangs on the shower door, and since I don't want to put my dirty clothes on again, I slip it on, making me feel like I'm at a resort. Hopefully the girl who lives here won't be annoyed that I'm wearing her robe, not to mention using her makeup and her curling iron, but I'm not entirely sure what choice I have. Maybe I can do something to make it up to her later. Maybe Teo will have some ideas on what to do. He always does— like when everyone kept freaking out about a return of the Living Rot. *Calm yourselves,* he'd said. *Emotional outbursts offer little help.*

Movement in the mirror tells me I'm not alone. Teo, still in his black suit, has joined me in the bathroom. "For you," he says, flinging a white dress at me, which brushes past the side of my face. When it lands on the counter in front of where I sit, I manage to grasp it just in time before it slinks to the ground.

He's giving me a dress. For keeps?

Teo sets an enormous arrangement of calla lilies on the counter, which makes me blush because it reminds me of a questionnaire I once filled out in school for prom décor. *Preferred flowers?* I had written calla lilies, my favorite.

I love that Teo knows. And I love how he never skimps on anything.

"Cheyenne," Teo says, inching toward me, the tails of his suit jacket flapping up as he walks. He brushes those warm, familiar hands on my trembling jaw and cheeks, the movement so unexpected I'm not sure how to respond at first. He's wrapping me in his arms and pulling my weary head into his chest. I close my eyes, disbelieving the embrace. Calculus is so far away. Then, it was them and us. Now, it's me and Teo and his familiar scent: Listerine and tobacco. The first time he wrapped his arms around me, I was surprised to find how he smelled, the lingering scent of tobacco on his clothes, until he showed me how he keeps unused cigars in his suit as a tribute to his deceased dad. *Rather sentimental of me,* he'd said, but that's what I love about Teo. At the right times, he knows how to reminisce over the past. At the right times, like now, he knows how to drape his arms around me like a warm, smooth cloak.

I want to kiss him again, feel that sensation of his mouth over mine, but I'm missing the final piece of information. I need to know why he's brought me here. We've danced around the issue for far too long. "Teo?" I ask. "What is this place?"

He holds me closer, breathing in the scent of my hair. I hope he likes the cucumber-melon shampoo I used. I don't think he's ever mentioned *not* liking cucumbers or melons, so I think it should be okay.

"Why, Miss Laurent," Teo's voice comes out muffled through my hair, "I have built our ideal world."

He's not telling me something. Heart rate picking up in speed, I push away from him. "But what about the old one?" There can't be something wrong with the world, with my family.

Teo's olive-toned cheeks flatten. His entire body sags as if in defeat. Holding his hands out to me, he says, "That is what I must show you. I am sorry, but you would have found out soon enough."

He's talking about the Living Rot. But it can't have returned. We were vaccinated, supposed to be safe. The mirrors swirl about me and I can't seem to find the right way to hold my head. I grab the counter to steady myself, and Teo supports me by slipping his strong arm around my waist.

The stubble of his beard bristles slightly against my quivering cheek. "Let us walk," he says. "Fresh air might do you some good."

But walking is the last thing I can do right now. My heart pounds in my chest and my fingers twitch. I shake my head, but he stops it from moving by placing a gentle hand on my trembling face.

I draw in a breath. Teo's reassuring touch is the only thing I need. The warmth of his palms, his slender fingertips. If I close my eyes and freeze time, then we can kiss again, and everything Teo's hinting at might go away. But he reaches into his suit coat pocket and pulls out a single vial with a clear liquid inside—and I'm so not ready to accept the fact that I need a vaccine.

My illogical impulse is to grab the flask and fling it on the ceramic tile, because in my mind not seeing a vial lets me keep lying to myself. It means the Living Rot hasn't come back.

"It has happened before," Teo whispers, stroking the hair above my ear, "and it was only a matter of time before it happened again." My nerves crackle, but not just because we're skin to skin. It *can't* be a repeat of Beijing. The Living Rot is in the past.

I watch our reflection: his black suit against my white dress, unable to believe our time together is because of this. This cannot be what has happened. They told us it was over. They told us we were safe, that the cause of the Living Rot was buried as deeply as the core of the earth. They said life would resume as normal. Teo can't be right.

3

Steering me from the bathroom and down the scorching street, Teo murmurs velvet-tinged words, but they bounce off my ears, my cheeks. I'm not really sure why, but I feel like I'm holding up a shield, blocking out anything that needs a vaccine. A sickness that causes people to eat other people? They promised it would be scoured from the earth. They said everything regarding the sickness was burned. Of course, it is possible for new viruses to be created or found, but our planet has already learned the horrific outcome of the disease.

"I am sorry to tell you like this," Teo says as he steers me past the third or fourth house, "but I need to bring you up to speed. The other couples know. It's the first thing I showed them when they arrived."

Vaccine. Couples. Rot. I can only think in one-word sentences, walking down the length of Elysian Fields as the sun over the horizon winks. Evening. Night. Lies.

Teo turns at the fifth or sixth mailbox. "Cleo has the footage," Teo is saying. "You know how I avoid watching TV." It's true. The only one at his house was in Marcus's room because, according to Teo, Marcus had a death-grip on his shows.

Somehow, Teo manages to pull me through Cleo's house, which I suppose is Egyptian-themed. Gold-painted baseboards, peach-painted walls, floor to ceiling statues of some Egyptian god—my stomach lurches. Whatever happened to beige? Even her couches are over-the-top with tassels and leopard prints.

Part of me acknowledges Teo pushing me up another curved, wrought iron staircase, and the other part of me trembles at the thought of everyone I know becoming sick. My mom. Mayor Tydal. Serenity and Josie, the other kids at school. Instead of peach walls everything would be broken, and the world would be colored in the stench of so much red.

Upstairs, Teo sits me down gently on a hieroglyphic-patterned bed, the foreign sprawl of symbols looking much like what's going on in my head—chaos and an inability to accept. The Living Rot, returned? But God would never again sour the earth.

Plucking up a remote, Teo clicks on the TV, and I don't want to look. Because real footage would show me the Living Rot *must* be accepted as the truth.

I train my eyes on the gold fabric of the bed, grit my teeth because I can't bear to see. But Teo's hand gently cups my chin and, with only a bit of resistance, I allow him to move my face up. Because maybe, just maybe, I can accept whatever it is with Teo holding me.

A cameraman we can't see is fleeing. The screen is bouncing and not quite up and down. The subject of the screen is a person, but gray, decaying, and diseased. It's a little girl. An orange dress hangs on her withered frame, and she's clutching a dismembered arm. She takes a bite from the wrist of the limb. The Living Rot, just like in Beijing.

"It's not over," the reporter shouts from off the bouncing screen. He yells and we see the reason for the yell—several arms are stretching toward him from the windows of a parked yellow car. And while only a low groan comes from the cars, the sound slices into my chest and curls up my spine. "There's nowhere safe anymore!" the cameraman shouts. Gasping for breath, he adds, "Protect yourselves!" The screen bounces, like the cameraman's just made a leap, and he curses before the screen crashes and goes black.

Teo clicks the TV off. "I wanted to spare you from that, but you gave me little choice. The epidemic leaked out, a mutated form this time. And when I got word from my contacts that the scientists already had a new vaccine, Jonas and I retrieved it from the hospital just in time. They were planning on giving it to government officials, scientists—people like that—but we knew those weren't the only people who we should protect. You should have seen it." He flashes a shy smile. "Jonas stood watch while I snuck inside."

Stroking my cheek, he bores his eyes into mine. "Do you see what I have given you? An asylum from the Living Rot."

My knees tremble where I sit, and I suddenly don't know what to do with my hands. Grab onto Teo? Hold him tight? Thank God the both of us are okay. Those groans were not human—at least, not anymore. What do you *do* with people like that? I'm not even sure they can be killed or how far the Rot has spread. I choke—on vomit or spit, I don't know—but what Teo has showed me has really taken place. The Living Rot has returned, and there's no telling how far it has spread.

Teo sits beside me on the bed. "I had to protect you. Your life means more than my own."

Teo's simple words make my panic still. It's somehow become a glorious moment knowing that, despite everything, he's unveiling how he feels.

My eyes sting—tears gather in the corners. But they're the best tears I've ever felt. And it simultaneously makes me feel guilty. How can I be glad that I'm cherished when everything about the world is at the cusp of so much death?

"So, you appreciate me?" Teo says, and I somehow want to laugh.

"Yes, Teo. Of course I do." Because we're together and he loves me and I love him and—

Dear God, how could the Rot be back?

Little finite details seem to shimmer in place. Now that I know how Teo feels, I need to know why he made this place. And how did he know about the Living Rot to make it in time? I know he is brilliant, but how would he have the connections to know something like that?

Teo moves away from me on the bed and starts pacing about the room. Even his walk has my attention fastened in place. His long, powerful legs only need two or three strides to make it across the room. "It was only a matter of time before something happened again," Teo says from across the room. "After Beijing, I knew I had to make a safety net, bring in friends in the prime of their youth."

Teo's comment jars me. It's silly, but I mostly think of us as the same age. True, he's twenty-four, but I don't think about it much. I've seen Cleo and Marcus, and I guess the others are my age, too. How did he pick us?

He takes another step toward me, an ebony fire simmering in his gaze. "There's something else," he says as he loops a finger through one of my curls, sending a current of longing crackling down my neck. "I wanted to tell you before, but I needed you to have the motivation to consent."

The word "consent" reminds me of my mom. That's the word she uses to remind me that *she* is the one who rules in our home. I require her "consent" for just about anything—

visiting a friend's house, ordering pizza. But even with her strict rules, I'm horrified I haven't thought earlier about my mom. He showed me a clip where animalistic humans soured the earth, and I hadn't thought about the safety of my mom, even if she does always tend to get a little crazy with the idea of "consent."

I can't stand the idea of her hurting, so I have to ask. "Have you heard from my mom?" I have to push aside the image of her cowering behind her bed—practically my twin, if you add a few sunspots to my face. Everyone says we look the same.

Teo's face grows cold, that spark of fire suddenly gone. "You are not listening! The Living Rot is already here." He clicks on the TV once again, and then points at the bottom right-hand corner of the screen where it reads, "Live in Austin." I look closer at the screen. Sam's Ice Cream Shoppe. The park with the old lady and the shop that sells handmade hair barrettes. This is all of Sixth Street, right downtown. Where I live.

I can't believe this has happened, can't believe this is my home. Where the street was once filled with bright memories, it's been poisoned by the worst kind of death. My home, those people, all of them gone. And not just the barrette store lady, but my *mom*. One of the Clarissa songs Teo recorded for me reels through my mind. I can't help her. I've been whisked away.

The inside of my chest withers; my fingers twitch on my lap. To calm them, I shove them under my legs, and force my face not to twitch, too. Because I know what happens when my face starts twitching. I cry. And the last thing I want is for Teo to see me emotional again.

Staring at my lap as I try to calm my twitching hands, I feel the bed shift next to me, and one of the hands I've come to love reaches over and pats my knee. "I do not mean to be unfeeling," Teo says. "I suppose I've had more time to digest the truth. But if you ever feel like you need time to consider all the ramifications, just ask."

Almost any other time I would appreciate Teo's offer to help me mull over the facts, but right now I can't help feeling like he's sweeping the world's greatest nightmare under the rug. Doesn't he know that eventually the mess leaks out?

But I'm wrong in my dismissal of Teo's offering. *He's* the one who's provided help. It's his foresight and careful planning that have allowed any sort of asylum from the monsters outside.

I take a deep breath and push my worries away. Sometimes it is better to hide away our hesitations and trust in those we love.

"And now," Teo says, moving to his feet and extending a confident hand, "allow me to introduce you to everyone. They are ever so eager to meet you." He tugs my hand and pulls me toward the door, and as we exit the bedroom, a soft ballad wafts up Cleo's sprawling stairs; I'm suddenly not so sure I want to be introduced. What if it's like junior year all over again, where everyone already has their friends and sees no need to make more?

Teo guides me by the arm and leads me across the upstairs hallway that's open to the bottom floor. I can see seven couples eating and chatting, and Teo has me stop where part of the staircase curves out into a semi-circular balcony over the living room, like we're on a stage.

"Everyone," Teo says, lifting his arm up, his baritone voice carrying easily over the music, "I would like you all to meet our last friend. The crowning jewel of Elysian Fields." He pauses briefly, nudges me ahead, and cries, "I give you, Persephone!"

Persephone?

My blood runs cold. I know that tale; I read about it last week. Persephone is paired with Hades, the god of the underworld. The god who abducts and imprisons her by force.

I thought he liked my name. I always liked it—my mom chose it specifically for me. After breaking down in a snowstorm in Wyoming while seven months pregnant with me, a lady took her in and fed her. For an entire week. In Cheyenne. It means something.

But Teo's hand holds mine still, like he's displaying a mannequin. I'd like to protest, but he squeezes my hand with reassurance and I know to follow his lead.

His hold on me is tight and I haven't forgotten that Teo has saved me. Saved us. He has provided us with asylum from the monsters outside, carefully built this world and invited me into it. So, really, what I should be feeling is gracious to him. Teo is honoring me. Here I stand above these other couples, supposedly as their crowning jewel. Their Persephone. While the implication is a bit ostentatious for my taste, Teo deserves my thanks. I should give it.

I turn to him then, allow him to lift my hand, and I graze my trembling fingers along his strong lips. And he holds them there like that, moving my fingers down his stubbled jaw. The strong lines and dark skin of his face make it hard to breathe; I wish I could pull him close for a kiss.

Teo's gaze warms me, making me feel like jellyfish and coals. "These are your friends," he says, breathing into my ear. He points down the stairs. "Do you see the blonds? They are quite amusing, don't you think?"

I see who he means; there are four people with long blond hair, two girls and two boys, by a counter jam-packed with food. But the girls wear elaborate medieval dresses, and the boys wear skater clothes—one with a pink and green streak of color in his hair. They seem to be playing a quiet, subdued game of charades.

"You've met Marc and Cleo." Teo gestures to where they sit on a tasseled couch against the wall. "They make a stunning pair, don't you think?" And it's true, though everything about Cleo tends to burrow beneath my skin. Her arms wrap possessively around Marcus's neck and she whispers something into his ear. Whatever. Maybe he has a thing for streetwalkers over heatstroke victims who come across his front porch.

A few other people cluster around a dining room table to the side, but Teo leads me away from the top before I can take a closer look. We travel down the curved staircase as everyone in the room stiffens. A plump girl wearing an orange sari and scarf on her head balances a plate of veggies on her lap where she sits on the other couch. She gropes for her partner's hand, but he jerks his hand back. What a douche.

At the foot of the stairs, Teo clutches my waist the way I have always dreamed he would. It's tight, possessive, and I am only too happy to be wanted by someone else. It reminds me of the two seahorses I saw at Sea World when I was little. My mom explained how their tails curl together when they've found their true love. It's nice to feel connected to someone. Plus, Teo's never held me like this before; our moments have been like captured fireflies—cherished, and much too soon released.

Someone mumbles from the kitchen table, an elaborate hunk of wood with hieroglyphics and large, clawed lions' feet. Two of the boys—one in overalls, the other in a plaid shirt—make me realize the women are the only ones wearing costumes. But the costumes are so random, so eclectic; it almost makes me wonder if Teo raided a high school theater's closet and said, "Here you go."

Teo grips my waist hard, which reminds me of how he hates mumbling in class. *It is time for you to learn eloquence,* he said as he had us listen to Gregorian chants. "Someone has a comment," Teo says. "I'd like to hear it. Perhaps you would like to comment on Persephone's name?"

I let my gaze shift over to the two blond couples again—they've discontinued their low-profile game of charades. They all look so shiny and alike. I think of one of those outdated Doublemint Gum commercials my mother laughed at when I was small, with sets of twins smiling in every scene. *Double Your Pleasure, Double Your Fun.* Only the two couples are missing their smiles. Teo has that effect on people—he makes them smile less and think more.

None of the couples around the table are talking, and Teo's fingers dig into my waist. The three couples at the table duck their heads, seeming to want to hide from Teo's question altogether. Some of my classmates used to do that, until they learned that Teo is much happier when you offer what you have learned, prove you've taken the time to study the material for class.

So I answer for them, knowing that sharing my knowledge of Persephone will ease Teo's mind. "Persephone was queen of the underworld." Married to Hades, I think inside, but I don't say it out loud.

Teo drops his head sideways, revealing the slight black stubble on his shaved head. He swivels his head back and forth, up and down, a stretch I've seen maybe a thousand times. "Is that all, Persephone?" he asks me like he's my best friend, or maybe the friendly checker at the 7-Eleven before I slap the counter with another pack of gum.

"Yes," I say, my throat constricting as it hits me that there will never again be visits to 7-Eleven. Barely five minutes have gone past and I have already forgotten this new fact.

I open my mouth to say something about the Living Rot when Teo says, "It is time to dance."

Immediately, everyone finds their feet. Everyone, that is, except for Cleo and Marcus. She's tugging his hands, trying to pull him from the couch. He'd better get a move on if he—oh, there he goes, trudging across the hardwood floor to dance with Cleo, who wraps her paws around his shoulders. I breathe a sigh of relief. No one speaks a word as the boys in regular clothes hold the waists of girls in fancy dresses.

With one hand squeezing my waist, Teo squints down at me as we waltz away from the stairs. "That went well."

I'm not entirely sure how he thought it would go—or how well differs from poorly—but I smile anyway and say, "Yes, it did."

The seven other couples mimic Teo's dance with blank faces and shoulders tight. How many of them are thinking about the monsters? How many are troubled by the fact that the Living Rot could—has—happened again?

Teo's masterful lead helps sweep me away from the horrors on the outside—he has given us our own protected world. It makes me wonder if there's some sort of barrier through the trees. The neighborhood seems isolated. I would guess no one knows we're here.

The couples stumble about with little grace, a few sneaking looks at Teo and me. The girl wearing the sari and her scowling, pencil-thin date are the clumsiest, both watching their feet before crashing straight into Cleo and Marc. There's a domino effect when Marc trips over a tassel-infested ottoman and falls awkwardly to his knees.

My heart leaps. I must be wincing, because Teo turns around to see the cause. He takes in the sight of his brother bent across the ottoman, and puts together the fact that someone in orange can't seem to find her balance in the room. This poor girl in the orange needs a rest, to put up her feet.

"You," Teo points to the sari-wearing girl, "and you," he points to her date, "tell Persephone your names."

"Ana," the girl squeaks, steadying herself on the couch. "And this is Sal." Her date bobs his head in agreement, wiping his hands on his jeans.

Teo narrows his eyes. "Tell me, *Ana,* do you enjoy looking like a hippo mashing feet with a giraffe?"

Everyone freezes. He did *not* say that. Whatever happened to my Teo, who's gifted with beautiful words? He must be tired, frustrated by our failure to contribute to his conversation before. Humiliation trickles into dear Ana's eyes. "You're right," she says, and I want to pull her aside and give her a hug, because we all make mistakes.

Her partner, Sal, though, *is* rather giraffe-like and does have an unusually long neck. He stares ahead, his miniature rectangular glasses perched neatly on the bridge of his nose. But his gaze isn't looking at anyone. He merely toys with a block of wood in his hands.

Teo sighs, glaring at Ana in her orange sari and slipping headscarf. "Let us see those mashed-potato arms in some type of position—"

My jaw falls open. "Teo!"

I've only spoken his name, but it's as if I've stolen a megaphone and wailed *Silence!* Seven couples hold their collective breaths. Even the air conditioning seems to pause out of shock and apprehension, and the musician in Cleo's music knows to soften her voice, her once-articulate stanzas becoming slurred.

I watch as Teo's shoulders rise and fall and hate that this party isn't going well. That's how class was sometimes with Teo. On the bad days, no one would speak a word, so fearful that he would snap. On the good days, though, no one could stop talking about his high spirits and how nothing was better than learning with him. And that's what I want right now. Those good days when everyone sees that what Teo does is for a purpose, and he's always thinking ahead so we can learn as much as possible. He is, after all, the reason we had the highest math scores in the state.

This is not one of those good days, not at all. Plus, I've broken Teo's cardinal rule: *never* interfere with what he says. I'm mostly mortified I somehow forget about that unspoken rule, but I can't help wondering why he thinks calling people names is okay. But that's Teo. His mind is so far ahead of everyone else's that he has a hard time being patient sometimes. My rebuke must have been embarrassing for him. For that, I can't help feeling a little dismayed at myself.

Teo rounds on me and sneers; rightly so, but it still hurts. "The others in this room have learned *never* to interrupt their Director." He grabs me by the arm and drags me past the massive Egyptian statues by the door. "Never interrupt me, Persephone. Never question what I have to say."

My face twitches again, and it takes all I have not to hang my head and weep. Teo expects a reply, but the singer in Cleo's music steals my focus. I can just now decipher what she's trying to say: *Little monkey, be my friend, be my friend, be my friend.* Pushing the sound away, I look Teo directly in the eyes and say, "I understand." My face doesn't twitch or anything.

Teo sucks in his lips, then swivels his head again. "Can't you see what I have here, Persephone? I've built our perfect world."

I shake my head; it's impossible to be perfect. Of course, Teo knows that, but who am I to challenge his authority? He's the reason why we're alive. He's the person who had the foresight to build this place. If he hurts people's feelings, maybe I can make it my own personal goal to swoop in and patch things up along the way—only *after* he leaves the room.

Before I can say that I see what he's trying to do, he grips me by the wrist, opens Cleo's front door, and pushes me out. I stagger; never has he shoved me like this. My fingers begin to twitch like I'll defend myself, but I force them to remain still. He pushed me because I didn't appreciate his work. I can't question him in front of everyone. I can't.

Teo follows me, slamming the door behind him, making me jump, but I force myself to remain calm and to still my twitching face.

Electricity simmers in Teo's gaze. I feel like he's stockpiled the entire world's energy and infused his gaze with it. I can almost hear the sizzle from all that power directed at me.

"Go inside, Persephone," he spits, making me flinch. "Learn the names of your neighbors. *All of them.* Then return to me tonight and show me you can pass this second task."

Second task? My heart slams inside my chest—Teo yelled at me. But I should have known to hold my tongue. While Teo was rude, I need to remember some things are better left explained away after he leaves. *He doesn't think before he speaks,* I could explain to poor Ana. *See, I'm twitching myself.*

Yet, Teo has provided safety from the monsters outside. We are protected against the Living Rot, and he has a vaccine.

"Wait," I call to Teo as he moves away from me to the street, his coattails billowing behind him, "what about the vaccine?"

Teo turns a cold look on me. "You have not earned it yet. Everyone must prove themselves first."

Prove ourselves—by learning everyone's names. At least, I hope that's what he means. But how can he hold onto the vaccine like a collateral while the sickness is mere miles away?

This echoes his reward systems in the past. He would say before the math meets: *Perform well and you can ride with me. Complete the extra credit and we can move on to higher things.* Like listen to him play the violin or meditate with Gregorian chants—activities like these were rewards for accomplishing the simpler tasks. *That's when we may enjoy a higher purpose,* he would say, and suddenly everything makes sense.

I learn the names, I receive the vaccine, and we can move on to him explaining his vision for Elysian Fields, his dream. Why am I always so obstinate? So unwilling to accept his direction? He *did* refer to himself as our Director, after all.

I watch Teo stride away from me, his powerful legs moving down the street. He even moves like he's in control. I need to show him I'm willing to learn his ways.

As his black suit coat disappears inside the house at the very center, the one where I woke up, I can't help wondering if it hurt him to be angry, if he realizes how much he hurt me. But it doesn't matter; I'll do anything to prove myself to him. Because I can show him I'm worthy of his love, his dreams, this place. He might have unrealistic expectations, but I can do better. He will see.

4

With the pointy-eared Egyptian statues flanking every nook and cranny of Cleo's too-warm house, I feel like I'm being watched. Like Teo's given the statues orders to report back to him. Part of me wonders what it would be like to see them move—to see their powerful bronze bodies marching about the room. Their footsteps would echo the drumbeats inside my chest, the never-ending pounding.

If I'm to learn the names of the couples, I must forget the oversized statues, digest everyone's faces as well as their names. It can't be that hard to learn fourteen names.

Leaning against the wooden door behind me, I watch the one person I know best—Marcus, with that black, floppy hair. He needs a haircut, because he keeps shaking his bangs out of his eyes. He's talking to Cleo, heads close together on the couch. But with Teo out of the room, I take the time to really study Marcus. The way his gray knit shirt actually has to stretch over his shoulders and chest, and how a shade of dusty plum enshrouds one eye. He must have been in a fight, though I can't imagine with whom. With those ripped arms, though, it's not hard to imagine him tearing someone apart.

Cleo's beads slap into his cheek, and he laughs like beads have never been more amusing in his life. I don't know—I guess I feel betrayed. I figured he would be an ally, but he wouldn't let me inside his house. And he's chitchatting with *Cleo*? I think I sort of hate her, the way her boobs are spilling out of her dress.

Marc's eyes dart to me and flicker before he looks away. His eyes always lit up when he saw me before, but today it's like he purposely pushes the light out. I'm suddenly finding it hard to stand.

It has happened before, when I ran into him at the grocery store. He was buying ingredients for lunch. I remember him balancing rice, asparagus, and cooking wine without a shopping cart. I asked him what he was making and he seemed to grit his teeth and wouldn't meet my gaze, which was really strange, coming from him. He didn't joke with me, didn't look at me the way he usually did. I left feeling disheartened, wondering what had happened to the friend who always tried to grab my ponytail at the math meets. The one who sang my name. Instead, he stalked off to meet Teo at the front of the store. I wanted to follow, but I didn't want to go where I wasn't welcome. And I didn't understand why he had left me like he was hurt.

And now all I can wonder is why he didn't tell me about the snake, why he wouldn't get me some water. He must have seen my sunburned arms, my lips cracked from the sun. I don't understand why he's grown so cold.

Marcus strides across the room with nothing like the prowl of his brother's. His is more automatic—nothing fluid, just a walk. When he reaches me, my knees stupidly buckle enough to make me lose my balance. He grips my arms and steadies me against the wrought-iron rails of the stairs at my back. My heart *thump-thumps* and I have to take an extra step.

"Careful there, Cheyenne."

I stiffen in his grip. Now he's my friend? He's so hot and cold—like when he was always playing around at the math meets. I don't know what he wants. I never know.

Cleo follows Marc's path, her beads swaying as she walks, a smirk playing on her full and pouty lips. "Well, hello there, Number Eight." She juts her bottom lip outward, as if in sympathy. "Did Teo-bear leave you behind?"

I scoff. I'm about to say something about *her* behind when Marcus cuts me off. "What did Teo say?"

I glance at Cleo, her mock sympathy shifting to disgust as she sees Marcus's interest. Her eyes narrow and she flips her beads as she huffs away, which almost makes me wish I had my own beads to swing for joy.

Marc wants to know what Teo said. But I'm not so sure Teo would like me confiding in his little brother just now. Besides, Marcus doesn't deserve to know after his little stunt with the snake. "Why didn't you help me before?" I ask, folding my arms.

He mimics my stance, folding his arms, too. "Look, Cheyenne, I couldn't tell you about the snake, but I was trying to help you out."

"By chasing me away?" What kind of an idiot thought yelling at someone was the same thing as, *Hey, you might want to come inside to get away from the anacondas hanging around my house?*

It takes all I have not to laugh. He's not the one terrified of snakes or charged with learning everyone's names. But Marc's eyes narrow into slits. "Do you think *I* made this place?"

And he makes a good point. I know Teo must have, but he has his reasons. He needs to protect us from the virus outside; I'm sure he knows what he's doing, even if his plan does include hidden snakes. It was Marc's job to warn me about the danger, and he didn't help me out.

At the same time, I know the relationship between Teo and his brother. How they didn't grow up close. In fact, the times I saw them interact at the math meets they were always distant. More like childhood friends who had grown into strangers, and nothing like brothers. I wonder what the catalyst for that was.

I focus on the lines creasing against each other on Marcus's forehead, wondering if Teo is hard on him, too. But that is only because he loves his little brother. He encourages those he loves to better themselves. "Okay," I say, deciding to be diplomatic, "tell me everything that's happened, right from the start."

He tousles the front of his black hair, pulling it down the side of his forehead. "You haven't missed anything. Teo asked me to grab fourteen people from my school. He showed up with his car, and we piled in."

I'm not sure about that. How could everyone fit? "Must've been a pretty big car."

"Who cares?" He throws his hands in the air, like what *I'm* saying is stupid. "He brought us, explaining the world was going to pot."

I throw my hands up like him, not really knowing why. "And it is. In case you haven't noticed, it's just like Beijing."

Marc's muscular chest inflates like he's growing powerful or something, but slowly he releases the air trapped inside. "Yes. And I—" He stares at me, the flash in his eyes receding. "I have no idea why we are arguing or what about. Are you always this difficult?"

We're both quiet as Cleo's music plays in the background. She laughs from across the room where she's leaning all over one of the Doublemint twin boys by the snack counter, and I can't help wondering why I should bother working on my friendship with Marcus when he sits around and whispers with the likes of Cleo.

I brush past him toward the couches, my arm clipping his, and I know he's offended, but he can take some time and think about the best way to help a friend. My fingers touch the place where my elbow touched him, and to my horror, it actually tingles; my body wants to "accidentally" clip him again. Which is ridiculous, because Teo is the only one who I'm supposed to want to touch. This must be a one-time fluke—I'm clearly craving some physical attention. I need to work hard to see Teo soon.

As I watch Marcus stalk away and find his place next to Cleo again, I find myself feeling a little sad. I thought he was my friend, albeit one I didn't always understand. Like his brother, he is the type of person who doesn't think before he speaks. Even his actions never make sense. Like when he asked the moderator at a math meet to repeat her question, "But with an Irish accent, please." Or how, minutes later, when buzzing in with an answer to her question, he recited the entire *Pease porridge hot, Pease porridge cold* nursery rhyme before bowing for applause.

Watching him tickle Cleo around the waist by the snack counter, I can't help wondering if Marcus thinks about any of the choices he makes, or if everything he does is merely to get the biggest rise out of people. Either way, he needs some guidance, some help. I know Teo wants to help him, but Marcus isn't what I would consider a malleable subject. He mostly avoids direct questions, laughing them off and changing the topic.

I don't have time to fix him.

Spotting Ana, the girl I defended before, on the other, non-Marc-and-Cleo contaminated couch, I take a breath and join her.

She picks noncommittally at some pieces of cucumber and celery—luxuries I'm sure we won't have for long with the Living Rot just outside—and smiles a little without looking up. "Thank you for helping me—before." Her face is round with eyes as clear as a child's, but this scarf is wrapped around her head that mostly obscures her face. Poor Ana must be hot.

I take a peek at Ana's bloodshot eyes, realizing I feel the same way. Everything's been such a whirlwind, from waking up on a street I've never seen to learning the Living Rot is back. My shoulders slouch and it's hard to find my smile. Even so, I find myself saying, "I can't believe it's happened again."

Ana draws in a quick breath. "I know," she whispers, setting a piece of celery on her lap. "I thought all of that was in the past."

"They promised it was over," I agree, and when I say *they*, I mean the scientists, the politicians, the reporters—everyone who said the cannibalistic disease would never leak. "Does anyone know how this happened again?" I ask Ana, watching her fiddle with the scarf on her head.

A girl in a bright red dress, slit up to *there*, joins us on the couch. Her red lips shimmer when she says, "Do you?"

I can't believe she thinks I would. "Of course I don't."

The girl laughs, a light-hearted twinkling. "Don't worry about it," she says, patting my hand. "I'm Bee. It was my house you were in."

Oh! Bee, right. "Thank you." I wish I could say something more, so I settle for, "Thanks for not kicking me out."

But Bee shakes her red-haired French twist, causing a few strands to fall loose. "I'm a dancer," she says. "Kicking is more for the jocks." She nods her head, indicating the dreadlocked boy I saw before. He's pumping his heels up and down beside a tiny, black-haired Asian girl who's positively drowning in a long skirt.

"Who're they?" I ask, eyeing them creeping around the dining table like they're playing a quiet game of cat and mouse.

"Abe and Eloise," Bee answers, flexing her rock-hard calves. "Probably the most fun couple in the bunch. Eloise was actually living with me before. A foreign exchange student from Hong Kong—our fathers worked together. Not that that matters now..." She trails off.

My stomach turns. I'm not the only one who left behind family. Part of me wants to ask Bee about her family. Not to mention Eloise, who once lived much closer to Beijing.

I could tell her about my mom, how most of the time she likes to seem perfect, but occasionally she'll dive into the ice cream and watch movies or read books with me. She isn't what I would call a happy person, but the happiest I ever saw her was when she was in a relationship. I wish she could see me with Teo—the depth that we share. How we can talk about literature, and I know Mom would have joined in. Talk about how she majored in English and how my obsession is probably a result of her interests.

"Did you get the vaccine?" Bee asks me, her eyes swimming, hopeful, and I have to force away the image of my mom meeting Teo.

The tiny-waisted Asian girl, Eloise, squeals in the dining room—her date's hanging from the doorframe, doing pull-ups, until he accidentally kicks the pink-and-green-haired boy in the head. *Ouch.*

Bee steps in front of my face. "Girly, did you get the vaccine?"

I shift my attention to Bee and look straight at her freckled face. "Teo said I need to prove myself first." A little part of me is still hurt that he yelled at me outside, but mostly I hope she understands the gravity of this task.

Yet Bee doesn't have a chance to respond to me, because Marcus has rejoined our group—with Cleo in tow. He smiles falsely, his grin stretching wide over his face. "There goes my brother and his brilliant reward system again."

I grit my teeth. How can he disrespect his brother like that? No wonder Teo has a hard time helping him. Marcus only finds faults with his brother, when Teo's only plan is to help. Teo can be harsh at times, but he has his reasons for being like that. Keeping my voice low, I say, "There's nothing wrong with rewards, as long as you understand the scope." Teo always has bigger plans.

Cleo rolls her eyes. "Right. Like holding onto the vaccine."

"But he's already given it to you guys, right?" I say, clenching my teeth.

Cleo throws back her head, the ornate beadwork in her hair swaying as she chortles. "That's a good one, Number Eight. Now I can see why Teo likes you. You make him laugh."

I consider saying a few choice words, all of which Teo would consider crass, so I decide the best way to deal with Cleo is to pretend I'm deaf. She's not worth the breath, anyway. Facing Bee and Ana, I say, "You mean you don't have the vaccine, either?"

Bee frowns, pointing her toes. "You're not the only one who needs to prove yourself first."

So everyone in Elysian Fields must do something to earn the vaccine. "I'm supposed to learn everyone's names," I say. "Is that what you're supposed to do, too?"

Bee sighs, watching Eloise and Abe hugging on the other side of the room. "Teo hasn't exactly told us. He was supposed to tell us tonight how we're to prove ourselves, but that was before he grew angry with you."

I can feel my cheeks burn with embarrassment. My row with Teo is affecting everyone in Elysian Fields. Not only are Ana, Bee, Marc, and Cleo all staring at me, but so is the guy wearing overalls, that plaid-shirted guy, and his date with the curly black hair. I'm supposed to learn everyone's names and they probably already despise me for risking their safety. So much for not repeating junior year.

The two sets of Doublemint twins are already a formidable clique, giggling together by the food-covered kitchen counter, and Cleo and Marcus seem like an inseparable pair as they move away from me to join the twins. But at least I have Bee and Ana. They seem like they could be friends.

I glance at Bee's feet while she points her toes again, like she's preparing to dance. Keeping my voice low, I say, "I didn't think it was possible for the Living Rot to come back."

She pulls a few strands loose from her French knot. "We've had overnight to let it sink in."

"So you came here last night?" I pick at a few tassels on the couch.

She nods. "Teo showed us the news report first thing. A few didn't believe him at first—like he made it up—but then," her voice cracks, "he got a few of our parents on the phone, and they pled for us to stay." I think of my mom and wish I had the chance to say good-bye. I can't believe he had Jonas—it must have been him—sneak up from behind me just outside my bedroom and knock me out with chloroform. I can still remember the smell of the acrid cloth on my nose and the blinding light when I woke up in Teo's house. Not that I would ever admit it, but Teo's methods for bringing me here were pretty bad. He should have run inside, explained everything to my mom, and I would have gotten to say good-bye or bring her along.

Bee looks so somber now, like she regrets a few things, then glances warily at the statues. "I had plans, you know? Break free of my parents' mold. But now, I—" she stops to wipe a bit of moisture from her face—"I'd do anything to do what they wanted and just dance."

My chest deflates. I suppose it really is Teo who's saved us from everything. The others, no doubt, feel indebted to him, too.

Bee picks at the old-fashioned belt wrapped around her red dress. "Teo's methods may not be my favorite," she says, "but we owe our lives to him. Dressing up a little is nothing compared to where we'd be without him."

What she says is true. I'm so excited for everyone to see what he can do, the things he can teach us—his mind is chock full, not only of math, but also the literature I love.

Deciding too much time has already passed—Teo's waiting for me—I turn to Bee and Ana. "I need to learn everyone's names," I say.

Licking ranch dressing from her fingertips one at a time, Ana says, "I would be more than happy to help you with that." She leans forward, awkwardly plants her short legs on the ground, and stands, the straining fabric of her sari ripping at the knees.

"Oh!" she exclaims, blood flooding her cheeks. "I—" She glances at me, embarrassment blotching her sweet face.

I try to make her feel better by shooting her my most compassionate smile, but the giraffe-like boy—Ana's partner—grumbles at my side, "We need to get her on an elliptical."

I freeze.

I didn't know it was possible, but Ana's cheeks flush darker. She gingerly sets her plate of veggies down on the couch and clutches the fabric closed with her fingers. "I'll be back," she whispers toward my feet, then scampers toward the door. Ana's champion of a partner trails behind. I'm tempted to ask him to let her be, but maybe Teo has a rule about couples sticking together tonight. Or keeping their clothing immaculate. Or maybe Ana actually wants her partner's help.

Bee frowns, her lip-gloss shining. "And that would be Sal." She pats a freckled hand on my knee. "So, do you think you're up to the task?"

I nod.

"That's great, Persephone."

This time it's my turn to frown. Picking at a tasseled pillow on the couch, I tell her, "I wish he would call me by my real name." Or at least pick a different story to name me after. He's comparing me to a girl imprisoned by force. My stomach squeezes, like I should try to read into that.

But Bee's laughing her musical laugh again. "Do you think 'Bee' is my real name?"

From the corner of my eye I see Bee's friend, Eloise, the one from Hong Kong, tiptoe around the lion-clawed dining table to sneak up on her dreadlocked date. She's carrying a flyswatter and cocks her arm like she's about to swat him on the rear when it hits me. "We've *all* been renamed." I can't believe I missed this before.

Bee nods, and Eloise's date is howling like Eloise just caused him searing pain. He's smiling, though.

"So that's why he wants me to meet you all," I tell Bee over the mock howls of pain. "There must be something important about our names—like a tie to literature, since I'm Persephone." *A higher meaning.* That's why I love Teo; it's always like that with him.

Bee rubs her hands together like she's brushing them clean, stands—her red dress has an intentional slit, unlike Ana's—and pulls me up. I'm a little sad to leave the comfort of the couch. But Bee keeps me focused when she says,

"That's just what I've been thinking. Maybe you can help us figure it out, and we'll all be one step closer to receiving that vaccine."

Exactly what I'm thinking, and I love how Bee spells it out.

5

When I explain to everyone that it will be easier for me to learn the names if we place everyone in numerical order like on the streets, with the girls standing across from the boys, everyone grumbles. One of the Doublemint twins keeps spouting off random acronyms, and I wonder if Cleo's eyesight is failing, because she seems to be fluttering her eyelashes an awful lot at Marc.

Apparently, I'm the only outlier; the only student from Khabela, while the others all went to Griffin. It makes me wonder what they're good at—if they sing or dance, draw or paint, or if anyone plays a musical instrument. The pink-and-green-haired boy looks like he might be in a band, and Bee mentioned dancing. I'd love to see her perform. Maybe Teo could arrange something. There is probably a reason why he invited these kids over his other students at Khabela. Even so, seeing them sort of makes me wish I had gone to their school. After spotting one of their flyers once, I asked Mom about going, but Mayor Tydal convinced Mom that Khabela was the more prestigious school. I always liked Mayor Tydal more when he and Mom were broken up. She listened to me better then.

Bee claps her hands, drawing everyone's attention. She told me she was the student-body president, and she must have been a great one, because they all seem more than willing to jump to their feet. She even fist-bumps Eloise's dreadlocked partner and glares at her own, gray jumpsuit-wearing partner for being too slow getting in line. What would I do without Bee?

Beginning at the back of the room, with its large windows decked out in golden drapes, I can't help smiling at the uniform lines of couples splitting down the center of the room. This shouldn't take much time at all. I'll be back to Teo in an hour, tops.

I face Bee's partner—it was his and Bee's homes I was closest to when Teo left me outside. I'm going to recite everyone's names out loud in the order in which I saw the men's signs.

"Ramus," I say, studying his Middle Eastern, diamond-shaped face. I can still see the scrawl of his messy handwriting on the sign on his door. Wanting to get to know him a little better, but not always at ease with idle chatter, I say, "So, how do you like Elysian Fields?"

Ramus only stares at me. I thought artistic people were supposed to be expressive. I try waiting for a response, but after a while, he looks away. Only a little hurt, I turn to Bee, laughing, mostly because I don't know what to do.

"No worries, Persephone," she says. "This one," she wheedles her arm through Ramus's, "is a bit frosty. But he's full of sunshine and daisies if you dig around deep enough." She winks at Ramus.

Ramus's cheeks darken; I think he's blushing. But when he looks up, he gives Bee a sidelong look, his eyes softening around the edges. It looks like Ramus doesn't mind being paired up with Bee. Not at all.

Not wanting to embarrass Ramus any further, and because I need to memorize the names of the others, I stroll to the next couple. "Boy number two," I say as I stop in front of the dreadlocked boy, who's somehow stolen the flyswatter from Eloise. Remembering the boxy letters on the sign outside his door, I say, "Abe." He nods, which bounces the intricate dreadlocks that are piled up in a ponytail on the top of his head.

Abe opens his mouth into the widest of grins. "Pleased to meet you," he says, extending a hand.

His cooperation already makes me like him. "Nice to meet you, too." I point at the flyswatter. "Planning to use that?"

Abe glances down, eyes widening like he had no idea the flyswatter was in his hands. "What? This?" he asks sweetly. Then, before anyone can stop him, he crosses the divide between the men and women and swats Eloise on the butt.

She squeals, but it's a happy sound, and when they start tickling each other there's a collective groan. Bee, beside me, makes a comment about how this is the last way she needs to waste yet *another* afternoon, and the boy on the end with the plaid shirt and a thick Southern twang shouts something about the couple getting a room. But it's hard to tell exactly what, because the acronym-shouting blonde mutters something with too many letters to make sense, and the pink-and-green-haired Doublemint twin sprints for the counter like he needs another snack. I'm losing them; I need to work, and fast.

I feel someone's eyes on me. Abe's looking at me, so I turn to face him.

"You're working to earn the vaccine?" Abe asks, eyes wide and friendly.

I try to smile because maybe he actually cares. No one else has asked why I'm doing this, but I'm sure they know. I expect Abe to say something else, but he looks toward the ground and shifts his feet. "Doesn't matter if I get it.

Nobody left in the world." His smile disappears from his face.

"Aww." Eloise shifts her massive skirts before latching herself onto Abe and wrapping an arm around his neck. She puts her lips together to say a word, but stops herself and opens her mouth to try something else. It takes me a minute to realize she's struggling with her English. Pinching her lips together, she says in a soft accent, "Don't say that. The world is full of poss—"

"—ibilities," Abe finishes, laughing. "I get that." He kisses her on the cheek.

I don't want to intrude, but I turn to the girl because the weight of my task is pressing. "So, you're Eloise," I state.

She waggles her eyebrows and black skirts, her lips spreading into a smile on her face.

"Well, it's good to meet you both." And not wanting the first boy, the Middle Eastern-looking one, Ramus, to feel left out, I smile at him, too. "It's nice to meet all of you. I can't wait to get to know you more."

The next boys in line—the Doublemint twins—have some breaded things in their hands. I need to move along if their cooperation lasts only as long as their snacks.

I take another step toward them, beginning with the pink-and-green-haired Doublemint boy, when Marcus yells, "And that is the conclusion to our night."

What? Why's he stopping me? First he didn't tell me about the snake, and now this? There's something seriously wrong with him. "But I've only learned a few of the names!" I find myself covering the five or six steps between us to reach him in the center of the room. I'm *this* close to popping him in the face.

Cleo snakes an arm around Marcus. "You heard him, chica. Time to scat." I've never been much of the violent type, but it takes everything I have not to smack her in the face.

But Marcus folds his arms, and it's a domino effect. Both of the blond-haired boys fold their arms, along with the plaid-shirted boy with the Southern twang. He actually looks familiar—I think he's one of Marcus's friends from the math meets—but right now I don't want anyone siding with Marc. We're all supposed to be working together to earn the vaccine.

"Why are you doing this?" I gape at Marcus as he turns away. To think all these months I thought he was my friend. From Mr. "Let me untangle your bracelets," to the guy who sang my name. Does he have a personality disorder, or did he only recently decide to be like this?

But he shakes his head as he walks away, and all I can do is stare at the back of his head, wondering why we're not friends anymore, where it all went so wrong.

Marcus grabs a few of those egg-roll wraps from Cleo's kitchen counter, and my stomach growls, but I don't have time to eat. He tosses one to Ramus, who's walking toward the front door, and then takes a bite out of the one in his hand. Talking around a mouthful, he says, eyes boring inside me, "You should be asking yourself why you want to be with Teo so much."

What is the matter with wanting to be with Teo? He should be happy for his brother and me. But the time Marcus noticed the connection between Teo and me flashes in my mind again, how he ducked down and scratched the back of his floppy hair like he was uncomfortable or something, and that's when I know the answer. "You don't like your brother being with *me*!"

It's strange. All these months I never would have dared say such a thing. Teachers are never allowed to get involved with their students. If anyone had found out, he would never have taught again. The world is changing, mostly for ill, but *this* is one of the perks! We no longer need to hide how we feel. And Marcus wants to take that away.

Marcus scrutinizes my face for several long seconds, his eyes narrowed, and it makes me feel uncomfortable to have him so close, like by studying me he'll be able to dissect all of my faults. Only a few seconds pass, however, before he grabs the long, floppy front of his hair and turns away. I'm not really sure, but I think he just cursed under his breath, and I have no idea why Teo's and my relationship would matter to him.

Everyone in the room is heading toward the door, stealing more of those stupid snacks, and the complete disregard for Teo's orders makes me want to scream. Teo *invited* all of them to come here. Well, I doubt he "invited" invited them, but the way they got here doesn't matter now. He's protecting us from the Living Rot. They shouldn't be disregarding everything he says. I can't—it's unfathomable to me that they can be so ungrateful. They should be showing Teo some respect.

Forcing my twitching fingers to grow still, I appeal to them with the most levelheaded question I can. "Don't you want me to accomplish my task?" I ask anyone who might hear some sense.

But Marcus and Cleo are too busy ushering the Doublemint twins out the front door, and the plaid-shirted boy is slapping Ramus on the back. I think about yelling at them to stop, maybe scribbling down their names and descriptions on a piece of paper, but I haven't got a pad. Or pen. My heart races and I think I'm going to be sick. I steal another look at Marcus, unable to believe he's doing this. It takes everything I have not to let my twitching fingers claw his face. "Marcus," I say again, because he needs to know it won't always go down this way.

The blue of his eyes lock with mine, but I can see that insubordinate flash of determination, like when he put his feet on the table at the math meet while winking at the old and crusty judge, and I know it—this time I won't win.

"Why won't you help me?" I plead, shocked I've lost my friend. I always thought he *got* me; he made that snide remark about Mayor Tydal and offered to slash his tires, just because. Everyone always thought I should love the idea of my mom and the Mayor being together, but Marcus saw what nobody else could see, that the Mayor was a fake, and he was making my mom the same way.

Marcus murmurs something to Ramus and the plaid-shirted boy on their way out, and then looks at me again. "Ask yourself if it's worth it, Cheyenne."

He's not making sense. Everyone should want to earn the vaccine.

Marcus's blue eyes flash and he turns for the door, but before he leaves, he stops, his hair flopping into his eyes. "Some of us aren't willing to play my brother's games," he says, the lines in his face softening. "The rest? Well, they're just pissed you get the first shot at the vaccine."

I take a few steps toward Marcus to explain that I'd like to be a team. We can all get along in Elysian Fields—enjoy what Teo has built. Teo will not like this rebellion, this little revolt. I mean to beg Marcus to change his mind when Bee grabs my wrist. "Let them go," she says. "I'll teach you their names real quick. Just don't tell Teo you didn't learn them all yourself."

But Cleo's already pushing us to the door. "Not in my house."

I want to protest—I figure Bee and I together would be able to take down Cleo and her little black dress—when someone presses something—a piece of paper—into my hands. I look up to see Ana smiling slightly at my surprise; she must have just snuck back in.

"You helped me," her voice is soft, in stark contrast to the loud orange shawl wrapped around her head, "so I help you." She's pressed awkwardly against the frame of the front door as Abe and Eloise, flyswatter flickering between the two, skirt around her.

I look down to see what Ana means, but the paper is folded neatly in half; I open it to see what's inside, and Ana—dear Ana—has written everyone's names with a few words of description in parentheses.

Ramus (overalls)

Abe (dreadlocks)

Everyone has a description, including the girls. I could kiss Ana, but Cleo's pawing my back, forcing me through the door. Bee, in her red-slitted dress, is right behind me, mumbling obscenities at Cleo, and I'll love her for that for the rest of my life.

The sun is melting over the trees—it reminds me of broccoli dipped in cheese—and I retreat from Cleo's Egyptian world with two new, potential friends. We're halfway down the footpath when Bee snatches the paper from my hands. She hoots at Ana, on the other side of me. "Lady, you are quick on your feet!"

Ana blushes, bits of red scampering across her cheeks. "It did take some quick maneuvering to get away from Sal."

Sal doesn't seem to be popular with anyone. Not that I blame Ana. He reminds me of a guy my mom used to date who kept a pair of tweezers in his back pocket to pluck random hairs from his nose and ears.

"'Pale skin'?" Bee groans, staring at the list. "How about 'radiant complexion'? Not a zit in sight."

But Ana's busy checking the rip in her dress, where a piece of duct tape now clings to the orange fabric on her leg—it doesn't look like it will last.

Now Bee's laughing, clutching her side. "*Love* your note for Cleo."

I snatch the paper from Bee, eager to be in on the joke. Scanning the list, I find Cleo's name, and next to it is only one word: "implants".

Oh, yes. It looks like Ana, Bee, and I will get along just fine.

The three of us sit down on the curb at the end of Cleo's pathway, and hover over Ana's notes. She's drawn two columns, the boys on one side, the girls on the other, so that it's easy to see who is paired. And instead of immediately scanning the girls' names, I read each of their names with their male partner's. I know some of them: Sal, Ana, Ramus, Bee. I'm not too sure of some of the others, though, so I scan the list in my hands.

Ramus (overalls)   Bee (pale skin)
Abe (dreadlocks)   Eloise (Chinese)
Tristan (pink & green hair) Izzy (big eyes)
Lance (drums)   Gwen (frizzy blonde)
Sal (glasses)   Ana (orange sari)
Marc (hot)   Cleo (implants)
Romeo (plaid shirt)   Juliet (black curls)

At first I can't help noticing she's labeled Marcus as "hot"—he isn't *that* good-looking—but then my gaze snags on the last pair. I chuckle. "Romeo and Juliet." I expect them to laugh, too, but they don't. Their faces are hard, without a trace of a smile.

Ana's voice is guarded. "We thought it was funny, too, until Teo warned us never to laugh about the names." She shivers, reaching for a piece of celery in the folds of her skirt.

While I had figured our names are somehow tied to literature, I can see a pattern taking shape. *Lance, Gwen: Lancelot, Guinevere. Marc, Cleo: Marc Antony, Cleopatra.* We aren't just classics; we're some of the most famous, romantic stories ever known. I am not entirely sure about a few of the names, like Ramus and Bee, and Abe and Eloise.

I open my mouth to ask Bee and Ana what their real names are as it occurs to me that, if Teo chose these names, their former ones must be forbidden. He, no doubt, wants to start over in this world, obtain perfection by starting again as someone else.

Bee's frowning at me like she wishes I'd share my thoughts, but I can't tell them now, so I smile at the girls, desperate to express my thanks. Without them, I would be on my own. Bee's willingness to help me meet the others, then Ana's quick thinking in creating this list, has enabled me to accomplish my goal. Teo will be so impressed. And with the pairing, I think I can remember everyone well enough. Part of me wants to grab the girls and swallow them both in a hug.

Bee seems to accept my little offering, because she says, "You'd best be off." She brushes her freckled fingers against the back of my hand. Keeping her voice low, she adds, "Be careful, lady."

Bee... *Bee*! Pyramus and Thisbe! I've just figured her out. She's from *A Midsummer Night's Dream*. Ramus is Pyramus. I love this story! But there isn't time; I need to get back to Teo, so I give her a look that says she has absolutely nothing to worry about. "Don't worry about me," I say. "I know Teo is nontraditional, but he cares for me in his way."

Ana leans in, her shawl slipping. "And you, him?"

I shrug, keeping my eyes on the list stretched out in my hands. "I can't help it. My feelings for Teo—they didn't happen because I wanted them to. I just do."

Both girls are silent for a moment before Bee finally speaks up, moving a stray curl behind my ear. "I hate that I sound like my mother, but just because you love someone doesn't mean you should."

There's a soft crunch as Ana works her celery between her teeth. I can't help thinking she must be wondering how I could care for someone who could treat others the way Teo treated her just now. I hope that, with time, Ana and Teo will come to love each other the way I am coming to love them all. Well, most of them, anyway.

Of course, I didn't like the idea of Teo and me at first. Those first few weeks my second year at Khabela, when I noticed my irreversible, growing attraction to my teacher, I tried to stop my feelings. I even tried talking the secretary at the front office into switching me to another class, but seniors were supposed to take calculus at my school. I needed it for college, and no other teacher taught calc.

And the longer I stayed in that class, the less I was able to look away. I was sure Teo knew of my obsession; it would have been futile to try to hide it. And none of the other students ever said anything, not that I didn't wonder why. Were they scared of Teo? Scared of me? Or maybe I really wasn't that obvious. I guess I will never know. None of my classmates are with us now in Elysian Fields, and who knows how long there will be survivors on the outside?

Reaching for both Ana's and Bee's hands, I offer them my most sincere thanks: "Anytime you need anything, just ask. I'll vouch for you with Teo." A twinge inside of me says I shouldn't have to vouch at all, but no one is perfect. That's just how Teo is.

The girls nod their heads a bit too eagerly, like bobble heads in a moving car. But neither of them has anything to worry about. With Teo, things take time. They will grow to love him soon enough. And Teo will give them the vaccine. I know he will.

With these reassurances, I jump to my feet, so eager to meet my Teo I fail for words. So I shoot the girls my best grin before sprinting off to meet our "Director." After all, I now know everyone's names.

And that will make Teo proud.

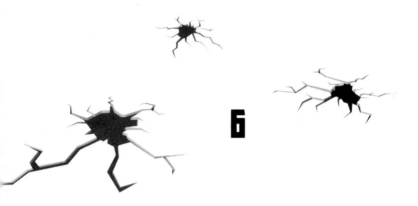

6

My dress whips around me like Teo has installed secret fans in Elysian Fields, and when I look up, the sun winks over the horizon, saying goodnight.

I'm so blessed Teo chose me to share this life. The neighborhood is amazing with its immaculate homes, the couples connecting with literature, and our safety from the Living Rot. I could be subhuman, living on other people's parts. But Teo saved me—all of us—from becoming that. He didn't just pick us up and dump us out in some random field; he prepared this place. Like the houses. Cleo's, for instance, is Egyptian-themed because she's Cleopatra. Bee's, or Thisbe's, home has cracks because that's how the girl talked to the man she loved. Everything, *everything* about this world makes sense.

Stalling on Teo's porch, I catch my breath. Seven men, seven women. But why would we be the eighth? And what about Jonas? We might spend the evening discussing these names and their stories. I want to understand everything about Teo's plans.

Lifting my hand up to his massive, wooden door, I knock. Boldly. Three times. A few seconds later, the door opens and Jonas stands aside to let me in. His chilling fingers scoop up my hand, and when he inspects my fingers, he frowns. "Your fingernails—" His clear gray eyes wind their way into mine.

I falter. I guess I sort of banged them up when I was digging up that survey stake. "Sorry about that," I stammer, glancing around for Teo, but Jonas makes it hard to see around the doorway, so I add, "Guess I wasn't really thinking." I hope Jonas won't always be the one to answer Teo's door.

Jonas drops my hand, frowning, and says, "You may follow." I watch the back of his white uniform as he strides away from me down the hall, and I can't help wondering how Teo knows him at all. Jonas, who seems so uptight, couldn't be more opposite from him.

I wipe my sweaty palms on my skirt as I shadow Jonas's steps, and when my heartbeats sprint inside my chest, I try slowing them with deep, even breaths. This is it. I have finally accomplished Teo's second task. We can be alone—I glance at Jonas and his stiff strides—at least, I hope we can be.

Stopping outside a closed door, Jonas knocks twice on what I guess is the door to Teo's room. Without waiting for Teo to arrive, Jonas spins away from me like a soldier moving out, and I find myself breathing out a huge sigh of relief.

Teo opens the door, and my knees buckle at the sight. One would think I would be used to facing him like this, but his olive-toned complexion combined with his slender, graceful form makes it hard to breathe—there's never been anyone more attractive to me in my life.

"Persephone," Teo says, holding his hands out for me.

I feel like frowning because I wish he would call me by my real name. "Miss Laurent," at the very least. But Teo is here, urging me in, and I can't think of a better arrangement where it's just him and me, so I fall into his arms and breathe in his musky scent.

He slides his gentle fingers down my arms, leaving trails of fire across my goose-bumped skin. Drawing me to his sinewy body, he cups my face, and he looks down at me like we're going to kiss. My heartbeats hammer, and the room's spinning around my head. I stare at his mouth and he closes the gap, and just before our lips connect, I let my eyes flutter shut. Tremors of pleasure curl inside my chest—this is our second-ever kiss. I hold myself impeccably still, savoring the sensation of his tender mouth on my own, but it's hard not to move because electricity crackles where we touch.

Seconds move much too fast, and too soon he drops his hands from my face and pulls away. I have to fight back the urge to grab him around the neck and kiss him again since he's not even looking at me; he's looking away. I want to be the lady he sees me to be—to be good and proper and check my behavior, because with Teo we can be so much more. He makes me more.

Slowly, he turns toward me, and I expect him to marvel about his world, but instead I find his black eyes probing inside my own. Not questioning or studying, but like he's hungering for something. And it takes me a moment, but I know what he's hungering after—me.

Warmth surges up and down my spine, and I reach out to touch the back of his hand.

That's all that it takes. Because his eyes are washing over me, and drinking me in, and he's gripping me by my hips, and slamming my body into his. My hips, my brain— everything's crackling. His lips are on top of mine, mine are on top of his, and we're dissolving into each other— nothing like a gentleman's kiss. My body crushes into his lean, toned chest, and his hands grip my hips tighter as our legs press into each other, hard. My veins implode, snip;

we're two people, but not, and I can't press into him hard enough.

When he weaves his fingers through my hair and trails them down my neck, my pulse pounds, so I grip the suit jacket on his back, yank it, and to my surprise, he rips it off and we're white on white—my white dress bleeding into his white shirt. The thin fabric between us simultaneously feels like nothing and too much. I want to keep ripping layers off, but my hands are too busy searching the lines of his shoulders, the small of his back. His hands are soaring up and down the length of my shoulders, my waist, my ribs. And when he forces me against the wall and presses his lips to my neck, my head falls back, my mouth opens, and I let out a moan.

Did I really just moan?

Teo nuzzles his face into my neck as blood rushes over my cheeks. I can't believe I messed up like that, but Teo's chuckling darkly, like he's never been happier. "You liked that?" he says.

He's never said anything so simple to me before, so I guess my slip-up is okay. I look up at him and find the ebony of his eyes lighting into my own. My lips travel down the stubble on his jaw and neck, and to my delight, Teo groans. It looks like he doesn't mind a little auditory feedback, after all. I guess it's kind of fun. Searching for another sound from him, I kiss his nose, his eyes, his lips, and soon he's crooning, "*Oh*, if you knew of the time I've wasted dreaming of this."

Wasted. Like he'd much prefer doing something else.

A bit of wall trim is suddenly digging into my back, and when I cast my eyes about his room, I find that it's empty—white walls, except for a full-sized bed pushed to one side and floor to ceiling bookcases jam-packed with books. Does he really feel that the time he spends thinking of me is a waste? But that can't be how he feels, because no one could fake a kiss like that. So maybe he meant that he's spent a lot of time thinking about me. Which is actually a compliment. I shouldn't get caught up in overanalyzing everything.

Teo holds the side of my face, and it becomes much easier to forget his earlier words. I close my eyes, savor his calm, soothing touch, and open them again to read the compassion I know he hides from the world. His bare shadow of hair mirrors his black, euphoric eyes, and I love how every time I look at him he looks different, but yet the same.

Cupping my face in his long, slender hands, Teo studies my eyes, my nose, my cheeks. And I study him back.

"Are you happy here?" Teo asks, his eyes pulsing into mine.

How could I not be? We've hit a few bumpy spots, like when he rebuked me in front of everybody else, but we're together at last. "Of course," I say.

Teo's face is somber. "But why?"

And the answer is simple. "Because you are here."

Teo smoothes his thumbs down the sides of my cheeks. "And that is enough for you?"

I swallow, and then I'm wondering about that swallow. Am I nervous? I suppose everything about Teo makes me shake. But that is love, isn't it? When our hearts scream out in response to someone else. My heart doesn't just *thump, thump* in my chest, but everywhere—the thumping pounds as an explosive force in my head, my feet, my shins. And through all this, I've somehow abandoned Teo's question. Is his being here enough to make me happy? Of course it is.

To prove my answer, I place my mouth over his, choosing instead to show him how I feel. I move away from the wall, and he meets me halfway, then more than halfway, because he's pressing me against the wall again and I'm welcoming the bit of trim jabbing into my back. He's kissing me again as warm goose bumps erupt across my flesh.

Burying his face in my hair, Teo breathes in deeply before kissing down the length of my neck. "You have learned the names?"

It's hard not to gasp as he skims the skin at the bottom of my neck. "Yes."

Holding his mouth over the hollow of my throat, he kisses me softly, sending tremors up and down my spine before moving back. "And you approve?"

It takes me a minute to catch my breath, so I breathe in and out, slowly, to clear my head. I want to be completely honest with him, explain I recognize *most* of the names, but I don't want him to be disappointed in my knowledge, so I let him know of my approval by clasping his hands and kissing them before I nod.

I expect him to reach for the vaccine. For him to say, "Well done, my love. Here!" But somehow everything shifts. Teo's bedroom door smashes open, smacking him on the back. His shoulders tense, his face grows dark, and he spins on whoever has come in.

Sparks fly from Teo's face—his eyes flash like obsidian and his jaw flexes several times, fast. His fingers grip me around the waist, then tighten, like he means to strike whoever's standing in that door. For them, I wish they'd disappear.

Three men stand in the doorway, bracing themselves against Teo's wrath: Marc, the plaid-shirted boy—Romeo?— and the diamond-faced, overalls-wearing Ramus. But Jonas stands behind them tapping a stick-like object. Is that a stun gun? Maybe it's in case the people infected with the Living Rot break through.

Teo studies them. All the lines of his face point inward—his eyebrows, his lips—and I'm terrified for the boys standing at that door. No one crosses Teo when he knows what he wants. What are they thinking, bursting into Teo's room? They could at least have knocked.

Teo's voice is impossibly low. "Why have you come?" he asks. His eyes bore into Marc's, but Marcus doesn't flinch. At first, I'm scared for Marcus—taking this action, standing up against his older brother—but then I look at his face, how his eyes are sparkling like there are fireworks inside. It's pent-up lava nearly erupting. But why is he so angry? There has to be something going on that I don't know about.

"You shouldn't be alone with her," Marcus says, eyes boiling, and it doesn't make sense that he would burst in on us for that. What is he thinking? That Teo has somehow become a monster and I should suddenly run far away? Marcus is so confused.

"Oh, what is this?" Teo laughs. "The chastity brigade? Well, isn't this fun?"

Ramus, in his janitorial overalls, pushes past Marcus, keeping his eyes on the ground. "We just wanted to be sure she was okay," he says, shrugging. Why's he here at all if he is so indifferent about everything?

Teo thrusts his hands out in front of him, a playful smile tilting his soft lips. "And what do you think, brethren? Does the fair maiden look harmed?"

Five sets of eyes turn on me: Teo, Marcus, Romeo, Ramus, and Jonas. Such a confined space for six people. I was just willingly kissing Teo, yet I can't deny that the protective nature of these boys touches me.

But Marc's eyes rage like a storm, and his arm is cocked, ready to throw a punch. I'm beginning to think he may need to see a therapist. First the math meets, now this. But I don't want the brothers to fight, so I step to Marc, place my hand on his elbow.

"Marcus," I smile up at him, "it's okay." I pat the muscles bulging beneath his shirt. He's awfully tense. Maybe someone said something wrong, like that I didn't want to be here, and this is all a big mistake. So I let him know that I want to be here as gently as I can. "Teo is a gentleman." I wipe away the memory of his brother throwing me against the wall, and the feeling of his lips on my skin. Feeling the blood rush to my cheeks, I add, "Thanks for checking in on us, though."

Marc's shoulders and his head look like an invisible baseball bat has pounded them. But why's he so sad?

Teo hooks his arm around my back, and it's beginning to be my favorite way he touches me in front of people, like he can't stand *not* touching me. "Gentlemen," he says, "I'd like to invite you to leave."

I look at the boys, trying to understand why Ramus is suddenly squaring his shoulders like he still means to throw a punch. And the plaid-shirted boy, Romeo, keeps looking from Ramus to Teo, like he's not sure which way he wants things to play out. But Marcus's reaction puzzles me most. He's staring at the ground. He should be relieved to see that everything with Teo is okay, that whoever made him believe I didn't want to be here was wrong.

Romeo discreetly grips Ramus's arm. He whispers something, and several seconds tick by before Ramus seems to let go of his instinct and turns for the door. The other boys do the same.

"Before you leave," Teo says, tilting his head to the side, "I have one minor question to ask of you."

The boys twist their heads around.

"Whose idea was it to come?"

Marcus and Romeo exchange looks like it was one of them, but Ramus strides to Teo, a look of defiance flashing across his eyes. "It was me. I brought the boys."

Oh, no. No, no, no. No one should ever openly defy Teo. This can't turn out well.

Before Teo says anything, Marc's jaw stiffens and Romeo grips Marcus's arm, like it never was Ramus from the beginning. And the way that Marcus seems to be shrugging Romeo off, it's like it *was* Marcus's idea to burst in on Teo and me, which makes perfect sense because, when I told him to leave, he was so sad.

"So, this was your idea?" Teo asks brightly, as if Ramus's claim to burst in on us is a good thing.

"Do you question my honesty?" Ramus asks, his diamond face widening. I wish I had a magic wand and could make him disappear. Is he *trying* to make his position worse?

Teo chuckles, his chest inflating. Clapping Ramus on the back, he says, "I suppose not, my friend." Teo chuckles a bit longer and then locks his black eyes on mine, and I know Teo is *not* simply happy. He's planning something. "What do you say, Persephone, shall we hold a meeting?" He gestures through the door. "You have a desire, no doubt, to learn the classical backdrop of our world?"

I do, and hopefully in the throes of Teo's explanation he'll forget about his anger toward Ramus and we can move on. And now I have learned the names, but I'm not clear on a few of their meanings. Ana, for instance, and her rude partner, Sal. Who do they represent?

Teo claps his hands together in two beats of dismissal, and my heart leaps. "Marc, my affectionate brother. Call a meeting. We meet in the street."

7

Street lamps dot the houses on the road like fireflies in the pitch of night. Teo looms above us, the porch light hollowing his face and eyes. He's like a specter, large and surreal, but those long fingers remind me he's much more than a phantom in the night. He's Teo—*my* Teo, who was just touching my face.

Stretching both arms high in the air, his baritone voice sings out, "And so we meet!" He extends his hand in my direction, several feet to the side of him on Ramus's porch. "And we are complete."

A few heads bob up and down—Abe's dreadlocked ponytail bounces in the faint light. He clutches Eloise's hand as she glances around, eyes open wide. It makes me wonder how much English she understands, or if she, too, is taken by Teo's presence. It's hard *not* to be taken by him.

Curious, I look for Marc's dark hair, but I don't see him; maybe he's in the back, behind the Doublemint twins, who shift impatiently on their feet. The tallest of the group taps on his legs, and it reminds me of Ana's note, how one of the blond boys plays the drums. Lance, I think. I hope they'll soon love Teo the way I do.

Striding to the front of the porch, Teo stretches his hands out toward the group. "Are there any here who desire to know the inspiration for this place?" he asks.

I feel as though I've backtracked to trig, the way he quizzed us in class; I'm tempted to launch my hand high in the air, but stop myself. He isn't asking me. If I gave all the answers, he wouldn't have the chance to connect with everyone, and I *need* for everyone to connect with him the way I do.

Raising his voice, Teo calls out, "Are there any here who desire to know the truth, the wisdom, the power of the number seven?"

I look to the others, hope to find someone as eager as I was in class to know the power of the number, though I can't help wondering why he's chosen eight couples. Well, eight and a half. But no one's hand darts into the air. Bee fidgets with her French twist, and Ramus keeps reaching for her waist, but she bats him away like he's invading her space.

Teo opens his mouth to explain anyway. "The simplest, most popular explanation is God's creation of the earth in seven days. But that was truly six," he clarifies. "He rested on the seventh. But we do not take that approach here. Is there anyone who desires to know the truth of our artistic world?"

I glance again at the other couples on the grass, how the black-haired girl standing with Romeo—Juliet?—keeps scratching her bare ankles on the grass. And her partner, Romeo, stares at the stars.

Someone raises their hand; five fingers stretch up behind Romeo's head. They must want to know the wisdom of Teo's world, too. If I could see who it is—

Romeo shifts enough to show me Sal, of all people, raising his hand. He pushes his glasses up the bridge of his nose, and I can't help wishing it was someone cooler, like Ana, or Bee, maybe.

Teo eyes the long-necked boy but doesn't comment on Sal's hand. Looking away, he says, "I would like to invite the first man and woman of our world to come forth." He holds his arms out for Ramus and Bee, who hunch together on the far side of the grass. Smiling at them politely, he adds, "If you please."

Slowly, they find their feet: Ramus still clad in his janitor's suit, and Bee more than a little conspicuous in her bright red dress. Ramus reaches for Bee's hand, and, though frowning, she allows him to take it. It makes me wonder if she doesn't like him or if she just likes her space. Ramus pulls her to our leader, though, jaw flexing, like he doesn't care if Bee wants to hold his hand or not. Now, if Teo can get on with their tale, and skip the part where he publicly rebukes Ramus for bursting in on us, we can see his vision of this world and put the Living Rot behind us.

Gripping Ramus and Bee by the shoulders, Teo turns them so they face the rest of the group. I'm ridiculously apart from everyone, standing on the far side of the porch. Bee glances over at me briefly, her eyes darting back and forth, but I know she'll be fine. Object lessons are Teo's specialty. I wish I could give her a hug, though, since I remember what it's like to face a crowd of classmates while trying to do what Teo wants.

"Allow me to share a little tale," Teo says, stepping to the side of Ramus, who reaches out for Bee's waist, but she's too far away from him so he drops his hand.

"Once upon a time," Teo says, "a beautiful woman fell in love with a man. Pyramus and Thisbe of ancient Babylon," he gestures at the couple, "were not permitted to marry. Their parents hated each other. Sounds familiar, does it not? Resembles the tale of Shakespeare's *Romeo and Juliet*?"

I remember this story. Pyramus and Thisbe—that was creative of Teo to change their names to Bee and Ramus. I can't wait to hear how he recounts the tale. Maybe he'll have them recite lines, like when Pyramus said, "O kiss me through the hole of this vile wall!" I love Shakespeare. I love all his plays. Teo knows that. I realize I'm grinning, and I probably look like a deranged idiot, so I force my face to go straight. But Teo must see that I'm happy because he winks at me, so I wink right back, which is something I've done—well, maybe never in front of a group.

It's hard not to bounce; the world is so beautiful at night, here in Elysian Fields. The night is warm and still, and I'm so happy to be a part of everything.

"Before we begin," Teo says, looking out at everyone, "won't you do me the honor of following me?" It somehow seems natural that he should lead us away from the porch to somewhere else. He steers Bee across the front of Ramus's gray stone house, and when they turn to go to the back, it's easy for me to follow, too.

Ramus, though, keeps glancing around, like he's unsure about following. Romeo mumbles something in his thick twang, clapping his friend on the back, so Ramus follows Bee and Teo, shoulders hunched. Patience, Ramus, patience. You just need to give Teo time.

Romeo and Juliet scamper behind Ramus, Juliet's curlicues bouncing as she bends over to scratch her legs. A quick glance tells me the other couples are following. The boy with pink and green hair—Tristan?—and his partner keep giggling at the way poor Juliet's scratching her legs, and the other Doublemint girl starts spouting off random acronyms again while her partner laughs. I wish everyone would focus more on the story; maybe wherever Teo is taking us will do the trick.

My eyes comb over the side-yard grass, spotting Marcus for the very first time, but he doesn't seem to notice me— he's too busy looking through the trees. I glance where he's looking, but there's nothing to see. The porch lights, moon, and stars offer very little light.

When I round the back corner of the house, I pause. There's this square platform off the back of Ramus's house, with a red curtain veiling the front of a giant box made of rock and brick. It looks more like a holding cell for something huge, like an elephant or a giraffe. But Teo's vision isn't waning—he's prepared us a stage. I almost wish I were Thisbe and got to recite some of the lines, but this isn't Persephone's story.

A string of lights dots the platform, casting a slightly brighter glow than the lantern on the front porch; besides that, the rest of the yard is cast in shadows, so I situate myself at the front of the group to have the best look.

Standing at the front of the platform, Teo cups Bee's elbow, and Ramus hunches awkwardly on the side with his hands in his pockets. I'd like to tell him to go stand next to Bee, but I'm sure Teo will handle this, so I don't say a thing.

As soon as the last of the couples round the back of the house, with Jonas bringing up the rear carrying that stun gun again, Teo rips the curtain to the side to reveal a wall.

"Ladies and gentleman," Teo says, "this is not your normal stage. Remember how Pyramus and Thisbe conversed through a crack?"

I step closer to see what he means. And he's right— there's a crack in the wall! Just like in the tale!

Releasing Bee's arm, Teo moves to Ramus and grips his arm. "Sir," Teo says, "converse through the crack." I wish I had a copy of the play so I could show Ramus what Teo means.

Ramus looks to Teo, eyebrows shooting up, so Teo elbows Ramus in the side. "Somewhat difficult when no one's on the other side," Teo says, laughing. I feel I should laugh, too, but his laughter is out of place. Someone kicks a rock or something from the corner of my eye, and I know what Teo needs to do—feed Ramus a line.

But Teo's frowning. "As the story goes," he says, "you were forbidden to love the girl you wanted." He gestures to Bee, who looks like she's trying to smile, but she only succeeds in hitching her upper lip. "Thisbe was your family's enemy," Teo says. "That's why you conversed through the wall."

Ramus and Bee stand there, like someone's snatched their voice boxes and their power to act. Maybe it would go down smoother if we'd all read the story first.

"Need I spell it out for you?" Teo throws up his hands. "Get to the other side!" he shouts, taking a step toward Bee.

Bee jolts the moment Teo rounds on her, and my own stomach lurches, too. Bee didn't understand that's what he meant; I barely understood it, myself. But Bee's staring at Teo, eyes open wide, and then she's looking at me, and I smile at her a little, wishing I could take her by the hand and help her out.

But Bee squares her shoulders and fixes her eyes on Teo. "You want me to crawl over the rock." She doesn't look down at her dress, but anyone looking at her could see her outfit's impossible for climbing a wall.

"I've asked harder things before," Teo says. I hate how heartless that makes him seem. He should be explaining why it fits with the tale.

Someone whoops, and when a bunch of dreadlocks bounces in the dark, I know it's Abe pointing at the wall. "There are pegs!" Abe calls, and when I look closer, I see what he means. They're two or three feet apart, wooden and round.

As if that's what she needed to know, Bee reaches up and re-twists her hair so that it stretches tight against her head. "How many other girls get the chance to scale a wall in a dress?" she says, grinning at me, and I love Bee so much right now that I grin back. As soon as I saw the pegs, I *knew* she'd be up for this.

Kicking off her ballet flats, Bee steps up to the first peg, secures her foot, and grabs the next. Her hands and legs move fluidly, like it's not difficult at all climbing in a dress, and I can't help wondering if her dancing has helped her be coordinated like this. At the top, Bee turns around and flashes that grin again.

"Thanks for the pointer, Abe," Bee says.

Everyone cheers. Abe, on the periphery, pumps a fist in the air. Bee, one leg on either side of the wall, sways side to side, and Romeo claps Abe on the back. But Marc's looking through the trees again. Why's he always so distracted? It's like he has ADD. He's missing all the fun.

The Doublemint twins are clapping now, and Eloise keeps letting out these random shrieks while swishing her long black skirt. I could be wrong, but I doubt Teo's pleased with the raucous noise they're making. Maybe I can help calm them down.

Sure enough, Teo's folding his arms across his chest, frowning. *I'm sorry they're clowning around like this,* I wish I could say. Maybe it's hard for them to know how to honor the tale.

I need to do something. If I just stand by, Teo might lash out at them again and further alienate himself from the group. If I help him tell the story, then I could bridge the gap between his knowledge and them.

I hold my hand out to him, locking my eyes on his. He must read my desire to help, because he offers me a faint smile, like he's embarrassed that I've seen him struggling with the group. So I smile back, let him know I know this isn't an easy thing to do. His lips twitch minutely, like there's something he wants to say, but he drops his gaze to the ground.

My heart warms. I know how he's feeling—it's an emotion I've felt many times myself. When you're drowning and you don't know if you'll survive, you *need* someone to toss you a life preserver so you can continue to float. It's an honor to do something like that for him, because he has always, *always* done that for me.

Clearing my throat loudly, I open up my arm toward Bee, who's still dangling her feet over the edge of the wall.

"Thisbe," I say, pointing to my redheaded friend perched high on the wall, "would go to her room and converse with her lover through a crack." I try glaring at Bee, but when she doesn't get what I'm trying to say, I jerk my head toward the other side of the wall.

This works, for she's sighing, "All right, all right," and I watch as she swings her pale leg over the wall. *Thank you, Bee.*

I wait, and maybe two or three seconds later there's an "Oof!" That probably means she's landed—is she okay?— but then she calls out, "I'm fine, I'm fine."

Smiling, I move on with the tale. "So the lovers conversed through the wall," I repeat what Teo said moments before. Only Ramus has somehow lumbered away from the stage, so I gesture toward where he should be standing.

"Ramus," I say, trying to be patient, "stand over there."

Like he has the next ten years to act, Ramus strolls impossibly slowly over to the crack in the wall, hands in his pockets.

Seriously? I don't have time for this. So I move on and say, "And what did Pyramus say?" *Crap*. How did that line start? Nothing's coming. Crap, oh crap, oh crap. Maybe he'll improvise or something.

But Ramus shrugs, and I could shake him by the shoulders now. He opens his mouth. I tense, waiting to hear the eloquence rolling from his tongue, when he offers, "Hey."

I groan. Really? That's the best he can do? I try to make a joke out of it. "Pyramus was *most* eloquent."

Teo laughs, slow and happy, and all I need is his warmth beside me. It may take some time, but together, we can teach the others to love the stories as much as we do.

Smiling, Teo continues for me, "Of course, Pyramus didn't speak alone. His Thisbe talked right back."

Everything falls silent when at last Bee answers, "Hey, Ramus, lover. I saw you checking out my legs!"

Eloise slaps a hand over her mouth again, and the frizzy-haired Doublemint twin, Gwen, hunches over, holding her gut. Even Teo and I chuckle together. But Teo, recovering himself quickly, says over the laughter, "But the couple soon discovered the wall was not enough."

I join him. "So the couple decided to meet."

"At a mulberry tree," Teo says, smiling at me. Releasing my hand, he walks off the stage. I can't tell why until a string of lights flickers on and, like Teo said, there's a mulberry tree. He reaches up to touch one of the branches, and like the other trees in the front yards, this, too, is new—slim and short. "Thisbe arrived first," Teo says, studying the delicate leaves of the tree.

It's sort of awkward. Shouldn't Bee be on this side now?

"Thisbe stood there," Teo's saying, "and along came a lion. A female—her jaws drenched in blood. Terrified,

Thisbe fled, dropping her veil. Our dear maiden would not want to be consumed by a lion!"

A few people on the grass laugh, but it's only a hiccup compared to the laughter before. The Doublemint twins, plaid-shirted Romeo, even Sal with his glasses slipping down his nose, smile. But Marcus isn't smiling at all. He's whispering something to Cleo and pointing through the trees. Ugh. Why can't he pay attention to the most exciting part of the tale? It's his own fault for missing everything.

Looking away from Marcus, I join Teo next to the tree, and from the corner of my eye see Ana fidgeting again with the orange shawl on her head.

"When Pyramus arrived," I join Teo again, "he found his lover's veil."

And to my delight, Teo pulls a bit of tulle from his pocket, the edges red like they've been dipped in blood. Teo thinks of everything. I take the veil in my hands, eager to explain to everyone.

"Ramus found his lover's veil covered in blood," I say, holding it high above my head. I walk over to Ramus, who's standing at the front of the stage, and place the veil in his hands. He holds it, staring, obviously unsure what to do. So I explain for him.

"Naturally, with blood on the veil, Pyramus feared the worst." I look to Ramus, wishing he could at least pretend to be scared, and I lean right into his face. "He thought his maiden had been killed."

Someone gasps—Eloise, with her hand over her mouth. Abe smiles at her like he knows what's going on, wrapping a protective hand around her shoulder.

Teo joins us again on the stage, standing right beside me.

"And so," Teo says, "our young lover found a knife and killed himself, and when the young woman found him, she killed herself, too."

Marc's looking down at the ground and pulling his hair out of his eyes, and Cleo, beside him, coos something into his ear. Even Juliet's still scratching her legs. I'm not sure why they're not paying better attention.

Smiling down on everyone, Teo says, "It all seems anticlimactic, does it not?"

I have to agree.

"Um, Teo?" someone's muffled voice calls, and it takes me a minute to realize it's Bee—still behind the wall. Poor Bee. I had totally forgotten about her. She clears her throat, loudly. "Is it okay if I come out now?"

Teo bobs his head sideways, like he's saying both yes and no. "I suppose that is an option," he says, looking around, "but that would ruin the best part." He winks at me, and I'm not sure why. I thought we'd finished with the tale.

Staring straight ahead, Teo's eyes lock on an invisible scene. "Pyramus," he says, voice unusually flat, "do me a favor, and bring Thisbe back."

Ramus narrows his eyes at Teo, but after being in his company, I'm sure he's learned everything's easier when you listen the first time. Luckily, Ramus inches forward to examine the wall. Stretching out his fingers, he looks like he's about to reach for the first peg, when Jonas breaks from the crowd, blue sparks shooting from his hand. Someone gasps. So do I, because Jonas has activated the stun gun in his hand.

Spinning, Ramus spots Jonas's charged weapon. He sprints up the wall, his feet slipping a little as he climbs. But he's quick, and apparently somewhat athletic, because he makes it to the top and disappears over it. What I don't get is why Jonas is threatening Ramus with his stun gun. Was it really necessary to bully him, just because he took a little while? Plus, we already reenacted the tale and Pyramus was never on the same side as Thisbe when they talked.

I reach out to pull on Teo's arm and ask what's going on, when Teo pulls something from his pocket. I look down at his hand to find him clicking a button on a remote.

A loud noise sounds, like the earth cracking open, as the entire curtained wall shifts. At first, I'm not sure what it means. There was nothing like moving walls in the tale, but when the wall shifts to the side, a gaping hole opens up with Ramus and Bee staring at us from the other side. Their legs and feet look dirty—like they're standing in wet paint, but the smell is worse, something acrid and decayed, like they're standing in a piece of road kill's grave, and a flash of fur springs from the hole, disappearing on the other side.

My blood freezes, knowing what I just saw. Teo's opened up a hole for a *lion* to spring out, and something tells me the stuff on Ramus and Bee isn't paint. They've been unknowingly standing in blood. The lion roars, and I cover my ears, because Ramus and Bee are inside. Teo's just set a lion on them.

Teo clicks the remote so the wall closes again, and siren-like sounds pierce my ears—Ramus's and Bee's screams.

I spin toward Teo, grabbing him by the arms. "What are you doing?" I scream. He must not realize what he's done. "They're on the other side," I explain, because my Teo would never purposely let loose a lion on two people in a cage. He would never stand by and watch as a lion chews them up.

A sound like the jaws of hell opening up rings in my ears. It's the lion, confined in a much too little space. Everything gets blurry—there're people running and too many limbs. Abe's dreadlocks brush my face as he runs past me. Romeo shouts his name, and I look around to see Abe trying to climb over the wall. But blue lights flash as Jonas presses the stun gun into their bodies, and there's hardly any sound. It's like they know they should be screaming, but everyone's gone mute. Thinking, running. Jonas swings his stun gun much too fast.

Teo smiles, and I'm choking. It feels like I've been shot in the chest. This isn't who he is. Teo would never do this. He loves and kisses me, saves us from the Living Rot, chats with me about the tales, makes me CDs, and helps me with my books.

There's a thud; Abe's body lies at my feet. I stare at him, at the dreadlocks fallen across his face, when there's another thud; Cleo lies unconscious next to Abe now. Why is Jonas shocking everyone to the ground?

Pounding sounds on the other side of the wall—I stagger closer—but two strong hands hold me back. I pull on the arms, but it's Marcus, his nails digging into my arm. A few paces off, I spot Teo, who's sighing, smiling. *Smiling.*

Wrenching myself from Marcus's fingers, I lunge at Teo's face. Because *this* face is not the one I loved, salivated over for months. This person is not him. As soon as I make contact, though, Teo's somehow grabbing my wrists, and his fingers are impossible to move. I try twisting, thrashing against his grasp, but he's death itself, hollow, wearing a mask. Those black eyes aren't seeing anything, only taking pleasure in the shrieks. Shrieks of living and breathing human beings, my friends, Ramus and Bee.

There's a crash behind the wall, and Bee's frantic voice drifts out, laced with fear and pain. She shrieks, the shrill sound imploding my ears, and I'm not sure how I'll do it, but I know I have to get her out.

Twisting in Teo's grasp, I scream, tears burning in my eyes, "Teo, you bastard, get them out!"

But he doesn't hear me. He's inclined his head a fraction to the right, in the opposite direction from me, as if purposely tuning me out.

So I dig my nails into his hands, and his grip loosens a bit, and I take the opportunity to wrench my hands away, racing straight for the wall.

I'm almost there, maybe two feet from the brick edge, when footsteps echo behind me. Bee shrieks a string of profanities before the lion roars and everything stops.

My heart pounds in my ears, my stomach clenches, and I can't accept the sound, refuse to let my stomach empty out. Why has the screaming stopped? Maybe she's found some cavity in the rock and is hiding—*that's* why everything's quiet now.

I reach for a peg; my foot finds another, and I'm just about to reach for another handhold when a large, calloused hand folds over mine. I try shaking the hand loose, but it grips harder, so I look up to find Marcus gently pulling me away.

"Cheyenne…" Marcus whispers, shaking his floppy-haired head. Liquid glistens in his eyes, but he doesn't let the moisture fall—it's trapped inside. Wrapping his arms around me, he pulls me away from the stage. Like a blanket around a hornet, he protects me from the elements and the elements from me.

I want to throw him, sting him where I stand, but I know he hasn't done this. Bee's no longer screaming, but not because of him. The man I thought I loved *killed* them. Killed. The word feels so wrong. It's not possible for someone to do such a thing. Turning to face Teo, I try to find the words, but instead the moment I shared with him inside his room flashes inside my head. The way he kissed my neck and how I shuddered in pleasure because of him. The caresses, the chats we've had about the tales. How could I never have seen this about him?

With one fluid motion, Teo pushes his brother aside and wraps his hungry fingers around my waist, searing my skin.

Raising my hand high into the air, he cries, "And so it has begun!" His call curls out to those inching backward on the grass. Romeo tucks Juliet into his plaid chest. Abe, rising from the ground, falls into Eloise's arms. Ana mauls her scarf with her hands.

A volcano rages in Teo's gaze. He looms above me; the spirits of the dead lurk in his face. "Seven men and seven women," he murmurs, scalding my ears. Running his thumb down my cheek—I am shrinking, shaking—he adds, "I am sorry to say there was not room for eight."

8

I stare at the red curtain Teo has used to cover his twelve-foot wall. It didn't take him long to get the lion back into the hole. Jonas tossed in a wad of meat and Teo hit the button on the remote like nothing ever happened. Nothing at all.

I try pushing aside the fear, the pain, the horrified way I feel about him. He *murdered* Ramus and Bee. And not with as much as a hint of remorse. He's disposed of them like used Kleenex. This isn't the same person I've known for two years, the man I wanted to be with.

Clutching my waist, Teo's fingers dig into my skin. I feel soiled, dirty for being near him. To think I actually *helped* him tell that story, took part in the murder of Ramus and Bee.

The other couples dot Ramus's yard like clustered clams washed up on the beach at night. They sit, shifting. Ana bites her nails, and Sal, next to her, rubs his sweaty palms on his jeans. Eloise and Abe hold each other, quaking. Little shrieks keep bubbling out of Eloise's mouth, and I know why. Bee was her friend.

It must be past midnight—it seems like years ago that I first came, but it's only been one very long day. Maybe if I close my eyes, I'll wake up, and laugh with Teo over my dream. I squeeze my eyes shut, and when I work the muscles in my cheeks, I know this isn't a dream; I'll never wake.

With the red curtain closed, everyone stares at the stage, as if contemplating what Teo has done, what other animal might spring from the hole. It makes me wonder how the lion got down there, and if there are more things, apart from the snake and the lion, trapped beneath the ground.

Trapped. We're all trapped, except for Ramus and Bee. I don't understand how Teo could kill them.

Teo releases my waist, and I swear he'll never hold me in that seahorse grasp again. Stalking toward the group, he's like a panther considering his next meal. "I shall now congratulate you on your faithfulness," he says over Eloise's cries as she floods Abe's shirt with her tears. "As of yet, no one else has marred my name."

Cleo studies the ground, gritting her teeth, and Marcus, beside her, leans over to whisper something in her ear. I watch numbly as she whispers back. Has Marc known of his brother's deceit all along?

Teo seems blind to the exchange. He's saying something about reporting any misdeeds we see in the future, when I realize I know why Ramus and Bee were killed. Ramus stood up to Teo for being alone with *me*. I have Ramus's blood on my hands. And Bee's.

I sway where I stand, with the stage behind me, and I find Marcus watching me. His mouth pulls down, like he can see the weight I feel, but he presses his lips together and nods, like I'm supposed to keep going. But how can I just stand here with Ramus's and Bee's deaths hanging over me?

Teo strides to the back of the group, encircling the men and women like they're his fresh kill. It makes me wonder if anyone else knew he had murder in his heart. Maybe that's why they all left Cleo's when I wanted to know their names. And Marc. He wasn't trying to stop me because he was jealous, but because he knows what his brother is. I try meeting his gaze again, but he's leaning over with his head in his hands. Marcus needs someone to nod at *him*.

"And now for our rules," Teo says, his voice stone cold. "They are, indeed, simple." He holds up one finger at a time. "First, never question me." He pauses for a moment, I suppose to detect any rebellion, probably from Marcus, but his head is down, and Cleo's staring at the ground.

"Second," Teo continues, "you must prove yourselves to me. The second is really a clarification of the first, but really, all the inner workings of our world adhere to these two rules."

I'm not really sure what Teo means by "proving ourselves to him," but after seeing Ramus's and Bee's deaths, I have no doubt it isn't good. And one of the Doublemint girls must be thinking the same thing because she's glancing around, her ponytail whipping madly around her face, the light of the moon highlighting her large eyes.

"And third," Teo smiles sweetly, "never forget that you're part of a pair. Commit to each other. You are part of a greater calling now. Embrace our world."

From the corner of my eye, I see Jonas skulking behind the group. He reaches into his pocket and hits something— probably another remote—causing the lights on the mulberry to flicker before going out.

Shadows fall more heavily across the crowd, draping over the contours of Teo's face, making his cheekbones stick out. He scans the crowd, I suppose searching for someone. I wonder who he's looking for—Marcus?—when Teo stops moving and he frowns. It's impossible to see who he's looking at, but someone's whispering, and when Teo says, "Cleo," the whispering stops. Raising his voice a few notches, he says, "Please, won't you stand?"

In the darkness, I watch as a beaded head rises above the others; Teo must have called on her because she wasn't listening just now.

"My dear Cleo," Teo says, "do you remember what I asked you all in the beginning?"

Cleo nods her head, beads clattering in the silent night. "Stay on your own gender's side of the street. Until the parties," she clarifies. "The men may enter the women's side for those." Part of me wants to offer reasons for why we shouldn't go strolling on the other side. Like snakes, for example. And lions. But I keep my mouth shut. No need to tempt Teo's wrath.

"Excellent, Cleo," Teo says. He extends his hands as if to embrace her, though she's much too far away. "I would like to reiterate what I said earlier. There are simply three overarching rules. What were they, may I ask?" Teo turns suddenly toward me and locks his deathly eyes on my face. It's like cockroaches are crawling all over me. Was I really just making out with him in his room? I should slash my wrists.

My stomach churns; he's waiting for me to tell him something—oh, yes, to repeat his "overarching rules," so I open my mouth. "Don't question you," I squeak, "prove ourselves, and—" Dear God, what was the other one?

A low voice calls from the crowd, "Never forget your other half."

I peer out at the couples sprawled out on the grass, and realize it's Marcus who's helped me just now. Despite what I thought about him earlier, I sort of want to run and hide with him wherever he was looking in the woods.

"That is right," Teo smiles, falsely, not bothering to turn his head. It looks like he's going to pretend I was the one who gave all the rules, and I'm not sure if that's lucky, or if he'll use the moment to hurt me later. I'm not sure which I'd prefer.

But I see it now, how he's really been selfish all along. He tells us he's our savior, but what he really wants is to rule a little cult where we worship him, fan his vanity. I used to think of him as handsome, disarming, but now all I see is a black, cold heart draped in the cloak of a much-too-thin man. The worst part is, there's nowhere to run. What am I supposed to do? Flee to the outside world without the vaccine?

"Some of you might question my methods," Teo is saying, "but to demonstrate my great brotherly love, my equal footing with you all, I announce a great change." Teo studies the wilting frames of the men and women on the grass, and I mean to study them, too, when his iron-manacled hand grabs mine and he laces his creepy-crawly fingers through my own. I want to vomit, hurl the kisses we've shared from my mouth. He wants me to remain beside him, but how can I when he's killed Ramus and Bee?

I look up to find Marcus watching me. It's hard to see in the faint light, but the set of his drooping shoulders tells me he's just as lost. He's not mentally unstable. His brother is.

Teo's watching the couples, his body perfectly motionless except for the grip of his fingers on my own. Voice measured and low, he says, "I will now be moving into Pyramus's house."

A chill scurries up my spine. He kills, then, "Oh, looky there! This looks like a wonderful house for me." I must not be the only one thinking the same thing, because Marc's shoulders aren't drooping anymore; they're drawing up tight. And one of the boys—I can make out a collar on his shirt, so it might be plaid, which would make it Romeo—walks around several of the couples to stand beside Marc. I watch as the boys tilt their heads toward each other and speak, but their voices are so low, and I'm so far away, there is absolutely no way I can hear what they say.

Teo's still talking, saying I'll be moving into Bee's. The bones in my fingers become so brittle that they might snap off, so I keep them in Teo's fist, though I yearn to pull away. I don't understand how he thinks it's okay for me to live in Bee's house. Bee was a leader and a friend. She was also their student body president—they had voted for her because they liked her so much. She spoke, they listened. She laughed, they laughed. And now she's gone because of him.

I watch as Jonas, in his bright white clothes, squirts something on the red curtain. My insides whimper. He's scrubbing off blood.

My nails dig into my palms, and I tense to lash out— claw Teo's face—but what would he do? Smile at me before punishing me by killing someone else?

Numb, I listen to whatever else Teo says. He tells us Jonas will be living in his old house, and something about the mailboxes, but I don't really care. His world is sick and twisted, perfect to cover up his greed.

"In *our* world," Teo's voice goes up a few notches, making it impossible to push him out, "perfection shall be known. By day," he glances over to the only person wearing glasses, so it must be Sal, "we shall live in study, modeling our lives after those we re-enact. Your homes are filled with the appropriate literature. Study the person you have become. There is a greatness in symbolism. An unparalleled truth."

I watch as Sal cocks his head to the side, as if considering what Teo is telling him, like he *wants* to experience this "unparalleled truth." And it makes me shrivel up and curse myself for knowing I wanted the same thing.

"At night," Teo prowls around the couples, "shall be our evening soirées." The Doublemint girls suddenly look up, eyes brightening. Teo smiles at them. "Each couple shall have the chance to host one, and dazzle us with your ability to bring your stories to life." The girls look at each other like they're excited about this part, and it makes everything inside me wilt seeing they're already willing to move past Bee.

Teo squeezes my hand, forcing me to tune in. In a low voice, he warns, "Do not fail in your soirées. You shall have the opportunity but once, for if you fail to impress your neighbors, there shall be no need for you to have the vaccine."

Spiders crawl inside of me; I was right. Yes, we will all bow to Teo and plant a smile on our lips, because otherwise we'll join Ramus and Bee.

"Until tomorrow!" Teo claps, making me jolt, and I watch as the other couples—six, now—scramble to their feet. Abe holds out a hand to help Eloise stand; Ana almost face-plants when she trips over her orange sari. I'm too hollow to have the heart to help, too busy feeling Teo's words drip into my head. Soirées. Artistry. Prove yourselves. Vaccine. My mind sputters as I think. The couples trickle away, with Marcus walking stiffly next to Cleo, and Jonas bringing up the rear, stun gun in hand.

Teo grips me around the waist and kisses me on the neck; roaches scurry across my skin. "It will take some time," he says softly, his breath suddenly rank against my face, "but you will come to love how I run this world. Greatness requires sacrifice. I am only relieved you are here."

As he steers me away from Ramus's and Bee's stage, my eyes snag on the red curtain and I realize something. Elysian Fields is nothing but a dark stage, and we are Teo's marionettes. He tips his hand to the right, we jostle our hands and feet; he flicks his hand down, and we're forced to bow low. We have no choice but to play along, because if we don't, he'll cut our strings and watch as we crash on the ground, shattering.

I'm not really sure which bothers me more: that I actually wanted to be his puppet, or that he clearly enjoys cutting our strings.

9

I lie in Bee's silk-sheeted bed, horrified that the girl whose home I invaded this morning, and the first boy to question Teo, are now gone, dead. I should have tried to defend them. Made Teo stop.

Staring at the painted vines on the walls of Bee's bedroom, I wonder what she thought when she looked at them. She must have seen how odd it was, but was willing to do anything to avoid the Living Rot. I hate the idea that she and Ramus might have been killed because Ramus busted in on Teo and me. It's all my fault.

Just because you love someone doesn't mean you should. Oh, Bee. You were right. When you woke up in the morning, you probably looked at yourself in those large mirrors, but now I don't think I can even look at myself. You should be walking through that door, telling me to scoot over in this bed, shimmying down in the covers and falling asleep next to me.

I flip my pillow over, struggling with the thought that I had actually loved this man. He's insane. I wish I could undo the last thirteen months. The last week, all the glances, the touch of his lips on mine. I can't believe I clutched my pillow, like this one but in my own bed, swooning over the time we first kissed. *He kissed me,* I had crooned, and marveled over the beauty, calling it the best moment of my life.

I may need to gargle Ajax tonight.

Forcing my eyes closed, I try pushing all thoughts of Teo aside, forcing the image of his face to the far side of the vined room. But it's impossible, because the only thing I can remember is the way Teo *always* dances with deceit. Like when he asked me to drive his car after the math meets, park a few blocks away from the school, and wait for him to come. When I asked him why *he* shouldn't be the one to drive his car, he'd chuckled, "What would be the fun in that?" And I'd enjoyed that rush from breaking the rules with him.

There was his insistence on "higher meanings," the way he bent the truth. *I'm not really your teacher right now,* he would say, excusing the fact that his arm was around my waist when I lingered in his classroom after calculus. *I'm simply someone who enjoys discussing literature with his friend.* I had always thought he lived on a higher plane, but now I see he likes to twist the truth.

Something clicks in the house. It's slight—I'm not sure if it's anything beyond the air conditioning or the window, but it makes my blood freeze. Easing out of bed, I tiptoe across my room to the square window at the back. But nothing's there. I hear something else—this time I can tell it's coming from down the hall.

Slinking across the carpet, I tremble as I move toward the living room in the dark, grateful Bee's house isn't as jam-packed as Cleo's. Please don't tell me Teo has returned.

A dark figure lurks at the back doorway. Spasms shoot through my skin until I spot the messy hair. It's Marcus, and with his shorter, broader stature, he couldn't look less like his brother.

I sprint through the room and whisk the door wide open. "Marcus," I breathe. But I don't know what else to say. Why has he come? Teo reminded us the men aren't allowed on the women's side of the street.

Marcus holds his finger to his lips and steps through the door. "Shh."

We stand there—bodies inches apart—and for some bizarre reason my heart rate reacts. It shoots around my chest. I'm excited to see him, but *why* am I excited to see him? I can't be one of those girls who gets all hyper just because there's a boy around.

"What?" Marcus asks, typically raging eyes calmed.

But I ignore him, unsure how he could also affect me like this. Instead, I study his somber cheeks, his flatter version of Teo's nose. The longer hair. And his scent: sheetrock, bark chips. And paint.

"He's dead because of me," Marcus says, and I know what he means. He's blaming himself for the death of Ramus. "Bee, too. It was my idea to bust in on you and my brother."

I remember the silent exchange between him and Romeo, how it really did seem like it was Marcus's idea to come.

"*I* should have done something," I eventually say. "Ramus and Bee—they tried to help me out." They actually told me their names.

Marcus looks away, mumbling a potpourri of four-letter words. But when he speaks clearly, he's nearly whispering. "Ramus and I spent every weekend together for months."

I grit my teeth. Ramus wasn't just the boy who died with Bee—he was somebody, Marc's friend. Once again, I think of us all as Teo's marionettes and of how helpless I feel tied to his strings. There's nothing I can do, and

I hate feeling useless. I like to help. But when Marcus scuffs the ground with his shoe, no doubt feeling the loss of his friend, I say what little I can. "I am so, so sorry, Marcus."

A second passes before a smile flickers across his face. "The thing that gets me is, Ramus just wanted to care about something. He's been in a funk for months. But then he gets concerned about you and Teo, and suddenly there's a spark in his eyes. So for the first time in forever, he stands up for something. And what does he get?"

I look away from him. What I could have done, could have said, replays in my head. Some say guilt weighs as heavily as a ton of bricks, but the truth is it weighs far less than you'd think—it has a way of eating up your insides until there's nothing left. How could I have let it happen? Both Ramus and Bee are dead. I think of asking him more about Ramus and Bee—how the boys spent their weekends together, how graceful Bee was when she danced.

Marcus studies my face like he's trying to figure out what I'm thinking right now, but there are no words. How can I tell him how sorry I am that they are dead? He must think I'm such a fool for playing along with Teo's game. Running his fingers through his shaggy hair, he looks away, and I'm not sure whether it's because he thinks my stupidity is contagious or not. My heart feels like it's stuffed with marbles, and my throat constricts, but I don't say anything, because there's nothing to say.

"You really were in love with him, weren't you?" Marcus asks, his eyes darting to my face again before moving away.

I laugh nervously. Open my mouth to respond, but end up closing it again. I'm not sure what I should say. It doesn't matter much since we both know I do—did. I'd like to know how he knew about Teo and me, and why his brother is like this. But I shouldn't wonder any of it, because Teo was right in front of my face. "I feel so stupid," I say, looking down at my feet.

Marcus shakes his head and reaches out for me, but his hand stops in mid-air. "It's taken me a few years to figure him out. And yet he still tends to surprise me. I had no idea he'd kill them."

So I guess I'm not the only one. A silence falls between us, and it's so uncomfortable I want to put my hands over my face and sob that I am *so* sorry I was wrong. But his shoulders are sagging. He's feeling guilty, too. Maybe he should, maybe he shouldn't. Maybe we've both done wrong, but I refuse to make excuses for us. I won't explain away the truth.

Marcus tentatively touches my arm, saying, "I need you to do something for me." When Teo touched me, it was electric and thrilling, but unsure; with Marcus it's all of that at once, but wrapped in a layer of calm, something steady and solid. And all from touching my arm. "I need you to pretend you love Teo still," he adds.

I step away from him, disgusted. Teo is *sick*. Marcus tousles the front of his hair again, pulling it down the side of his eyes. He does that when he's uncomfortable, I've noticed. "You've seen my brother when he doesn't get what he wants," Marcus says. "He's chosen you. Unless he chooses someone else, you have to pretend to love him back."

I shake my head to let his words fall away. I don't want Teo to have chosen me. I don't want to pretend. I want to go back to yesterday, when everything made sense. "You think he might choose someone else?" I ask with a flicker of hope. It's a selfish wish, but maybe it's just what

I need. He could like Cleo, for instance, and that would make me free.

"You never know with my brother," Marcus says, running his hand over his stubbled face. "Sometimes he can be faithful, but other times it's like he feels entitled to help himself."

Before, I thought I could do anything for Teo—fly if he asked me to. But now that I know who he is, the responsibility weighs me down. It's like I'm holding twelve-ton crates, and I'm tired, and it's only been one night.

Marcus seems to see the weariness in my face, because he says, "Just keep doing what you're doing. So far, it's worked great." He doesn't meet my eyes, and I wonder if it's because my feelings for his brother sickened him before. I wish he knew that I could never love a man who kills.

But now that I know who Teo really is, Marcus and I will hopefully see things more eye to eye. This morning, which seems like an eternity ago, we didn't, but thinking about our constant disagreement reminds me of when we argued over how everyone got here, so I have to ask, "Why did you bring fourteen other people here when you knew your brother was like this?"

Marcus opens up his palms defensively and takes a step back on the hardwood floor. "It was that or be killed by the Living Rot. It's more widespread than Beijing ever got. It's taken all the southern states since we arrived here, so it's lucky we're safe."

My heart jumps to my throat. I can't believe we didn't know any of this was going on. How was Teo so ready when we didn't have a clue? And how long until it took the whole US? "I didn't see that footage…"

Marcus nods. "Cleo has a few other tapes. Teo left them with her since everyone tends to pay attention to her house."

They pay attention to her tight-fitting dresses and implants, he means. I may just need to mutter a few profanities of my own.

"Not that I'm into her," Marcus stammers, looking sideways at me. "She's a little too obvious for me."

I raise my eyebrow; Marcus was flirting with her last night. But it doesn't matter, so I let the comment pass. If he likes her, he likes her. That's that.

Marc's eyes are all over the house—the benches, the plants and painted arched windows, the cracks on the walls. He's looking anywhere but at me. "About my brother," he says, staring at the closest stringy-looking plant on the floor, "don't beat yourself up about him. *Everyone's* susceptible to his charm. But when he left you outside today, I don't know. I kind of snapped."

Something inside of me melts, and I stare at the plant, too. Not that snapping seems that irregular of an occurrence for Marcus, but the fact that he wanted to snap, makes me want it, too. Even though I'm not entirely sure how.

Grabbing the handle of the back door, Marcus looks back at me. "Promise to pretend to love him back?"

I nod, wishing I could see an end to this madness. But what if we're trapped here for the rest of our lives? What if Teo expects me to *do things* with him?

Marc's eyes flash like he knows exactly what I'm thinking. His hand reaches toward me and pulls up my chin. There's that crackle of electricity again, jolting through me. He lets go quickly. Too quickly. "Don't worry," he says to me, a gentle smile resting on his lips, "you'll only need to put up the act until we find out how to grab the vaccine and leave this place."

He's right. We'll play along until we earn the vaccine. No, we can do better than that. We find the medicine, then bolt. If we're lucky, we can skip out earlier than I thought. I'm feeling lighter. "So, what's stopping us from leaving tonight?"

"We can't," Marcus reminds me. "There's some type of fence. But don't worry—we'll figure it out. I think it's electric or something. Ty—I mean, Romeo, says he saw some type of control panel in Jonas's house. Maybe it's just a matter of turning it off."

"But the Living Rot—maybe they knocked the power out."

"Oh." Marcus frowns. "Teo has a massive generator with some sort of underground wiring that connects us to the regular power grid. He told us before. He also said to enjoy the produce since it's not like we can get any more."

I'm gaping at him, not believing he's talking about produce in a time like this, and then I'm bowing my head, unable to utter a word. I can't register this. I can't be stuck here forever with him and—

"Cheyenne."

I look up, and suddenly Marc's eyes are planted firmly on my own, which makes my chest tremble, not from fear, but because it's nice to have someone looking at me with so much warmth, like hot chocolate in a snowstorm. But the warmth is fleeting, because Marcus looks away. He must be remembering how I loved his brother. He must think I'm so stupid for loving him.

Marc's shoulders hunch as he opens the back door. He's leaving, and I don't know what to say.

"Study your books," he tells me, but I want him to, I don't know, walk over to the bookshelf with me and help me find the right books. Not because I'm incapable of looking by myself, but because I like this feeling between us—warm and comfortable. Not just hot chocolate, but a snug, downy quilt.

Marcus closes the door behind him, and as I listen to the soft crunch of the grass as he moves away, I can't push away the thought that I don't want him to leave.

10

I've been reading Greek mythology for over an hour now, and I feel like I know what I need to know about my character. Persephone was just a girl who was abducted from her mother by the god of the Underworld, Hades, who tricked her into eating a pomegranate seed. Anyone who ate or drank anything in the Underworld was required by the Fates to stay. Because she ate several, she had to return to the Underworld for a season every year. Wonderful.

Not that Teo would want me to leave. He would never want me to face the sickness. Marcus desires to go; I do, too, but maybe it's safer inside. If we go out there we're definitely dead—and in here we're maybe dead. The odds almost seem equally weighted.

Someone knocks. Please, God, don't send Teo over to me this early. Tossing aside the book I've been studying, I run to the door, open it a crack, and look outside. But God is kind to me this morning. It's not Teo, but a girl. I open the door wider and see her smile, her blonde hair. Gwen or Izzy. I don't remember which Doublemint girl is which. Not that it matters.

"Breakfast," the platinum blonde says, pointing to a basket on the ground. Plucking it up, I invite her in, and while we walk to the kitchen I peek inside. Muffins. Cranberry orange—my favorite. Digging beneath a red cloth, I find something else—lime yogurt. Again, my favorite.

"I brought your invitation," Doublemint girl says, waving what looks like a roll of aged paper in her hand, and I'm completely lost as to where she'd find something like that. "You forgot to check your mail, but then I remembered how last night it looked like you were zoning out."

I hold out my hand—she was watching me? I'll need to be careful not to let Teo see me blocking him out.

She hands over the scroll and I notice the wax seal, like the invitation comes from royalty. "Whoever hosts the party sends out invitations," she says. "I don't think you were paying attention when Teo asked Romeo and Juliet to host the next soirée."

Okay, I really need to start paying better attention when Teo speaks. Even if the words coming out of his mouth are worse than cockroaches—fire ants, maybe.

Staring at the aged scroll in my hands, I slip my finger under the wax and break the seal. Opening up the parchment roll, I find an invitation written in calligraphy.

"Wow," I muse. It looks like Romeo and Juliet are off to a good start, with the flourishing writing and perfectly phrased prose.

The girl—I'm still not sure which Doublemint twin she is, so I stare at her for a moment to see if anything pops. *Big eyes.* Yes! This girl definitely has large, green eyes. The bug-eyed girl is Izzy, I'm pretty sure.

Smiling confidently with a piece of gum sticking out between the side of her teeth, she points out the time. "Seven o'clock. Teo's particular about no one being late."

"Thank you," I say, wondering slightly why she's helping me. I haven't a clue, but maybe I can return the favor. "Is there anything I can do for you?"

Izzy pats my hand, her green eyes bulging. "I just wanted to chat," she says, prancing into the living room. Her green dress skims the floor behind her as she runs, and I haven't the slightest idea why she's running farther into my house. I just want to eat my muffin.

"That's so unfair." Izzy frowns at the two benches that form an L in the great room. "Where's a girl to lie down?" She glares at the benches like they're made of old socks, then flippantly turns away from them, causing her ponytail to slap her in the face.

"So… Izzy, right?" I ask, wondering why she's staying now.

She nods, petting the chocolate-colored hardwood floor, and I'm wondering if she's lonely or something.

"You know," I say, because I don't have anything else, "if I were you, I'd go by Isolde." *Tristan and Isolde*—one of my favorite tragedies of all time. The way Isolde tended to Tristan's wounds, so far away from everybody…

Izzy smacks her gum. "You *so* did not call me that."

"I'm sorry?" What could be her problem with the name? I've always loved it. I like the spelling, too.

"Is. Old." Izzy folds her arms across her chest, chewing her gum loudly. "I'm only seventeen."

This is what I call missing the point of the story completely. One of the great things about the old tales is how they let you forget your own worries and put yourself in the characters' heads. "Isolde," or "Iseult," is an Irish name. Much cooler than Persephone.

Izzy stretches across the hardwood to touch her toes. It's a common enough stretch, but she does it with such ease, such enthusiasm, I have to ask, "Cheerleader?"

A large smile spreads across Izzy's face. "How did you know?" Even her green eyes are popping now.

"Just a random guess." I plaster a winning smile across my face. But just because Izzy's a cheerleader doesn't mean we can't be friends. Maybe if I show her something about the stories, she can embrace her name and we can get off to a better start.

Reaching for the book I was studying before, I thumb through, find a picture of Isolde, and hand it to her. "Just so you know, there's a reason two men fought over the original Isolde."

Izzy leans over, her platinum ponytail staying perfectly intact. She scrunches her forehead up in thought, then looks to me, green eyes shining. "She's *way* cuter than me." Okay, not exactly the *let's bond over Tristan and Izzy* moment I was looking for, but her vulnerability is almost something. Better than Cleo, at least.

I lean over and pat her hand. "Izzy, you're gorgeous," I say. "You have nothing to worry about." I mean it. Marc's school was quite the opposite from mine; the math team at my school, Khabela, didn't know about breath mints or tweezers, but Marc's school, Griffin, must have drafted supermodels.

Dabbing at her mascara, Izzy hands me back the hefty book, and I set it next to me on the floor. "I'm sorry," she sniffs. "I can't tell you how difficult it is living in this place. I mean, there isn't even a gym!"

"You're kidding." And now we're back to square one.

"I've been on the squad since fifth grade," Izzy says, mauling the gum in her mouth, "and I *need* my exercise."

Because the rest of us don't?

Izzy leans forward, eyes wide. "Don't you think Tristan's smokin' hot?" I'm pretty sure Tristan's the one with the pink and green hair—I think I'd spend too much time worrying about it rubbing off on me. So, no, I don't really think he's "smokin' hot," but I smile encouragingly anyway.

"And for the life of me," Izzy flips her ponytail, "I keep thinking I should call him Kyle, since that's his *real* name, but I gotta tell ya, I like 'Tristan' better. His mom lives in Florida, and he flies out there every summer. He teaches *surfing* and snorkeling and even swam with sharks. Not to mention his break dancing…"

I tune out Izzy. Snorkeling and sharks. If Ramus and Bee were killed by a lion, what does that mean for the rest of us? Teo, no doubt, has hidden deadly animals or weapons relating to all of our tales all around the property.

Taking in a breath, Izzy leans in, not realizing my mind is somewhere else. "And you wouldn't believe what he says he shaved."

Whoa. I feel my eyes widen. "Hey, Izzy," I say, thinking fast, "what do you think about this place?"

"We're alive," she says, blowing a bubble and letting it pop. "Give me a gym and I'd be great."

"But…" Isn't she scared by what happened last night? Or maybe working out was her coping mechanism. Like if she ran a couple of miles, she could take Teo down. But I'm not sure anyone can take Teo down. Not when he has someone like Jonas around.

Izzy leans toward me, shooting me that bug-eyed, conspiratorial look again. "Look," she whispers, "I know what you're asking. Teo fr-*reaks* me out, but I can't show that face. If the others hear about it, they might tattle. Remember what he said? We're to report anyone who doesn't live by his rules. We *all* wanted to leave. Trust me. But nobody's willing to try anything now after what happened with that lion."

I shiver, thinking of Bee. Izzy's right. The others might turn us in if they catch wind of any type of revolt. Maybe if I understood more about who they are, I could learn what it'd take for them to go from protecting themselves to protecting each other.

Leaning back again, Izzy examines her nails. "Pity your manicure didn't hold up as well as mine."

"Just tell me," I keep my voice low, praying there aren't hidden cameras, "who likes this place? And who doesn't?"

Izzy wiggles her manicured fingers on her lap. "A few of the guys tend to waffle back and forth, but Cleo, Ana, and I wanna get out. Ever since Bee…" Her smile falters, but she quickly picks it up. "I have to keep up a good front—especially if I'm ever gonna snag Tristan. Can't you just *see* us making out?"

But I'm back where she listed the girls who object to Teo's world. "That means the others like it?"

"Unless they're faking," Izzy says, inspecting a hangnail on her thumb, "but who knows if they're acting? From the beginning, Teo has been pretty good at shutting us up."

I wait for her to explain, and Izzy doesn't bat an eye. "You weren't here," she whispers. "You didn't see how he lit Gwen's dress on fire for crossing to the men's side of the street."

"He—*what?*" My stomach roils. Why didn't anyone tell me about that?

"The dress was fire retardant," Izzy says, shaking her head. She swallows. "But Teo lit her up to prove a point. 'Never disobey me,' he said. Needless to say, we shut up pretty fast after that."

I'm reminded of how Bee seemed so somber at Cleo's party when she told me about getting here. No doubt she was sparing me these details. Oh, Bee. You should have told me.

"But enough of that." Izzy pats my hand. "Let's get back to that acting part. It was pretty clear last night, after what happened to Ramus and Bee, that you don't quite feel the same way you used to about Teo."

She can say that again.

"If you wanna live, Persephone, you'd better put up a good act. I've decided to be the cheerleader!" She pops her gum again as she stands. "Now you need to decide what part you'll play."

I blink. *Oh.* So how much of this conversation was an act? Izzy seems like she is naturally energetic. Maybe she isn't typically so enthused. I slouch. She said I can't act. *I* know I can't act, but I couldn't have been that bad. "Was I really that obvious?"

Izzy nods gravely as she stands above me, her eyes never looking so huge. "Afraid so. But there *is* a secret to covering up your real feelings when around a less than desirable guy."

I don't ask, pretty sure I don't really want to know.

Popping her gum, Izzy tells me anyway as she walks to the front door. "Kissing. Lots and lots of kissing."

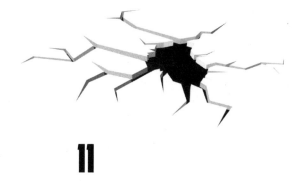

11

"Welcome to Verona!" Juliet beams, filling my wine goblet with sparkling apple cider. I study the wide smile plastered on Juliet's face and realize it's a nutcracker's smile: enormous and, much like everything here, completely fake. One real fact is that I can breathe a little better—Teo and Jonas decided to hang back by the front door before entering the room. They may be plotting which weapons to use with whose murders, but at least for the time being I can enjoy standing by these wrought-iron stairs without him.

A sheen of sweat shines above Juliet's chest and trickles across her tired face. Even her long black curls are matted down, wet. I'd like to tell her not to worry, that she will earn the vaccine. But in truth, I don't know if she will; I don't know if any of us will. I'm not even sure how impressed Teo will be with this soirée. The invitation said it would be a ball, but the only indication of that so far is the Renaissance-style music playing over the speakers hanging on the walls—some slow ballad with a lute, and what I'm pretty sure is a harp. This song doesn't sound very dance-worthy; we need a beat.

"You doing okay?" I ask Juliet, noting the vines wrapped around the wrought-iron staircase and spiraling down the twisted columns throughout the room. The floor plan is identical to all the homes in Elysian Fields, only the décor fits the stage for Romeo and Juliet. Rose petals dot the chocolate hardwood floor, and one or two fake birds peek out from the ivy on the stairs.

"Just peachy!" Juliet says, pulling up the front of her lilac scoop-necked dress.

I try a few reassuring phrases in my head—*just be yourself; flatter Teo, he likes that best*—but by the time I've settled on something promising, Juliet's already across the room by the windows, filling Sal's and Ana's glasses; they remain mute, like I have. Ana's absently munching on another piece of celery, lost in thought.

I look around for Marcus, only to find him sitting on the red chaise lounge pushed up against the east wall. Naturally, Cleo's sprawled across his lap, decked out in a paper-thin gold wrap, "reading" his palm. Tristan and Izzy hover over the chaise lounge, and Izzy keeps glancing at it like she wishes Cleo would move away so she and Tristan could cozy up. But Tristan's rubbing his finger over what looks like a surfboard keychain, and I'm reminded of Izzy's comment that he loves to surf. Without the ocean close by, he must be feeling especially caged in Elysian Fields.

Seconds later, Juliet crosses back toward me by the stairs. Not wanting to lose her again, I grab her arm. "Own your couple's story," I say as fast as I can. When it comes down to it, that's what Teo wants. For us to show him we can be who he needs us to be. Most of us don't like who we have become, but if it means obtaining the vaccine, we must do everything we can to convince him we love this place. No one wants to be killed, or fired up like Izzy said happened to Gwen.

Juliet shifts the bottle of sparkling cider to her other hand. "How are you doing?" she asks, narrowing her eyes.

I blink, startled that she could be worrying about me. *She's* the one hosting the soirée. She's the one who needs to breathe.

"Teo's kind of a control freak, isn't he?" Juliet talks through her teeth.

I stammer for a second, unsure what to say. The last thing I need is for Teo to suddenly show up in the room.

Locking her charcoal eyes on mine, Juliet says, "If you need anything, any time, you only need to ask. Let's just say, I understand." She glances at Romeo, who's managed to pry Marc and Cleo apart. Whatever he and Marcus are talking about doesn't look pleasant. Marcus keeps shaking his head, sending his black hair into his eyes, and Romeo's gritting his teeth; I thought the two of them were friends.

"You mean Romeo?" I try to picture the cowboy treating Juliet wrong. But he seems like a likeable guy—even if he and Marcus are disagreeing about something now.

Juliet laughs, softly. "Ha, hardly. My boyfriend from before. The jerk controlled everything I did." She then laughs heartily, as if we've just shared some secret joke. I join in, impressed by her act. But she goes further—holds her side, as if it's the funniest thing she's heard in her life. She braces a hand on the wrought-iron rails, gestures wildly, ever the perfect host. "I love this house," she nearly shouts. Then she walks away from me to tend to everyone else. Poor Juliet. I wonder if she, too, thinks Teo won't be impressed with her soirée—hopefully she'll do something impressive, like some Renaissance-era dancing, soon.

Teo sneaks up behind me and snakes his arm around my waist. With his hand gripping the white fabric of my dress, I have to focus my entire concentration on not recoiling from his touch, the same touch that pushed the button on the remote to kill Ramus and Bee. How can he possibly think that was okay? He must not think of people as people, but as things.

When I don't say anything for a while, Teo says, "You are rather quiet tonight, my love."

I burrow my face in his neck to stall for time. Yeah, because everything I can think of to say involves avenging Ramus and Bee. But Izzy told me I need to act, so I take a steadying breath and dive right in. "I suppose there is so much to drink in. Your world is so elaborate, you know."

Teo caresses the back of my arm, causing the hair to stand on end. "Mmm," he murmurs into my goose-bumped neck. "You do know how to stroke an ego so. Did you notice the detailing on the baseboards? I signed William Shakespeare's name myself."

I force myself to stand up straight, to study the baseboard below the stairs, because that's what Teo expects. And he's right—a black signature lies at the very center of the eggshell-colored trim. Eggshells—that's how I feel with him. Walking on eggshells. I never truly understood the term until now. But Teo is no doubt awaiting a compliment, so I lather it on thick. "Even your writing looks like his."

The compliment works beautifully, because his lips press against mine, his stubble bristling across my sensitive skin. And I hate it; I do. The way his tongue thrashes against my own, causing me to wither away like a daffodil in a frost. But then he lowers his mouth, repeating what he did before when we were in his room. He brings those tender lips to my neck and brushes my skin before kissing my throat.

I should *hate* it, and I abhor myself that I don't. My mind shrivels, but there's this little part of my body that quivers at his touch. Like it hasn't gotten the memo that Teo's a deranged killer who enjoys snipping marionettes. I wonder if there's a way to murder that part of myself.

Apparently I'm blushing, because Teo chuckles softly. "You liked that?" he asks, just like before, and I tell all my feminine hormones to jump off a cliff. What did Izzy say? *Lots and lots of kissing.* I want to strangle myself.

Teo's ironclad seahorse grasp softens, and I feel like I can breathe again. I wonder if he noticed I was different beneath his touch, but he doesn't say anything as he looks around the room.

The Renaissance music has shifted; now it's a song heavy on the drums and bells. A few paces away, by the refreshment counter of apples and cheese, Eloise and Abe are struggling with Eloise's skirts, but it appears they're making a game out of her dress, arranging it over her shoulder, or pinning it on her hip. They laugh as if they can't imagine a more amusing game. On one hand, I'm glad they're finding some fun in Teo's dark world, but on the other, I feel they should be mourning the loss of Ramus and Bee, since Bee and Eloise were close friends.

One of the longhaired blond boys—Lance—is lightly tapping wooden spoons on an upside-down bowl in the corner by the chaise lounge, and I remember Ana wrote that he plays drums. His partner, Gwen, the Doublemint blonde girl with frizzier hair, taps her foot to the beat.

Marc and Romeo don't look like they're talking anymore, because Romeo is suddenly walking away from him and striding into the middle of the room.

"Juliet!" Romeo shouts in a twang that jars my ears. "Will you give me the honor of the first dance?"

Juliet bows like she's been waiting for Romeo to ask, but my pulse quickens, because Romeo's already ruining his tale. Romeo stole into Juliet's ball—he was a Montague, therefore hated by all Capulets. Didn't the couple do their reading? He needs to sound more Shakespearean and less redneck.

The couple, now facing each other on the dance floor, reach out for each other, and I'm relieved to see them lift up their hands but leave a slight gap between their palms, like they want to touch, but can't. I'm not sure if it's actually from the Renaissance era, but it works.

Romeo and Juliet move seamlessly to the beat, their footsteps light on the dark floor. When percussion trickles through the tune, they switch palms; as if on cue, both sets of Doublemint twins join them on the floor. Izzy's green eyes swim with pleasure that she gets to dance with Tristan. Lance and Gwen don't seem all that hesitant to dance with each other, either, and it makes me wonder if Teo is noticing this—that his couples are "uniting" as he required us to do in his third rule.

Each couple holds out their palms, and when the music increases in tempo, the girls sashay their skirts.

Eloise squeals as she pulls Abe onto the floor, and Cleo's paws are not only on Marc's hands, but his back, his neck, and, for a split second, his butt.

My teeth clamp shut. Not that it should matter—Marc can be touched by whomever he wants—but then he pushes Cleo's hand away, and I know there is a chance Marc and I can be friends.

Glancing sideways at Teo, I try to see if he wants to join the others in the room, but his eyes are fastened on the front door. He must be thinking their "devotion" is pretty bad. They started off shaky, but I'm thinking this dance actually works. Surely he's willing to give them a little more time to earn the vaccine. And no one is clowning around, like they were before Ramus and Bee died. I can't imagine Romeo and Juliet doing more to enhance their tale.

Teo cocks a playful eyebrow at me, saying, "I do believe I know how to improve this tune." And without another word, he brushes past me and out the front door. I'm glad he's not killing anybody, but then again, maybe he is. Maybe his idea of "improving things" is finding a dagger and some poison and smearing a bit of blood with those rose petals on the floor.

I look to the couples, thinking maybe I should warn them or something. But what am I supposed to say? *Quick, run for your lives! Teo says he's going to "improve" your song.* My evidence is as flimsy as those vines wrapped around the iron rods on the stairs.

Ana clomps over to me in her orange sari, that bit of duct tape still fastening together her skirts. She sees me looking and laughs. "Needless to say, I'm glad Teo left the room. Sal would shrivel up and die if we touched."

I could say the point of the dance is to *not* touch, but Ana's little comment makes goose bumps sizzle over my skin. How bad must she feel about herself? Sal is an idiot. *He's* the one nobody wants to touch.

Teo bursts through the door again. My slamming heartbeats ease since there's no weapon in his fist. Instead, it's his violin. I've marveled at Teo's abilities many times, but I won't let his playing affect me.

The red wood gleams off the high light of the room, and Teo wordlessly strides up the stairs. When he reaches the top, in my mind he leans over the rail and claims, *your dance moves beg to be improved,* but instead Teo simply tucks his mahogany instrument below his chin and plays.

His slender arm sways gracefully like it did in class. The instrument hums the pitch of a tenor, and the bow *flick-flicks* just as the women kick. He's mimicking the music and dancers in the room. Even Ana and Sal have found the dance floor, not dancing with as much grace as the other dancers, but staying in time with the beat.

When the women twirl, Teo's bow glides like an ice skater whirling on a lake, and when the tambourines *ding* over the speakers, Teo stitches all the sounds together like the embroidery on Juliet's skirts.

Part of me wants to join in and sing a cadence, too, but the other louder, more fearful side of me remembers what happened at the end of another one of Teo's plays. He tricked Bee into going over that wall and had Jonas chase Ramus onto the other side. Jonas isn't anywhere I can see, but that doesn't mean he isn't hovering on the periphery, readying himself for the moment when Teo says, "Leap."

Eventually, the music dies down, and my heartbeats grow louder, cracking over the flat silence of the room. Juliet's crimson cheeks and chest are drenched in sweat, and I watch as Romeo deftly hands her a glass of water and a dishtowel for the sweat.

As Teo lowers his violin, it's impossible to look away. From where he stands on the balcony, his hungry eyes devour the couples below him, and even from here I can see his chest heaving up and down. I silently cheer Romeo and Juliet for arranging this ball and inspiring Teo to make it his own, to take part.

Tentatively, Abe brings his hands together for a clap, and Eloise joins in, swishing her skirts. The Doublemint boys grab the girls by their waists and lift them up, and Teo, high above, laughs. "I knew the addition of my violin would enhance the tale!"

Gwen giggles and tosses up a few rose petals from the hardwood floor. As if the rose petals aren't enough, she then moves on to tossing up a fake bird. The little fowl slices against the ceiling fan's pull-string before dropping down to Gwen's hands, and when I can see she means to toss it higher, I fear it will hit Teo, so the muscles in my mouth unhinge.

I've just opened my mouth, uttered a "N—," when the feathered dove smacks Teo right on the side of his head.

My heart, my organs jump inside my mouth. She didn't really just hit him. How will he react?

Six men and seven women look up at our leader, Teo, far above. He's trailing his fingers across the side of his head, seemingly too startled to know how to speak. It's like he can feel the imprint of where the little bird hit, like the white fowling has seared its shape into the side of his head.

Licking his lips, Teo grips the high banister with both hands, leans forward, and...laughs.

The sound is impossible to categorize. Disbelief? Or shock? He's going to ask for Jonas to take care of Gwen now. Because she just *hit him* with a bird. He's laughing because he will kill. Looking down on us, Teo cries, "Our reenactment has awakened the birds!"

An unsure chuckle echoes Teo's reaction. Two or three people full out laugh. But Gwen, maybe only two or three feet from me, cowers in her green medieval dress and keeps muttering the acronyms, "OMG. OMFG." I think I'm with Gwen.

But Teo has that look in his eyes he got when he played for us in class. Forty minutes would get swept away, and none of the other students minded because it meant we just had to watch. Teo's classical violin classes were my favorite, too, not because we didn't take notes, but because I got to watch him play.

Eventually, Teo turns his fierce ebony gaze on all of us far below. "Romeo and Juliet—"

Someone clears his throat.

As if he's purposely trying to ruin the moment, Romeo breaks away from the group, wearing a sequined mask. Extending one hand to Juliet, Romeo cries in his thick twang, "Though I wear this visor, the Capulet let me through. And, though you do not see me, I can see you."

Juliet's grin is so fierce it makes my chest hurt. Her fingers twitch, and beads of sweat trickle down her neck. In a voice that's a little too high-pitched, she replies, "What satisfaction canst thou have tonight?"

I watch in amazement as Romeo pulls out a ring. With trembling hands he says, "The exchange of thy love's faithful vow for mine."

This is precisely *not* what I think should happen. Teo, no doubt, will find this absurd. We are far too young; he'll find it a mockery in his world. And yet—he did set up these fourteen homes. The men and women are paired, so maybe that's what he wants. Maybe it makes sense for Romeo to take this leap. If the couples don't die, maybe Teo wants them to prove their devotion to each other first, but we shouldn't be forced to pledge ourselves to each other like this.

Romeo and Juliet stand awkwardly together like some Renaissance Barbie and Ken, and I can't decide whether Teo will smile down on their work, or give a flick of the bow, signaling Jonas to take care of them. What would Teo do to murder the couple now? In the story, Juliet takes a sleeping potion, but Romeo thinks she is dead, so he kills himself with poison, then Juliet uses Romeo's dagger to take her own life. So would Jonas be hiding poison or daggers, or both? But Teo remains precisely where he stands and doesn't flick his bow for Jonas to come.

Gripping the banister of the balcony, Teo stares down on Romeo and Juliet. "Well?" he asks. "Do you promise to wed?"

Romeo twists his mask in his hands, his face drenched in sweat. Marcus, a few paces off, keeps looking at him, moving off the chaise lounge like he wants to stand with his friend.

"Sir," Romeo says in his twang, "I would like to clarify. The ring is more of a promise thing. We're not exactly thinking of *marrying* right now, but we commit to each other and to this place."

Where before it might have been said that Teo's face was sublime, now the contentment erodes, and two ebony eyes with fangs lash out. "You either commit or you don't. There is no halfway." He ignores Romeo completely and turns to Juliet. *Please, Juliet, say something to calm the fire in his gaze.*

When Teo says, "What do you have to say?" Juliet shifts her feet, and I can't help feeling like I'm inside her body, answering Teo instead. Because I know what it's like to be put on the spot, to have all the pressure mounting on you and to want desperately to please him. Juliet looks around the room, like she might get help from the other couples somehow, and when she looks at Izzy, Izzy's green eyes pop, like she's saying, "You can *do* this."

But Juliet seems to be consumed with self-doubt. She's biting her lip and pulling on her curled hair, and I can't help remembering how she told me of her boyfriend before, how he tried to control her life. Her voice as small as a child's, she says, "I don't really know if I'm ready to wed."

Teo's voice grows stern. "And why is that?"

She blinks, like she's trying hard not to cry. "We're not ready," she says. "Like Romeo said."

In my mind's eye, Teo plays his song again, and the women's dresses whip around the figures of the plain-clothed men. How can he waffle on her verdict like this? He can't really believe he has the authority to decide whether or not they deserve to die or live. I hate that we do nothing, merely watch as he reigns. But Juliet must know she's hanging on by a thread, because she closes her eyes and cries, "I wish to wed!"

I feel like crying and covering my head.

Teo's eyes are like two black holes. The spirits of the dead have returned to his face, but eventually the darkness scatters. He's staring at his violin, no doubt remembering the music he played while they danced. While Romeo and Juliet have been clumsy with their ending, Teo must be remembering the connection he enjoyed. And Teo, the Teo I have salivated over for these past thirteen months, loves artistry above anything else.

Reaching inside his suit pocket, he retrieves two needle-tipped vials. But what if that's not the vaccine, but poison? My heart's in my mouth. Teo stares down at Romeo and Juliet and says, "You honor your stations well. Come!"

I should join the couple, demand he prick my skin first, but now I'm convinced it *is* the vaccine, and my intrusion would only sour his mood.

Romeo's eyes fasten on the ground, but he manages to secure Juliet's hand. Together, they ascend the stairs. The muscles in Marc's jaw look like they're working so quickly they might explode, and Ana, standing the furthest from everyone, wrings her sari's shawl in her hands.

As Romeo and Juliet reach the top, Teo has them pull up their sleeves. He pierces their skin, a needle for each. Gwen gasps, frizzy tendrils of hair whisking around her face, and Eloise chants, half-whispering something to Abe. Marc, though, is doing what I noticed he does when he's uncomfortable or scared—pulling on the front of his hair again, gripping a fistful at the side of his head.

For me, it all feels wrong. Or maybe it's right. Because Romeo and Juliet aren't falling down, dead. There stands Romeo, head hanging, and Juliet, trembling with flushed cheeks. They should be celebrating, relieved they won't get sick. The couple has earned a spot in Teo's world, two polished pieces of treasure placed neatly on a shelf. They might not want to be his treasures, but they've passed, sure enough.

Izzy, in the center of the room, bounces her head up and down, which reminds me of her decision—to act like the stereotypical cheerleader who's happy with this life. But she's convincing. She's leaning over to her partner, Tristan, and stroking his pink and green hair.

"Let this be the standard for all of you," Teo says, eyes resting thoughtfully on Tristan and Izzy, who sit so closely that Tristan's leg rests several inches over Izzy's. Oh yes, Izzy, you're doing fine.

"Though you are young," Teo smiles, "there is no reason for this to be prolonged. The homes have extra bedrooms, ideal for the little ones when they come." *Little ones*? He can't possibly see us as baby factories to rear up the next generation of Teo Youth.

Teo studies Romeo and Juliet, who stand below him on the hardwood floor. "Become your stories," he says, "*and* pledge your allegiance to wed. When you do," he lifts his arms out to the couple, "you shall obtain the vaccine!"

Teo pauses dramatically, and it's like he expects us to clap, so Abe and Eloise quickly slap their hands together, and the rest of us dutifully follow suit.

When Teo moves down the wrought-iron staircase, he reaches out for me, lowering his voice. "It looks like the Shakespearean couple has escaped its fate." He chuckles darkly, and I have to fight to control myself. I want to claw the eyeballs right out of his face, so I look away and try to still my twitching fingers.

But Teo's just staring at me, probably waiting for some sort of indication that I adore his sick game. So I try formulating a decent question for Teo, show him an unchanged Cheyenne—or Persephone. "So," I flutter my eyelashes as I gaze up at him, "what is your vision for the remainder of these parties?"

"Eager, aren't you, my dear?" He rubs his lips on the top of my head. "Very well, how about I make you a promise?"

The word "promise" makes me cringe. I don't want any of his promises. He'll say something horrific, like I could kill someone next.

But his eyes don't flash. Instead he says, "Tomorrow night, *you* may host the next soirée."

Every millimeter of my body crumples. The last party I hosted was in fourth grade, and we played *Monopoly*, *Twister*, and *Clue*. I can't measure up to this. Frantic, I search for Marcus, but he's moved on from Romeo to chat it up with Cleo. I feel Teo's eyes on me and will Marcus to look up. *Marcus, forget Cleo and exchange serious looks with me.*

But Teo's gaze is intense on me, so I reply, "Of course, my Hades." It's a risk mentioning Teo's new name. He's never openly admitted it to me.

I'm lucky. Delight, sheer happiness, ripples from Teo's throat. "*Oh*, my dear. I cannot tell you how happy that makes me."

Folding one arm around my stomach, he uses the other to squeeze my back. Locked inside, I can think of nothing but prison. I'm not merely trapped in Teo's world; he has bonded us together. My life is his in every way to create, build, and destroy. My heart wrenches as his hold on my waist pulls me closer.

He'll never let me go.

12

I close my eyes, trying to force my exhausted body and racing mind to sleep, but all I see is Bee's smile, that florescent lip-gloss shimmering in delight. And Ramus, his diamond face and drooping shoulders. Seven men and seven women. I was the eighth person. It should have been me.

I can't believe I came to this place. Of course, I didn't choose to be knocked out, blindfolded, and drugged to come to Teo's utopia, but there must have been something I could have done. A distraction I could have made. Not falling for Teo would've been a good place to start.

Small. I feel so small. Like the hamster my mother bought me when I was a child. Lila? Lola? I don't remember, but she was always getting trapped in her wheel.

I roll out of Bee's bed to my feet, and the touch of the carpet reminds me of home. It's so different than what we had, not as plush and cloud-like—Mom's relationship with the Mayor paid for things like that. Mayor Tydal. He had this way of looking at me sideways while putting his arm around my mom. It was like he could see my useless wish that my real dad was here. But my dad, who mom called "the flighty flight attendant," never stayed in one place for long. I used to think he'd come and get me, take me to Hansel and

Gretel's house. We'd eat giant-sized gumdrops and licorice and mints. Maybe that explains my initial attraction to Teo; deep down, I needed a male to look up to, and there Teo had been with all his wisdom and charm. I need to stop thinking about him.

I head to the kitchen for a drink of water before I sleep. Maybe I'll get inspired as to what to do for my party tomorrow night.

The cool tile stings the pads of my feet, and I jump a little when the shadows spilling into every corner seem to form Teo's shape. I really feel like he's watching everything. One of the shadows in the kitchen moves. *It's Teo and he's come for me.* My heart races inside my chest, and I grip the side of the counter, trying to steady my nerves. But the shadow looks wrong—it's short, has floppy hair. *Marcus* is visiting me.

He tosses back the little liquid left in a wine goblet and sets the glass down. I exhale, forcing my twitching fingers to grow still.

"Hey, Cheyenne," he says, smiling slightly. It's so nice to hear my real name.

He walks closer to me, and I immediately pick up his scent—the sheetrock, bark chips, and paint—always that combination. Such ordinary objects shouldn't make me want to breathe him in, but they do. They're comforting.

"You do realize," I say, "if your brother knew you were here, he would not be thrilled." I shut my eyes and close the thought from my mind. *Teo wouldn't murder his own brother— right?* I walk to the cabinet to retrieve a glass with trembling hands, lift the faucet, and fill the goblet up. Trying to calm my fluttering heartbeats, my twitching fingers, I tell myself Marcus and I are safe—Teo won't hurt us tonight.

Gripping the goblet, I lift it to my lips and let the cool water soothe my throat. I'm glad to have something to do, because my penchant for screwing up small talk may take front and center again.

"Funny." Marcus stretches out his fingers to touch the knuckles of my empty hand. "Teo shouldn't be the only one who gets to be thrilled."

My stomach flip-flops. What does he mean? He likes the thrill of potentially getting caught visiting me? Or that he should get to have his own private moment with Cleo by picking up where they left off on that chaise lounge?

Marcus draws his hand back, then walks to the sink to refill his cup. "Stupid glasses," he mutters under his breath. "Gotta refill them twenty times to get a decent drink."

I laugh, both excited and nervous. Maybe he would like to spend a little time on that chaise lounge with *me*.

Oh, Cheyenne. What are you thinking? He's Teo's *brother*. Nothing more. That's it.

I clear my throat. "Yeah, I know. At first I thought it was just Cleo who had the cups."

He turns the water off and turns to face me, laughing. "That would fit her, I guess."

I hate how my heart's bouncing around like a ping-pong ball in my chest, so in an attempt to calm myself, I push myself up onto the counter to take a seat. Marcus does the same thing. His gray knit shirt stretches over what I'm suddenly realizing are *very* ripped shoulders and chest. I would never describe Teo as ripped. Teo is lean. I look away.

We sit knee to knee with only about an inch of space between us, and it takes all my concentration not to stare at the gap. I want to close the distance, make contact, but I shouldn't want to do that. I was just obsessing over his brother, trying to force the image of that olive-toned skin out.

"So," I say, circling the rim of my glass with my thumb, "what was it like, growing up with Teo?"

Marc eyes me suspiciously, that black eye I spotted earlier nearly healed. I could ask him about how he got hurt, but I figure I can save that conversation for another time.

"Not to know *him* better," I explain, "I just want to know what it was like being raised behind a madman."

Marc grunts; I may have just used a touchy word. Maybe mental illness runs in their family. But Marcus doesn't look grumpy; in fact, the grunt almost sounded happy. Friendly. Something I could scoop up and hold in my hand. He's always friendly, though, and I don't understand why. I've never been anyone to him besides a girl at math meets, one he jokes with a bit, but certainly not anyone he'd really care about.

Marcus rubs his hand over his face, like he's searching for a memory. "I have a story for you," he says, and my mind momentarily darts to the fact that I haven't planned anything for my party tomorrow, but right now I listen to Marc. "It shows that Teo has pretty much always been the same." Marc smiles at me. "Our mom told it to me once." He glances at me to make sure this is what I mean.

"Okay."

Marcus sets his glass beside him on the sink, and once again I think about my party, but I push the little worry away. I have time.

"There was this one time," Marcus says, lacing his fingers behind his head, "when my mom took Teo to the zoo. I don't remember it; he was, like, nine or ten, so I was only three. Anyway, they were looking at the anacondas—"

I shudder. Anything but them.

But Marcus smiles. "Teo thought he needed one."

"What?" I grumble something unintelligible, even to myself. Remembering the snake from yesterday, I kick the pale-colored cupboard behind my feet. "Figures."

"Hey, you know Teo. He kept bugging our mom, whining he needed one for a pet, so my mom finally talked to a worker."

Okay, I'd say their mother sounds off. But I may be misreading things, so I double-check. "You're kidding. She actually asked for an anaconda for him?"

Marc laughs, a simple, unreserved sound. "You never knew our mom—she died when I was ten—but she had a plan to wise up Teo. Paid the guy fifty bucks to stick him in the cage."

"*No.*" My mouth drops open. I can't decide if his mom was extremely cool or just demented. Maybe this is the reason Teo went nuts.

"The snake was in a cage within a cage," Marcus says. "It never could have really reached Teo, but he didn't know that. Scared the crap out of him."

All I can picture is a much shorter Teo with ebony eyes bulging from fright. I wrinkle my nose. "He stopped asking for the snake?"

"Yup." He nods proudly, like he's hell-bent on defending his mom.

But Teo had to get messed from somewhere, and putting your kid anywhere near anacondas seems pretty messed up. Marcus seems proud of her, so I ask about her as delicately as I can.

"She was a good mom." I say it like a statement, but I'm digging around.

He drops his hands from behind his head onto his lap. "The best."

But the way Teo turned out doesn't make sense. "So why tell me this story?" I ask, looking into his eyes, but I don't know about locking gazes with him, so I look away.

Marc leans forward, our knees lightly touching. "To show you Teo can be beat."

I take in a sharp breath, suddenly overwhelmed by the touch. It's warm and nice, but almost too much. I want his leg to come closer, *and* I want to push it off.

Looking away from our legs, I sigh loudly. "He was nine, Marc." But Marc's looking across the room, like he's not really seeing anything.

He rips his eyes away from wherever he's looking and glances at me. "You also need to understand my brother. He and Mom had the same mind—they were creative to a fault. She used it to teach him, and I think he turned out like he did because she died. She didn't get to finish her work."

"So she was a good person?" I ask, unable to help it.

"The best kind."

"What about your dad?" I pause. Teo has warned me never to talk about their father—said something about Marcus getting worked up ever since he died last year. I never really thought about it this way, but Teo and Marc are orphans. I suppose I always thought of them as okay because Teo always seems so grown up.

Marc leans forward as the air conditioning kicks on, and the skin on my knee cools from the breeze. I can't believe I'm so pathetic that I want him to come back to me again.

Marcus's eyes rove over my eyes, my nose, my chin, and I can't help but study the faint scars on his cheeks. The largest runs down the length of one side, almost luminescent, a pale, pale white. It makes me wonder how he got that one—probably battle wound of an active boy. Which leaves me wondering if Teo ever roughhoused, or if his olive-toned complexion covers up any scars he might have. Marc's skin tone is fair despite his black hair, sideburns, and growing beard.

Marcus jumps off the counter, apparently needing to move around the room. Watching him pace across the tiled floor, I decide to try one more time. "So, Teo is like your dad?"

Marcus grabs onto the front of his hair and pulls it down at the side. "Pretty much." I know that tone. Marcus is minimizing things. When he says, "pretty much," he means, "in every possible way." I know because I tend to do the same thing. Minimizing things is a coping mechanism. A way to handle whatever threatens you by making it small.

He keeps closing off. I have questions about how his dad died exactly, and how he made Teo turn out the way he did, but I decide to let them drop. We can talk about this another time, when Marcus is ready to open up. Besides, for the first time being here, I can revel in the fact that this particular boy has chosen to visit *me*. Not Cleo, not any of the other pretty girls from his school. It's just Marcus and me, and there's nothing preventing us from getting to know each other better, from talking.

Fully preparing myself to launch into whatever topic he likes, my eyes snag on the bulge of his bicep beneath his short-sleeved shirt. To think I'd been so obsessed with Teo that I'd missed *that*. Marc's arms look like they could snap Teo in half. Now, if Jonas wasn't around…

I scoot off the counter and try to decide where to go next. Marcus has planted himself halfway between the kitchen and the great room. It's time to stretch out on the floor. Carpet would be better, but I'm not about to invite Marcus to my room or upstairs, so I move over to the hardwood and sit down.

An uncomfortable silence falls between us—no, not uncomfortable. Tentative. Marcus is careful around me. I'm sure that's what he must be thinking, because he's glancing around the room, then at me.

Eventually, he says, "Let's go into the dining room—it's more comfortable in there."

I'm not really sure how he thinks a dining room table would be more comfortable, but I follow him anyway. He saunters toward the front door, slowing a little like he wants to be sure I'm checking him out.

When he veers left into the dining room with a little more bounce in his step, I can't help teasing him. "Think you have an audience or something?"

He twists his head around and shoots me a grin. "Obviously." I hate that he's right—that it's impossible not to notice how his pants hang just a teensy bit too low on his hips. But I quickly look away as I watch him move a few chairs to give us room to sit on the carpet.

"So," I nudge him on the arm, "what do you like to do in your spare time?" I only ever saw him at the math meets or grocery shopping.

"You mean, besides playing dress-up with Cleo?" Marcus cocks an eyebrow as he moves a chair onto the hardwood.

I smile. "Besides that."

"Well, you know I like math—that and literature are the only things Teo and I have in common, but he disregards everything else." He waves away the "everything else" like his other interests shouldn't matter to him, too. Minimizing again.

I wait for him to explain, and when he doesn't immediately say anything, I nudge him again. "Like…?"

"Like—he thinks I should have gone to Khabela." He sighs, moving another chair. "Says I don't have the talent to pursue art."

I feel my jaw unhinge. I can't believe Teo would say such a thing. Well, I can believe it, but to squash someone's dreams before they have the chance to try them is the mark of a royal douche. "How can he say that?" I finally ask.

Marcus shrugs again. "Says I study too much."

"Teo doesn't approve of you studying?"

"Well, the idea of it, yes. But the practice of it, not so much. Everything always came so naturally to him. The idea that it takes some of us a few extra hours to soak up the material is crazy to him."

I nod, knowing what he means. I was the lucky one—had a knack for math—but my friend Josie didn't have the same gift. She never did understand why I was in love with Teo. *Josie, like Bee, you were so right.*

"How about you?" Marcus asks, settling himself on the floor. His head smacks uncomfortably against the chair rail slicing through the center of the wall, so he slouches a little, and I decide to sit and do the same thing. Not that I'm as tall as him, but it feels good to slouch. No, this is awkward; we're sitting side-by-side. So I move to the front of him and lie on the floor with my tummy down, cradling my chin with my hands. I kick my legs up.

"I really want to get into college," I say, crossing my ankles, when a cry escapes my throat. There won't *be* any college. The world is crawling with the Living Rot. If we escape, we'll have to break into old college campuses to find our own books. I can see myself sneaking into the University of Texas wearing something like an astronaut's suit and bungee cords, ducking in and around the Living Rot.

"The world is a pretty big place," Marcus says with an extra spark of color in his eyes. "How many governments are out there? Hundreds? You'd think at least one of them would find a way to ward off the sickness."

My mind reels, picturing more people wearing that astronaut's suit. "But the coverage I watched took place in Austin. That must be the closest city. How could we get around them, if we could even get out?"

Marcus taps the vined wall behind him in thought. "The Gulf of Mexico is probably only a couple hundred miles south," he offers. "We could get anywhere from there."

I don't respond. He has to know what a stretch that sounds like. Like catching a yacht to Florence, or Kiev—not to mention getting around the Living Rot. I'm picturing myself in those bungee cords again and foolishly seeing Marcus and myself using them as ropes in trees, swinging our way to the Gulf of Mexico like Tarzan and Jane. But Marc's eyes are closed, like he's thinking, with his head resting against the wall. I'd like to share my little picture with him, but don't—he'd think it was dumb.

But I like what Marcus is thinking. Even if it makes me stupidly think of Tarzan and Jane. I always knew he was Teo's playful little brother—I just never knew he'd subconsciously bring out that side of me, too.

"What I don't get," Marcus says, stretching his arms above him in the air, "is why my brother 'rewards' us with a vaccine when we live in a society that's supposedly impenetrable."

The question makes me stop. "You're right. Maybe it's his final defense. Like if the infected break through, we're safe."

Marcus's forehead is wrinkling, but he nods like he's not completely sure. I don't know what Teo is thinking, and it looks like Marc doesn't have a clue, either. But he's trying, gripping the front of his long, dark hair again and scrunching up his face. When nothing seems to come, he shakes his head, letting his hand drop to his lap. "Do you know what you're going to do for your party tomorrow?" he asks.

Part of me wishes I could announce this awesome plan. *I've already sculpted a Hades and Persephone scene.* But I don't sculpt, dance, or sing. So I let my shoulders sag. "I don't know. Bob for pomegranates?"

Marcus snorts this low-pitched sound, which is almost cute, when I notice a little box and wire peeking out from the bottom of his shirt. "What's that?" I ask.

"What?" he looks down as if he's spilled something down the front of his shirt.

"No, that," I say, nearly touching the wire, but I don't want to push his boundaries, so I don't.

"Oh." He leans his head back against the wall as if it's nothing. "Insulin."

Wait. "You're diabetic?" I hadn't had a clue.

"Since I was five." Marcus shrugs. "In the scientific world they call it type one." He taps the pump on his side. "I'm dependent on this stuff."

A horrible thought occurs to me. What happens when he runs out? Does he think he has to be the *expert* on minimizing things? He should have brought this up way before now. I don't know where to find more insulin, and I hate how helpless this makes me feel, so I slug his arm. "You should have said something!"

"It's not like you can do anything." Marcus rolls his eyes. "It is what it is."

My mind is reeling. "How much do you have left?"

This is when the shrugging stops. Marcus winces. His eyes partially shut, and he turns his head away from me to the window. "About a week's worth," he says.

"But Teo has to have more," I cry, suddenly on my feet. Where would Teo keep it?

"It's possible," Marcus frowns up at me, "but I don't really know for sure. If you can't tell, I try to do things without my brother."

The air around us thickens as the air conditioning shuts off with a click. I must *do* something. I could run outside and make some sort of distraction so Marcus can steamroll Jonas, and then together we could search his house.

I'm pacing, just like I saw Marcus pacing before. But it doesn't really work because the chairs he moved act like a barrier, blocking me in. I grit my teeth and walk to the window in the room. How are we going to earn the vaccine, escape, evade the monsters, *and* find a supply of insulin, all in a week? Part of me wants to disregard what Marcus just said, to ask Teo where he keeps Marc's insulin—he *has* to have some. Teo thinks of everything.

But Marc's sad eyes find my face. "Don't worry, Cheyenne," his sympathetic smile is so wonderful, and so horrific, my insides feel like slush, "we've got big things to look forward to here. Like throwing parties. And bobbing for pomegranates."

At first I can't respond, his last suggestion seeming to echo around the dining room—bobbing for pomegranates. An enormous tub, red fruit floating within. Seven men and seven women lining up to play the game. But the image shifts. In my head, Jonas dives in, frantic to win. And an absurd giggle escapes my throat. I crash to the floor.

It's like Marcus is reading my mind, because he's smiling, too, and before I know it we're echoing each other, laughing back and forth, our knees knocking into each other. I feel like we're chatting at the math meets again, but back then our conversations were always cut short. This is the longest we've ever had, and I don't want it to stop.

"Chey-yi-yi-yenne," Marcus sings softly, just like he did before, only it's a reminiscence, a reminder that so much has changed. He's sitting closer to me than he ever has before, his knee resting comfortably on my own. I want him to move closer, for the contact to spread. He's warm and fun, like his arms are perpetually around me, holding me close, but allowing me to move. His hand brushes my leg, and I'm frantically clinging to this new idea of Marcus and Cheyenne, him and *me*.

My heart squeezes inside my chest, and embers of fire rush up my cheeks. He's facing me, and his eyes are fluttering so close to mine. His lips are two or three inches away, and—

I look away. This line runs through my head where I say something stupid like, "I can't." Which means nothing, because of *course* I can, but it's because he's here and I'm here and it's much too easy right now. I'm *liking* him, and I don't know if I should like him. This is Teo's brother and he's warm and nice, but those are the exact things I thought Teo was. How do I know there isn't something about Marcus that makes him the same?

Marcus leans back against the wall, the crown of his head hitting the sheetrock. He's quiet for a moment—I can hear him scratching the back of his neck—when eventually he says, "So, assuming you're Persephone and he's Hades, how do you 'prove your love'?"

This is exactly why I like Marcus. He knows how to veer onto another topic when things start to get weird. I could hug him right now; he just might be for keeps.

I take a deep breath, trying to pretend nothing happened just now. "Propose." I shoot off the obvious answer, because that's what Romeo and Juliet did. And Teo loved that.

Marcus jumps to his feet. "Wait—you doodle!"

I look up at him, confused.

"At the math meets," he says, smiling, "you always doodle on your pad."

Ah. I look down at my lap. "So?"

"So, they're pretty good." He holds his hand out to me and pulls me to my feet. "Almost gothic."

MARY GRAY

"Please, they're pathetic." My foot's fallen asleep, so I shake it out. "You're the one who goes to the artsy-fartsy school."

But he's not listening to me, looking toward the back of the house. "You present him with a gift. A drawing. Of you, Persephone, kneeling in subservience, as if to propose."

My stomach lurches; Teo would love something like that. He's the type of guy who makes only the *women* dress up. "But where would I find the paint?"

Marcus beams at me. Veering around the dining room chairs, he walks through the great room to the back door.

I watch him, lost. Does he have his own little stash? "Where are you—"

Opening the back door a few inches, Marcus leans over to pluck something from the ground. He turns around to hand me a strip of acrylic paints.

I stare at them. "You planned this all along?"

"Luckily for you," he places the paint in my hands, "I have resources."

"But from where?" Not only can Teo play me like a fiddle, but Marc can, too? I can't possibly be that gullible. And dumb.

Marc knocks my shoulder, playfully. "Knew you'd be happy."

If only happy were synonymous with mad. He'd planned this all along. "Where did you get them?"

Shoving his hands in his pockets, he smiles. "Had them in my backpack. Like you said, from school."

I try giving the paints back, but he won't budge his hands from his pockets, and the set of paints knocks lightly into his chest.

"Nuh-uh," he stares at the paints, "Teo could spot my style anywhere. Besides, my brother likes gifts that make an impression." He turns to face the largest wall in the room. "I think you should paint your picture on that."

I stare at the painted arches, the vines and the cracks— all reminders of Bee. Part of me wonders if painting over Bee's story is disregarding her existence, but I don't think so. Thisbe wasn't even her real name. She had an entire life apart from this. Keeping this shrine untouched somehow soils her name. Even so, I hesitate. "You don't think Teo will be mad?"

Marcus shrugs. "It's possible."

"Thanks a lot for your help," I groan.

"No problem," Marcus says, like he knew his answer would sweep me off my feet. He can be so overly confident, like he's just fixed my entire life. Which he has, but I wish he didn't know that.

"Paint brush?" I hold out my hand.

A funny expression creeps onto Marcus's face. He looks like he's about to say something, but he changes his mind, digs deeper into his pocket instead. "Here," he says, handing me a brush before practically bolting for the door. "Good luck painting. I'd wait 'til it's light." He means to walk away, but I stop him.

"Marc?"

He turns back.

"Do you really think we can beat Teo at his own game?"

Marcus chomps on his answer, and I imagine he's construing how many ways he can say, "No." I could make my own list, but I'd rather err on the hopeful side. With the tragedies we've already witnessed at Elysian Fields, I'm searching for the smallest hope, but I need Marcus to tell me, logically, that it will be okay.

"It all comes down to strategy," Marcus says. "As I see it, we have two paths to explore: escape, or find a loophole inside. I'll focus on the fence—you're hosting the 'soirée' tomorrow night. But you can wine 'n' dine Teo the way he likes, earn the vaccine, and all the while be scheming how to best him."

I'm not sure what he means. My confusion must be evident on my face, because Marcus adds, "Just watch for your moment. I think he cares for you too much to do away with you like he did Bee."

Marc's reminder of her sends shivers down my arms and legs as my mind keeps repeating the awful sound of her screams. The confusion. The fact that I helped Teo tell the story from the start. Teo "did away" with Bee, and I helped him. I helped him wipe her and Ramus from the earth.

Marcus steps forward and cups my elbow in his palm. I feel the rough callouses of his hands, and I would take this a million times over Teo's seahorse grip. It's comforting and steady. Teo doesn't touch me without an agenda bubbling up somewhere in his mind.

"You know my brother's smart, but you're smart, too. Mix that with your conscience and there's no stopping what you can do." I giggle as he mumbles something indiscernible under his breath. "I sound like a frickin' Dr. Seuss book."

I laugh some more, and Marcus presses his finger to his lips, so I cover my mouth. He's laughing silently, too, his blue eyes dancing in the darkness of the night.

I love the feeling between us, this layer of innocence and calm; every day I spent with Marcus would be like building sandcastles on the beach. Which is infinitely better than the fireflies I used to catch with his brother, who no doubt left them in the jar to die.

"Good night," Marcus says, walking backward several steps, his eyes locked on my own until I can't make out the familiar tidal wave of blue. Eventually he turns to walk straight ahead. I watch the faint outline of his back, how the moonlight catches snippets of his shirt, and I don't look away until all I see is darkness. I start to close the door, sad that we're apart, as Marc sings out my name in the breeze: "Chey-yi-yi-enne."

It might just be four syllables, nothing to get excited about, but something like hope starts to burrow inside me, and while it's terrifying, I don't want it to leave.

13

At seven o'clock, I pull at my dress, wishing I had something else to wear, especially with the snags my uneven fingernails have made. Why does Cleo seem to have a closetful when I have one dress? Probably something to do with Cleopatra's role as a queen.

I pass by the counter and straighten a plate layered with ham and bread. I wish my hands would steady themselves again. We're having fondue for dinner—the ingredients arrived in a basket mid-afternoon—and I got it all ready, perfect, like Mom always did when she entertained her colleagues who also worked for the city. *Don't let them see the brushstrokes,* she always said. And she didn't. Her parties never had issues—that's probably why Mayor Tydal liked her so much. That's probably why they got back together all the time. They'd break up, Mom would host another one of her gatherings, then he'd fall for her all over again and I'd be stuck with him in my life.

I'm not sure yet how to beat Teo or if he can even be beaten, but I will do what Marcus told me to do: allow my sense of right and wrong to steer me toward ending his reign.

I walk through the living room, and while I didn't rearrange the furniture—the two white benches make that

L-shape, greeting visitors as they walk inside the house—I moved all the plants to my room. For my Persephone theme to work, I think I need to abolish the Thisbe and Pyramus story and start my own. I'm not hiding Bee's memory, merely trying to move past it so we can escape. The lighting from a lamp I brought in from Bee's bedroom is bright enough to display my painting but dark enough to match my artwork's tone. The Underworld cast in the light of shadows. I pray Teo doesn't make me flip on all the lights, because then hiding Thisbe's tale will be nearly impossible. I didn't get the chance to cover all the arched windows and leaves on the other walls, though I pushed a tall dresser from Bee's bedroom in front of a large painted arch and lit candles on the floor under my painting to highlight the main part of the room.

I steal one last glance at my work from this morning painted across the east wall. Persephone's eyes, darker than my blue, fit the painting well. And Hades's ebony stubble, on both his head and chin, mirrors Teo's. Passing between them is that pomegranate. I hope I was right to make Persephone smile. Hades's portrait works—the sallow, impassive expression almost perfectly mirrors Teo's face.

I hid a secret in her and my hair—greenery from an olive tree, a symbol for victory—my hope that our confinement in Elysian Fields will not last. A hidden hope inspired by Marcus, the only reason I'm as calm as I am. My fingers may be twitching, my heart may be suffocating inside my chest, but like Marcus said, I can get through this. Just as long as Teo doesn't freak out that I painted over Bee's Babylonian theme.

Someone knocks at the door, and I wish I didn't have to answer—the last thing I want to do is host a soirée. But Marcus and I have decided on a plan—besting Teo and earning the vaccine.

"My dear Persephone," Teo says when I open the door. I feel much more like Pandora opening her box of chaos than like Persephone, goddess of spring's bounty. He plucks my heavy hand and brings it to his lips. "Pray, tell me, what is in your hair?"

It's unnerving how quickly he picked up on the one little rebellion I'd stashed away. I think how to answer him. *It's pretty, don't you think? My mom always did fancy things to our hair when we invited guests over.*

Good fortune arrives in the form of Eloise and Abe. Eloise hikes her pilgrim skirt up nearly a foot so she can waddle up the three steps. She grins at me once, revealing a large gap in her front teeth, then moves past the dresser I shoved in front of the painted arches and walks to the great room. Eloise is always smiling—she and Abe never seem to have a complaint about this place. I wonder if she doesn't mind Teo so much because of something she told me last night—how she's supposed to marry some old guy her dad picked out once she returns to Hong Kong. *A traditionalist,* she'd called him. It's amazing the things you can pick up on at the latter end of parties when Teo leaves the room.

I tap Abe on the arm as he passes by Teo and me hovering by the front door. "Thanks for coming," I tell Abe, then, remembering a comment he made after Eloise and I talked about loving to run, I add, "Have you tried running around the neighborhood? At least on the boys' half?"

Abe opens his large mouth to answer my question, but Eloise squealing loudly from the great room interrupts him—no doubt she's found my painted wall.

I usher in the other couples—trying not to stare too obviously at Marc's arm around Cleo's waist—before trailing after them to see Eloise, who's oohing and ahhing over my work.

"Well, what do we have here?" Abe asks from the center of the room, now standing by Eloise, who's moved on to quietly clapping her hands. I should take this as a compliment, but I remember Eloise only attended Griffin because, as a foreign exchange student, that's where Bee's family sent them both.

The other couples drift to their various parts of the room, and I realize they're beginning a pattern: Ana and Sal drift over to the windows like where they stood at Juliet's, and Marc and Cleo take over one of the benches instead of the chaise lounge. Luckily for Izzy, there's another bench for her and Tristan, and the remaining three couples hover together by the food.

The broad smile stretching over Gwen's face looks like a carbon copy of Juliet's, like she's trying to prove to Teo that she loves his world through her grin alone. I picture holding that expression for longer than three seconds and imagine it hurting my face.

Hovering by the staircase again, I feel Teo's presence beside me—how his breathing is labored and has deepened, almost like the room's suffocating him and he needs to sit down.

I turn to see why. He's studying my painting; my breaths quicken. There's no way my painting can measure up. Artwork takes *years* to perfect; how could I think I could impress him with a few brushstrokes completed in a single morning?

Tilting his head to the side, Teo studies my picture as if considering a piece of art in a museum. He can't possibly like it. He probably thinks Hades is too much like him—or not enough.

And my technique. He has to know about painting. I've never taken an art lesson in my life; how could I have had the audacity to paint his wall? Maybe I should run away while I can, into the still, hot Texan night. But I can't; when Teo is near me I am cemented to the ground. I hate myself for the fear I feel, that despite all this, I still want to please him. Why isn't he saying anything? He must hate what I've done.

Teo leans in to whisper in my ear, his warm breath tickling my skin. "We shall talk about this tonight." He spins, his suit tails slapping my hands, and strides out the front door.

Everyone in the room falls silent.

Tears sting my eyes; I won't let them loose again. Blinking them away, I think of my mother—her strength, how she never cried when Mayor Tydal left, no matter how rejected she felt.

"Thank you for coming, everyone," I say, mimicking her happy voice, though everyone's a washed-out blur around the room. "I made fondue," I force myself to say. "Please, help yourselves in the kitchen. Otherwise, I will eat it all myself."

Someone chuckles. Abe, I think. What a pleasant boy. He knows how to diffuse tension in a group.

Drifting over to my painting, I crouch down and start rearranging the candles to give my twitching fingers something to do. I try placing them two by two, but that doesn't work. Two by three by two by three? A varying pattern might be what the room needs. Because the tears stinging in my eyes make me realize I'm not like my mom at all. I still care what Teo thinks.

I glare at the chocolate-colored hardwood floor, forcing the water in my eyes back. I need to suck it up and act more like my mom. A pair of Doc Martens blocks my line of vision and I wish they'd move on, but when the person clears his throat, I look up and find Marcus smiling down on me. Funny, I didn't know those are the shoes Marcus wears. For some reason I pictured sneakers. I love that he wears this kind.

"Hey, Doodler," he says with half a smile twitching his upper lip.

I don't know what it is, but there's something light about his tone. A lilt, a caress, like he's wiping the hair out of my eyes after a storm; it makes my face twitch. *No.* It's so simple for him to call me that and act like we're normal and safe. He's so unchanging, confident in all this, and I don't know what I'm doing. My face twitches again, and the rivers I've been holding back flood right over; I have to concentrate not to sob. The last thing I need is a scene.

"Cheyenne?" Marcus's concern washes over me as he crouches next to me on the floor. Discreetly, he touches my waist. "What's wrong?" He lowers his voice. "I mean, is he worse than usual tonight?"

I stare at the flickering candles and try to force my hands not to shake, my chest heaving in and out. I had better get a grip on myself before everyone sees. Marcus is right—Teo affects me like salt on ice. I shouldn't let him bother me—I don't know *why* I let him bother me—but he does and I can't help it, and I want that stupid part of me to leave.

I stammer over my words. "I...it's stupid." What can I say? There's something about your brother? I can't push him out?

Marcus leans into my ear. "It's perfect, Cheyenne," and his voice is so soothing and warm. "You just took him by surprise. I don't think he realized you could paint."

I'm desperate to believe him, but how does Marcus know that's how Teo feels? He's seen his brother's erratic mood swings, where he can love something one moment then hate it the very next. There's no telling if or when I will earn the vaccine. I may have sealed my death tonight.

I start to speak again, but Cleo knows just when to step in. Her beads brush Marcus's face as she worms her arm around his waist. I rub my palms into my eyes and heave in a breath. I don't need her to see me like this.

"Oh, Marc," she says. She traces the line of his jaw with her manicured fingernail, and I wish she'd keep her grubby paws to herself, "it's so nice of you to be there for Number Eight. She has such a vulnerable shell." I blink back the tears, because no one actually says things like this in real life.

I scramble for something brilliant to spit back in her face, but Marc's eyes lash out like Teo's do when he's mad, only there's this righteous indignation that flickers along his jaw. I could wrap my arms around Marcus right now.

While this one look should be able to melt down ore, Cleo bats her mile-long eyelashes innocently as she turns toward me. "Need a tissue, honey?"

There's no way in hell Cleo and I might be friends, not unless I can pin those batty eyelashes of hers to her head.

Unsteadily, I move past Marc and Cleo, flounder through the great room and out the front door. It's raining—God's crying for me tonight. It's fitting, really, because both of us need our teardrops to fall. For Him, to save these coarse, dry trees. I need a certain person to stop affecting me.

Staring across the subdivision as the porch lights flicker on each of the men's homes, a wave of self-pity washes over me as I remember what Cleo said. *She has such a vulnerable shell.* I hate that there's truth to what she says. Teo likes me because I've *always* had this vulnerability. I suppose he's my Achilles' heel. I used to pride myself on not letting others change me, but Teo knows how to burrow inside my heart and squeeze. Around him, I'm this pathetic, whimpering child. Fragile. Breakable. Like I'm obsessed with what he thinks. Not because our lives are on the line, but because seeking Teo's approval has become this sick goal. And I've lived this way for so many months, it's like I need to be rewired. The problem is that I don't know if I can be. Teo was always there for me, even at the worst. Like when I was stuck riding the city bus to school.

Oh, how I hated riding the city bus to school.

Especially because I had to cover those last few blocks on foot, even when the sky opened up and tried to drown me. And the road, how it smelled—rubber, trash, mud. I used to clutch my bag closed because the zipper had broken, and walk on the shoulder of the road since there were no sidewalks.

One morning, there was this convertible, then a BMW; both swerved around me, spraying puddles on my shirt. I could have turned around to change at home, but that would've meant waiting around for the bus, and I couldn't afford to be late to school again.

Slogging on, I noted the tins of tobacco, condoms, and liquor bottles littering the shoulder of the road. The rain drizzled harder, and I remember wishing I had a friend to wave down, or at least an umbrella.

My bag felt light. Checking inside, I found a gaping hole. While my textbooks clung to the sides, I was missing three of my favorite paperbacks—*Dracula,* an Edgar Allen Poe compilation, and *Jane Eyre.* Heart racing with the rain, I retraced my steps.

By then, the rain wasn't drizzling, but pelting my pounding head. My hair stuck to my face, my skirt was glued to my legs, and water pooled into my sneakers as I sloshed back to the stop. By the time I found my books strewn across the side of the road, they looked like they'd been dropped into a tub. Retrieving them, I tried wiping them on my skirt, which made *Jane Eyre's* cover rip.

Blearily, I made my way back to the school, pulled those heavy doors open, and slipped inside. It was clear class had long since begun; the entryway was clean, silent. I tried tiptoeing down the hall, my sneakers *screech-scrunching* against the checkered tile.

I was veering around the corner, aiming for my biology class, when I nearly ran into the school secretary. She had a walking stick and gripped it like she was Moses or Gandalf, wielding the greatest power on Earth. She looked me up and down. "What are you doing out of class?" she asked.

I was obviously soaked and hadn't even *been* to class, but she didn't look like she cared. Shifting my books in my hands, I tried stating that I needed to get to my class. But she held out her hands. "Give me this."

But I didn't want to give them to her. They were my own copies, and they might tear again while wet.

The secretary tapped her walking stick. "Why are you late?"

I tried making the books disappear into the crook of my arm. "The bus was behind schedule," I lied, glancing around her to biology, only a few paces past.

"Sorry, but policy is policy," she said.

I paused, unsure what to do.

"I'm afraid I'll have to confiscate those until I know you can be on time."

"What?"

"Your paperbacks." She pointed. "It's obvious you care about them, so I would like to hold onto them until you can prove to us that you can be punctual to school."

What sort of a school *was* this, where even the secretaries were allowed to confiscate items?

I don't think of myself as a trembly sort of person—my entire school experience prior to this had never given me a reason to shake—but it must have been the anger combined with the rain, because my hands started trembling. I didn't want to hand them over, I couldn't hand them over; those books were how I got through lunch, through free time at school.

The secretary ambled closer, reaching out her ancient, chalky, veined hand, when a voice sang out like an instrument, "Why, Miss Laurent, you remembered my books!"

Dazed, I turned. I knew it was my trig teacher's voice, and when I saw his fluid walk, I knew I was right. The suit coat he normally wore was gone, and his cornflower blue tie flapped up while he walked. Opening up his palms, Teo smiled warmly at me, and thinking of the CD he had made for me, I flung the paperbacks into his hands.

The secretary huffed. "You could have told me they were his books." I wasn't watching, but it was only a few seconds before her cane *tap tapped* away from us down the hall.

Feeling like a vulnerable, wet dog, I scrounged around for a "thanks," but found myself worrying whether or not mascara had run down my face.

But Teo was studying the title of the ripped book. I expected him to frown at the condition of *Jane Eyre,* but instead he said, "I hear Mr. Rochester is more mouthwatering than words."

"Y-yes," I laughed, appreciating that he didn't chastise me for ripping it.

Teo tapped his lean fingers thoughtfully on Mr. Rochester's book. "I have an affinity for the classics. It pains me to see them wet. Would it be too much for me to ask to air them out?" He glanced down at *Jane Eyre.* "And get this one fixed?"

It's impossible to say what it was—the rain, the bus, or the secretary snatching at my books—but the way Teo pled, like *I* was the one helping him out, made the tears I was holding back tremor frantically inside my eyelids.

Turning away before he could see, I mumbled a "thank you" before scurrying toward class.

Teo called after me, "Anything to make you happy, Miss Laurent."

14

With my hand on the doorknob, I move to step into Bee's house when footsteps slap the wet pavement and a voice I always recognize calls out.

"Miss Laurent—Persephone!" Teo's double naming stills my hand. It's so nice to hear my real name again, I have to turn.

He's running toward me, fresh rainwater running down his cheeks. The drizzle of God's teardrops soaks his white shirt through, and I'm left staring at that lean body I've come to know so well—those square shoulders and powerfully built legs, like he's actually a runner but takes too much pleasure in his reading to use them much.

I shouldn't look.

But it's impossible to turn away; he's like a vision from God—tall and shining. Even his white shirt seems to glow beneath the raindrops, and his lips are turning up slightly, like the only thing that can make him this happy is seeing me.

Moving across the porch in two powerful strides, he reaches out his dripping wet arms and wraps them around me. His warm wet shirt bleeds into my dry white dress, and it's like he's melting into me. Gently, he weaves his fingers up and down my back, runs his fingers down the side of my face, and even with all this touching, I can barely feel a thing.

But then he's holding me closer, pressing his leg into my own, and my thigh feels like it's next to a torch. He's brushing my hair away from my face, tendrils of fire groping for my eyes, my cheek. He's whispering to me, "You are my everything."

My shoulders twitch, and my breath rushes from my chest. I'm tingling inside—I feel like someone's sprinkled faerie dust inside me. These words—they're just words. I can't let them affect me.

I don't know how, I don't know why, but I'm suddenly running my hand down the length of his face, trying to read those death-black eyes. Does he mean it? He's further unveiling his feelings. My heart hiccups, my fingers twitch, and I flounder for some way to not care what he thinks.

"You're trembling!" Teo laughs and pulls me closer into his warm, wet chest; he's right, because my hands, my lips, my legs—everything's shaking.

He rubs his hands up and down my arms, lighting little coals within me, and I hate how, in this instant, I too easily remember how I've always loved him, how he so frequently saved me from everything.

No. I back away. No, no, no. This is wrong. I shouldn't allow myself to be alone with him. He *kills* people. He is the enemy.

But Teo follows me, backs me into the cool wood grain of the front door. Running those slender fingers over my arms, those coals I felt before burn, begin to glow. So I open my mouth, trying to think of a reason why we should go back inside, but he cups the side of my face, and he's just *looking* at me.

Eyes never more gentle, soft and round, he tells me, "You didn't tell me you could paint. No one has ever done something like that for me."

His fingers trail down my jaw, and my stupid girl feelings are cheering. *He likes it! He loves it!* But I tell myself not to be happy. Because this is Teo. I shouldn't care how he feels. I should be glad that I've passed the test, that I've earned the vaccine. But then he's kissing me, and those soft lips are melting into my own, and I'm reminded of those times he looked at me in class, and, when no one was around, how he brushed the hair out of my face.

His mouth is on top of mine, and it's impossible not to shrink back because his kisses are gentle and slow, like he's singing to me. His lips gently nudge my own, and when I nudge back, he opens his mouth so I follow him, unable to stop. Ripples of pleasure tear through me, and I may be cast out to the farthest reaches of hell for reveling in everything. I shouldn't be kissing him; I don't want to stop kissing him, so I touch his arm, and his strong hand grips me on the back.

It's like his hand lights me on fire. I'm glowing, breathing shallowly. I shouldn't be out here with him; I don't want to be out here with him, but my heart is exploding like it's been dipped in gasoline. We're so close; he pushes me against the front door, and I can't stop feeling his mouth moving over my own. His lips move so tenderly, and then they're skimming the length of my neck, and when he finds the base of my throat, a gasp rips through me.

I pull away. He's smiling, but my head is pitched at an odd angle against the front door. I shouldn't be enjoying it. Not like this.

I think how I can explain. How the way he's kissing me is both everything I ever wanted and the most horrible thing I have ever experienced. How he's both much too appealing and poison. That I'm supposed to pretend to love him, *and* learn not to love him. None of this is easy.

I've never been very good at lying, so I let one word follow the other. Tell him truths without letting him know all the lies. "You're fire," I choke out, unable to deny the forest fire raging within me. "You are ice," I say because I'm visibly shaking. "You're smooth and dark and so much more than I can express. Teo," my voice cracks, "you are destroying me."

Teo's somber eyes watch my lips quake, and an emotion I've never seen in him before wakes; his eyes are still dark, but soft around the edges, sad but smiling. I know that expression—Teo Richardson is empathizing with me. Reaching for me, he again cups the side of my face. "Let's get you inside," he murmurs, smiling. "There's something I need to tell you," and I haven't a clue what that means.

Tucking my hand into the crook of his arm, he steers me through the door, and though there's a party, Teo silently leads me past the couples, the hardwood floors sprinkled with their shifting feet. Keeping my eyes fastened on the chocolate-colored floor, I don't look up at any of them. Because I know Teo's kisses are painted on my face, and Marcus, Izzy, Ana, and everyone else will see the brushstrokes across my cheeks.

I've just reached the hall when Izzy, eyes wide, plants herself right in front of me. "Take some of these!" She beams at me, handing me a couple of plates of ham, bread, and cheese. "The fondue is delicious, and you haven't gotten any," she adds, smiling.

I take the plates from Izzy, feeling the blood rush to my cheeks. Surely she will detect the traitorous kisses on me.

But Izzy's smile doesn't falter, and Teo takes the plates from me. "Thank you, Izzy," he says, almost gallantly.

I don't believe I've ever heard Teo thank someone without being ironic. Forcing my breaths to even out, I let him steer me down the hall to my bedroom, barely acknowledging the painted vines and cracks on Bee's walls, or the fact that I still like him touching me.

Once inside my bedroom, Teo releases my arm, gesturing ahead. "Jonas brought these for you."

Feeling my skin cool where he just removed his hand, I spot the stacks of dresses perched neatly on my bed. No, *Bee's* bed. Teo has forced every single one of us to come here, and this moment when he is gracious and kind is merely a precursor to something else.

"Well, what do you think?" Teo asks, holding the plates of food. There isn't anywhere to put them since I moved Bee's dresser by the front door to block the painted vines on the walls. What do I think? I think I need to find a guillotine. Because what I've just done outside means I'm beyond repair. There's no rewiring me.

But Teo's expecting a response, so I give him some words. "It's too much." I try to smile but I don't. He's lathering me up with too many dresses, and I shouldn't be finding the gesture sweet. I stalk over to the nearest stack, pick up the first dress and hold it up to me. It's blue with long strips of ribbon that make up the skirt and shimmers in the light. I think it's pretty, naturally.

"Try it on," Teo offers, and part of me wishes he'd growl or yell at me, but with his voice so soft and low, it's impossible to refuse him. I nod and take the dress into the mirrored bathroom I've come to know as both mine and Bee's.

Peeling off my wet dress, I can't help noticing the fabric of both of these dresses is thin, flimsy. Perhaps that's how he pictures his Persephone. Moldable. Easily blown over. If I don't snap out of it, that will always, *always* be me.

Teo calls through the door, "I had Jonas order only the dresses that I could picture Persephone wearing. I hope you like them—I chose them myself."

I couldn't have been more right. Bits of sheer fabric comprise me.

When I step out from the bathroom, Teo whistles, which actually makes my cheeks warm. *You should be impaled, Cheyenne. Sliced through the gut. Hop in a time machine, and ask Vlad the Impaler to lend a hand.*

Standing in the doorway, I find that I can't move—sitting next to Teo on that bed could be a very bad thing. He could move my hair behind my shoulder, bring those lips to my throat, and I'd forget everything. How he kills, and twists, and laughs when it hurts most. It's better not to move at all.

But Teo holds out a plate, like he means for me to sit. I stare at that food, my stomach growling. I should have thought to eat before the party.

Bits of laughter come from the front room. Someone's squealing—probably Eloise. But the seconds are ticking by, and I can't leave Teo waiting, so I reach out for that plate of fondue and sit on the bed, leaving a reasonable amount of space between us. Four or five inches, maybe.

Holding the plate carefully on my lap, I decide on a piece of bread, pluck it up and set it in my mouth. It immediately melts, and I decide I *won't* be like the bread. I'll be steadfast and immoveable when it comes to Teo. I can do this. I'll be everything sturdy.

"I have something to tell you," Teo says as he sets his untouched plate on the bed, "but I do not quite know how it should be phrased."

That doesn't make sense. Teo knows how to put everything. Like the time when my bra strap was showing, and instead of pointing it out in front of everyone, or making some snide comment like the other goons at my school would, he simply rubbed a little on his shoulder and smiled at me. I looked down and saw the problem immediately.

Okay, he didn't necessarily have to *say* anything, but he conveyed his message and it helped. He *can* be delicate when he wants to be.

Breathing raggedly, Teo moves to his feet, looking at my plants strewn across the room, and now I wish I'd stashed them somewhere else. His mouth twitches before he clamps it shut, and I've never seen Teo flustered like this. It gives me this sick sort of satisfaction that I can do that to him, but then I remember I'm not supposed to care how I affect Teo, so I grab a piece of ham and shove it in my mouth.

When he moves to the window, Teo's breathing slows, and when he turns his obsidian eyes down on me, my old Teo is back. He shows his teacher face—his gaze is hard, but nothing fierce, and his forehead is crinkling slightly. "There are times it is best to be weak," he says eventually.

I stare at him, unsure why he would say such a thing. I can imagine the way he would answer me in class. *It is good to identify the weak so they might be squashed and we can feel peace,* or, *weakness provides a way of improving oneself. You have ever so many weaknesses, Persephone.*

Unsure whether or not I really want to know, I give him the question he obviously wants: "Why do you say that?"

Taking a step closer, he says, "Let me answer by asking you something. What would you say constitutes strength?"

"Endurance," I say. Why is he asking this? "Compassion," I add, just to throw out something. And then, remembering the new way he kissed me in the rain, I add quietly, "Willpower," because that's a strength I clearly need.

Teo smiles, maybe two feet above me. "What an odd combination you present." Extending his hand, he brings me to my feet so that the bits of blue fabric on my dress flutter up. "Would you say the most evil men and women on the planet possess these traits?"

"Absolutely." A spark of humanity is in everyone—at least at first. But why compare us to them? Is Teo admitting he is evil, or that he is far above the corrupt?

"People do not become evil from strength alone," Teo says, running his thumb and finger over the sheer fabric of my sleeve. My arm and shoulder quiver. "They possess something else."

I stare at him, as blank as the white ceiling above my head.

"Pride," he answers. "Not just honor, but selfish conceit, when your own ambitions are the only whims you heed. And what is the inverse of pride, Persephone?"

"Humility?" Where is he going with this?

"That is right," he smiles, nodding. "Humility is a trait for which many of us stretch but can never quite grasp. For once we state we have it—"

"We really have pride," I finish, seeing the answer easily.

Teo laughs, an almost pleasant rumble in his throat, and I don't know whether I should be *proud* of myself, or if my comments would make any lunatic happy.

"And so we come full circle," Teo says. He turns to look out the window again. "There *are* times it is best to be weak—admit our failings to enhance an ultimate strength."

I watch the drying back of his shirt, how the fabric's lifting from the contours of his body. "I could suggest," I say, "such an act is really a strength from the very start."

He turns his eyes back on me. "But that would defeat the purpose of our little debate. The thoughts of mankind are some of the only true pearls we have. There is a complexity to our minds. At times, the strength of daggers is needed to fortify our world, but occasionally the tender morsels of humility are the key to unlocking our greed."

Sitting next to me on the bed again, Teo turns his somber face toward me. I study the growing stubble trickling near his ears, and the slight dip of his chin—not quite a cleft, but almost. I have to fight the urge to touch it—

Oh, dear God, have mercy on me, because what I really deserve is for my brains to be splattered on the side of the street. I can't let him get to me like this. I am flint. I am steel—

"And that is why—" Teo breaks off, lips twitching. He closes his eyes, but reopens them again. Letting his eyes smolder into my own, he says, "That is why I love and need you, Persephone."

Just how long have I waited to hear these words? He always offered tidbits. *I care so much; I only want to see you happy.* But love? I didn't know he would ever *say* that word. I've thought it maybe a million times, but even *I* haven't told him that's how I feel—felt. Of course, it's obvious. Every glance, every touch has dripped *I love you.* But he's saying it right now. Why's he saying it right now? And—

DEAR GOD, WHY IS HE KNEELING?

With one leg barely touching my knee, Teo plucks up my hand like he's holding a rose petal. Boring his ebony eyes into mine, he says, "While you do not arm yourself with the callous strength of swords, you empower us all with the fertile seeds of fragility, the divine weakness—humility— we cannot do without. And while mythology has us believe Hades gave Persephone the six seeds of the pomegranate, I know the truth. You, in fact, gave them to me." Without another word, Teo reaches inside his pocket, pulls out the vaccine. Holding it out to me, he asks, eyes round and innocent, "Marry me?"

There are no words.

The man I have daydreamed about these past thirteen months is proposing to me.

It must have been our kiss in the rain. Or that awful speech about how he is fire and ice. No. No. No, Cheyenne. Teo was planning this all along, because of these "seeds of fragility."

When I look down at his hand, I have to blink. *Blink, blink.* One hand holds the needle, the other holds a gold ring, and a thrill of pleasure sweeps through me. I have to throw my hand over my mouth to stifle a squeal. *Teo's proposing to me.*

Teo's offering me the vaccine.

Teo is giving me everything.

I slap my cheeks, shake my hands; there's too much confusion and shock not to be happy. He wants to marry me. And I *wanted* to marry him, but now I'm just insanely happy. If I was a quick-witted sort of person, I'd have grabbed that vaccine and jabbed it into my skin seconds ago. Searched his suit pocket for more vials for Marcus and the others, too. But I can feel my eyes, no doubt stretched as wide as the moon across my face, and it's like I've been struck with paralysis, because my mouth is stuck in this ridiculous grimace that's halfway smiling.

Extending a trembling hand, I invite him to place the ring on my finger. And when a flash of gold, warm from his pocket, slides on my finger, it's all I can do not to let out a gasp. *What is wrong with me?* I shouldn't be happy. Smiling.

When I extend my arm for the vaccine, Teo doesn't move his hand. "You have earned this," he says, voice suddenly flat, like he's lost, and this moment's come much too fast. Well, welcome to the club, my dear. You're not the only one feeling about ten million different things. Exhilaration, shock, disbelief.

"If I give this to you now—" Teo starts, but seems to change his mind because he doesn't finish what he was saying. Lifting his hand, he gently pierces the skin below my shoulder with the needle, which stings like the old vaccine did after Beijing.

Since I came here, I've been working toward this moment. I've actually acquired the vaccine; the Living Rot can no longer hurt me. Now Marcus and Izzy need it. All the others. Ana, and those silly other girls, too. Cleo can get it last—if she decides to keep her paws off Marc. But what am I doing thinking about Marc? I'm engaged! Not *really* engaged—because I don't love Teo; Teo is bad—so I can't tell Cleo to keep her paws off Marc, because that would sound stupid coming from a girl wearing a ring—

Teo brushes my cheek with his hand and asks quietly, "What are you thinking?"

My heart plummets thirty floors. I close my eyes, push the idea of Marcus away, and allow myself this moment with Teo, because that's what Teo wants, *needs*. What was I even thinking? He told me he loves me *and* proposed to me.

He's probably waiting for me to say I love him, too. But is it weird that I don't think I can do it? Though everything hinges on the hope that I can *stop* loving him, I can't bring myself to tell him those little words. They're supposed to mean something, and I can't offer them up falsely.

"Let us save the announcement," Teo says, brushing my cheek with his swollen lips. "Tomorrow, Tristan and Izzy entertain us."

The lost look on Teo's face makes me believe he finds our engagement out of whack. He really must be waiting for me to tell him I love him. But I can't. It's what I feel, but I don't. I love him, but I *don't* really love him, because how can you love someone who kills?

When Teo finds his feet again, I don't watch him leave; instead I focus on the consistency of my breathing. *In, then out. Breathe in—breathe out.* He didn't just propose to me; he didn't, he didn't—

The door gently shuts behind him.

Falling back on the cool, silken sheets, I stare at the pale white ceiling. I can't believe I let myself be alone with him. He could snap my spine, sneak his way inside my heart at any moment. I shouldn't allow him to do that. Not now. Not ever. What must Marcus have thought, seeing me come through that front door just now? And then, when we moved to my bedroom, how I could only stare at my feet. It must have been hard for him not to burst in on us again.

I stare at the simple gold band on my finger, trying to decide how I should feel. Moderately happy that I earned the vaccine? No, I should be screaming that I won. But not everyone has received it, so that would make me a jerk, so I should be moderately to heavily happy, and indifferent that I now wear Teo's ring.

The ring is simple, a gold band without a stone, but the intricate cuts in the band and squared edges makes me draw in a breath. It's perfect, exactly the type of ring I could see "Persephone" wearing. Bits of leaves trickle along the outside surface, and when I slip it off and study an engraving on the inside, I find, "For Persephone. My only."

There are no other ladies for Teo; just me.

This is not some random, throwaway ring. It's not a trinket he impulsively plucked, but something he clearly thought about. It even fits perfectly. Like the CD, Teo personalizes everything, because, like he said, he loves me.

It's difficult to breathe, so I stand and pace about the bedroom. In my daydreams before, Teo and I would leave town, be together, but it was always just that. I never allowed myself to think about a future—kids, a house. This. I suppose that's what I get for liking an older man, but I do not like him anymore, I cannot like him anymore. He's a disease.

Teo is poison. Darkness. Yes, he understands poetry, analyzes attributes of the human heart, but everything about his perception is skewed. Just because no earthly being has ever looked so ethereal in the rain doesn't mean he should affect me.

Teo kills, and that's something I must always remember. I must think of Bee, honor her memory by using the shield of the vaccine. Because I will escape. Not just from Teo's world, but from his hold on *me*.

15

This is getting ridiculous. All I've done this morning is stare at the ring on my finger, not believing that it's really there. I alternate between wanting to snap a picture and wanting to cut my finger off to get myself to look away. Someone's yelling in the street again, but I'm too busy to go see. A few minutes ago it was Tristan and Izzy play sword fighting, and the voices sound the same, so I'm pretty sure it's them.

I need to see Marcus, have him tell me how horrible everything is. He needs to remind me how Teo's a killer and how he's using me. I need good, decent conversation, and I need it today.

Rushing out the back door, I decide to do what Marc's probably doing on the other side of the street—studying the fence line. He's not the only one who can look for a breach. I study the trees surrounding our yards—compact and mature, they block all light from the outside world. What type are they? Oak or elm, maybe. I should have listened to Mom when she tried teaching me about shrubs and trees. The trunks split early, giving the illusion of a "v," and the leafy tops umbrella outward, creating rounded splotches of shade.

I run past the women's yards, in too much of a hurry to stop and think about each girl, though a few anthills block my way. Behind Izzy's or Gwen's house, I find a pack of hornets working on a nest high up on the brick of the house. I need to feel closer to Marcus, remember the way he looked when he wanted to kiss me in my dining room. I wish I could run into him, but no doubt he's not dumb enough to cross to our side of the street during the day. That would be a death wish. Maybe Cleo knows where he is. I can't believe I'm considering talking to Cleo. I may need to gouge my eyes out first.

Maybe I could make up some lame excuse. *I didn't get any breakfast. Do you have any extra muffins lying around?* Then I could casually slip in my question about Marcus. *You haven't, by any chance, seen him in or around our street? Did he ask about me?*

I'm lifting my hand to knock on Cleo's back door when a slight noise behind me, like a twig snapping, makes me turn. Tree branches sway slightly, and a gust of wind gathers my shoulder-skimming hair, whipping it around my face. The fences have been breached. The Living Rot! Someone's gotten inside. I'm not sure how protected I feel even with the vaccine.

But it's Marcus who steps out from behind a short and extra-knobby tree, holding a finger to his lips. My stomach flip-flops. *Marcus—I've missed you more than I thought.* I remember the feel of his knee against mine, how it seemed to warm that skin the entire night. He's smiling at me, but he quickly darts his eyes left and right, clearly careful about us being watched. I'm not sure what Teo or Jonas would do if they found out he was in the woods. I don't think Teo would kill his own brother, but how many times have I been wrong when I've made a guess involving him?

A ring of sweat on the front of Marc's T-shirt has a funny way of making him blend in. Now I'm wishing I hadn't chosen to wear this yellow dress. One of the green ones would have camouflaged much better. All I know is I can't think of anyone I would like to see more.

As I step into the forest, the trees I once thought of as giants seem to shrink in size. When I look up, they tower high above my head, but they're maybe only two or three times my height. I reach out to touch the knobby warts on the trunk when Marcus stops me.

"Careful. They're sharper than you'd think."

I glance up at him, then back at the knobby trees, thinking they stand for Teo in some small way. They lure you in, if just for curiosity's sake, but once you trust them, they'll only cause you pain. I'm suddenly not so surprised these are the trees Teo's chosen to surround his community with.

Glancing away from the tree trunk, I look up to Marcus to see what he thinks, and smile a little because it's impossible not to smile when looking at him. I don't know if it's how he never intimidates me, or because I know it's just a matter of time before he will make me laugh. Either reason is fine with me.

"You caught me," Marcus says, mischief playing on his face, and it's the face I remember from the math meets, always plotting something trivial but fun. Like when he tied two of the contestants' ponytails together. You wouldn't think it possible with the moderators close by, but both the girls' hair ran all the way down their backs and peeked out the backs of their chairs. He was sitting right behind them, and I watched him tie the knot before he disappeared. Naturally, when the girls stood up the ponytails went taut, and everyone burst out laughing.

Eager to help, but not wanting to risk Teo finding out, I find myself asking, "Do you really think we should be out here during the day?"

Marcus shrugs, and it's such a comfortable look, like the last thing on his mind right now is Teo. "Better than at night. I think that's when the infected come out."

My arms and chest freeze. "You mean—you saw them?" I don't know if I can stand to look at them with their blood-dripping teeth.

But Marcus shakes his head, a quick, jerky movement, so very opposite from Teo. "I think I heard them, though."

I imagine the sounds of their moans. That low rumble in their throats, like they are breaking out of a coma. That was the sound of the Living Rot on the TV. Suddenly my ears are pricking, tensing for the moment I hear that low moan. I look past Marcus into the dense woods. "Do you think they saw you?"

"Maybe." He shrugs that carefree shrug again. "I was dumb the first night—too loud. But then I figured no one would think I was stupid enough to crawl around here in the middle of the day."

Good point. I'm not sure whether he's brilliant or really, really careless. I might be considered careless the way I'm planning to run from Teo, but I'm trying to be discreet. And I've found Marcus, who can help me forget about this ring. "I don't suppose you've found the exit?" I ask, gesturing through the trees with the hand that doesn't wear the ring.

Marcus shakes his head. "That's the thing. I thought it would be behind the albino's house, but there aren't any breaks in the fence." Naturally.

It does make sense that Teo brought us through a discreet gate. The blindfolds were in case we woke up. "How about behind Ramus's place?" I ask. "Where Teo moved in?"

Marcus shakes his head again, and my chest tightens—I need some sort of hope, some escape route from Teo's clutch. "I don't think so. I covered that ground pretty fast, but I didn't see anything that looked like it could open up."

I glance through the trees—no squirrels, no birds. It's like everything's dead. Either that or these trees have only arrived, which with what I've seen from the rest of Teo's little compound, could be true.

"What about Teo's SUV?" I try. "You said he packed everyone inside when you first got here."

"Yeah, but then he and the albino asked us to blindfold ourselves 'for our own safety' before drugging us." Marcus scuffs his Doc Martens in the dirt. "Wish I never listened to that."

My chest deflates as he crushes my last hope. And that's not to mention his limited supply of insulin. How many days does he have left? Three? Four? I start to ask, but Marcus is already clicking something on his pump. He's well aware of his insulin depletion. He doesn't need me making it worse.

Deciding that searching the perimeter is our best option for escape, I finally ask, "Which way were you heading?"

"Well…"

"What?" I ask, annoyed, "Don't you trust me?" I thought we were beyond that. I don't know, ever since he visited and we had that talk in the dining room, I thought we were on the same page.

"I just don't want you to get caught." He's studying the strips of fabric that make up my skirt and I blush, because now I feel dumb, like I look like Tinkerbell.

But I can't let him see me looking self-conscious, so I spout off, "You haven't been caught." Because he hasn't. Gosh, Cheyenne, you're showing your smart genes today.

"That's because I have mad skills," Marcus plays along.

"Seriously?" I groan. "And you think I don't?"

Marcus grabs my wrist, raises it high in the air, then drops it, as if that's the way to assess my potential. He shakes his head, regretful, a smile on his lips. "Sorry, Cheyenne. Not so much as a spark."

"What did you expect?" I huff. "For my hand to hover *magically* in the air?"

"Actually," Marc's face grows serious, "there is another way."

I don't know what he means until he stares at my lips. My throat constricts, and my heart pauses between beats. "And what is that?" I ask, unable to resist staring at his lips, too. I hate that I'm suddenly desperate to know whether or not Cleo knows what they're like.

"It goes like this." Marcus moves toward me and his face is suddenly inches from mine, his lips maybe three inches away. He's going to kiss me. My heart's thrashing because I really want him to. I thought he was going to kiss me when we were in my dining room, and like an idiot, I stopped him. But now it's going to happen. He's really going to place his lips on mine.

He leans in minutely, and my eyes flutter shut, my pulse thrashing inside my neck. Because he's going to kiss me, and I'm going to get to know how those lips feel on mine. I'll bet they're soft, but not too cushy. Just as I think his lips are going to connect, a breeze washes over my face.

He's laughing.

I open my eyes to find him staring at me, but now he's more like a solid foot away. His lips are smirking in a crooked line and his eyes are darting all over my face, as if saying, *What? You thought I was going to kiss you? There's no way.*

Now I feel like a complete idiot—I was positive that's what he meant. I'm pretty sure he was inches away from me before because that *was* his intent. So I decide to go for clueless and shoot him the most puzzled look I can. To which Marcus shrugs like *he* doesn't know what I'm talking about. But I can tell he's disappointed I'm not begging for that kiss, because his eyes dart back to me when he thinks I've looked away, and our eyes lock for a split second before we both become so flustered that we look away.

Teo has never tried something like that. Playful isn't quite Teo's style. Erratic mood swings, anger, obsession. Those are the personality traits Teo knows best. Not smiling just because, and never little touches meant simply to buoy me up.

Marc weaves his fingers through my own, and I immediately tighten my hand against his. I love the strength he gives—the hard callouses, the large, wide hands that make me feel safer just having him around. Plus, *he's holding my hand.*

We walk side-by-side in the woods, and he watches the ground, probably to walk quietly. I watch the ground, too—all the little twigs and roots and groundcover masking the dirt—when I stop watching closely enough and my foot crunches a pile of leaves.

"Sorry," I mutter, glancing up at him in time to hook the front of my shoe under a tree branch. I try catching my balance by dropping his hand, but that only makes me succeed in swiping at the air like a lunatic before falling on a hard tree branch, right on my knees.

Marc's voice is soft. "Mad skills, indeed."

I glare up at him. Really? He's joking about that now? But he's staring lower, and when I look down to see at what, I find blood smeared across my knees. Beautiful.

Marc crouches down and gingerly presses his palm to my bare skin. "So, what other talents do you possess?" he asks with only a flicker of laughter now.

"Oh, I don't know." I roll my eyes. "Prostitution, gambling." There's no use in trying to come up with something real, because now I'm staring into Marc's eyes and my brain's sort of turning into slush.

His eyes are sparkling at me, and I hate to be the girl who says the boy's eyes are sparkling, but they are. He looks happy. And I feel the same, like I've just chugged two Red Bulls and am ready to ride on a rollercoaster at Six Flags before buying a funnel cake and stuffing my face. I really can't look away, because his eyes are so *blue*, like the indigo mushrooms in my mom's garden—the exact shade she says mine are.

Marcus is studying me as much as I'm studying him. He lifts his finger and traces my jawline. "You're really pretty, Cheyenne." I try not to blush, but I know I'm failing as he rests the tip of his finger in the dimple of my cheek.

My heart becomes a Ping-Pong ball in my chest, and standing with him now, I *feel* like I'm pretty. I don't know what it is, but when I'm with Marcus, I feel pretty inside *and* out. Not that I'm going to say that out loud.

Marc's fingers trail down my shoulder, my arm, until they find their way into mine. Finger, by finger, by finger, by finger. I never imagined I could shiver in the hot sun, but I'm trembling, happy.

I think he's going to trail his fingers up my arm and shoulder again, but then he does something absolutely unforgiveable. He squeezes my hand.

I pull my hand from his and move away to a mass of thistles. Hand squeezing is one of my biggest pet peeves ever since I saw Mayor Tydal do it to my mom. Ugh. "You did *not* just do that."

Marc's eyes widen, like he hasn't got a clue. "What? I thought you would, uh," he clears his throat, "like it."

He doesn't get it, so I decide to spell it out for him. "You squeezed my hand. That's what old people do."

"So?" His dark eyebrows perk up.

"So, there are plenty of other ways to get my attention. Hand squeezing is just so…" I can't find the right word. Blasé. Cliché. There has to be a word for both, but worse.

Marcus folds his arms over his chest, that sparkle dances in his eyes. "So, you'll never squeeze my hand?" He reaches up and breaks off a gnarled tree branch.

Not in a million years. I shake my head.

"Even if you really want to?"

I shake again.

"Huh." He thinks for a moment, then smiles, a wide grin cracking open his face. "You will," he says before chucking the branch he broke off into the woods.

He may *think* I will, but he's inexperienced with the Laurent family stamina. My mom's so stubborn she *forbids* the guys she dates from opening doors for her. And not just after they're in a relationship. She bites their heads off on the first date.

Something crunches in the woods, maybe twenty, thirty feet from us. *They* have broken through. Or Teo has found us. I drop to the ground, and Marcus does the same, though I catch myself with the palms of my hands, which land right on a twig of thorns. *Crap*—I grit my teeth, force myself to swallow the pain.

Gingerly, I pick up the twig with my other hand and toss it to the side before catching Marc's eye. He winces too.

We're shoulder to shoulder, Marcus's body heat pulling goose bumps from my skin. My heart *thump-thumps*, and I'm afraid he can hear how much he affects me. I want to be closer, am sort of glad to have this excuse not to pull away. He makes me feel so safe and warm, and it's not a feeling I have by myself.

Someone trudges through the trees, the sound of breaking twigs and rustling leaves cracking through the woods. I think they're coming from the fence. But no.

The footsteps are going farther away, away from Teo's compound. A slight clinking sound—the gate?—someone grunts and the clinking sounds again. My legs twitch to follow, to jump up to the sound, but Marcus's steady arm has me planted to the ground. I yearn to shift, because even though Marc's here, it's hard to find a comfortable position with thistles and thorns digging into my hands and feet.

We wait for what feels like hours; the brown-green seeds littered about me give the illusion of grenades ready to explode. Some already have—the casings split open wide—and I tense, jittery, waiting.

Eventually, the crunching grows softer before silencing completely. My instinct is to run, but I force myself to stay on the ground and count slowly to twenty. One, three, six, eleven. I've just hit nineteen when my mouth flies open. "What do you think—?"

"Come on." Marc grabs my hand and pulls me up. It's nice to stand again after lying so long on the ground. Pulling me past a cluster of thorny spikes jutting out from a handful of trunks, we tread past rocks that threaten to trip me. But Marc's directing me. We weave in and out of the trees, and I'm so glad to be with him.

And then I see it. A multilayered, barbed-wired fence cuts us off from the outside. The barbs are so close together that nothing much bigger than a toothpick could fit through. It's twelve feet high. There's no way we can hop the fence, and at the bottom where we might dig a hole, the barbs scratch the surface of a three-foot high stretch of cement. I stare at the wires, trying to detect a break in the fence, when something black and human-sized launches my heart into my mouth.

Body bags.

Two of them.

I try not to look, but I can't help it. I cover my mouth with my hands to stifle a shriek. *Bee.* And Ramus. Ramus and Bee. Deposited like rotten produce or sardines. I saw the body bags that first morning, knew what Teo said, but I never really thought I would see them again, never believed real bodies would be sewn up inside.

Marcus looks away, his face turning the color of the beige carpet in Bee's room, and I step to the fence and stick out my hand, but he catches it. "It's electric, remember?" he chokes out. Of course I remember, but I have to feel closer to Bee.

I shudder; the body bags don't look all that filled—there wouldn't be much of a body left after that lion. But it's like if I can reach my hand through that barbed wire I can reconnect, bring them back to life.

I feel like a ninety-volt battery has already been in direct contact with my chest, but I lower my hand a few inches, know electrocuting myself won't do any good. I stare at that three-foot stretch of cement below the fence and wish I could turn myself into a jackhammer to break through.

"Didn't you say *they* come out at night?" I ask, the little girl in the orange dress from Cleo's TV flashing in my mind.

Marc pushes my hand further down. "When the sun goes down," he says, and my hand tingles where he touched, long after he moves away.

I can't stop staring at the body bags. "How well did you know them?" All I can hear are Ramus's and Bee's screams.

"Ramus and I—we went to preschool together," Marcus answers, and the idea of watching someone you've known your entire life die becomes a new pain. Sharp and biting and dull at once.

Here Marc's been joking around in the woods with me when, really, he's been grieving over the loss of his friend. But that's what Marc does. He jokes to forget the pain. That's what he did when his father died. He screwed around at the math meets when he should have been seeing a counselor instead.

I turn to him, study the lines running under his eyes. Did he have them before Elysian Fields, or did watching his friends get murdered do that to him? Where there was once a faint outline of a bruise, his skin has healed completely to a fair brown, but a bruise seems like nothing compared with the death of our friends. If we're going to move their bodies before the sun goes down, before *they* can get them, we'll need to leave before the party at Izzy's ends.

Marcus doesn't look at me, merely studies the intricate wires of the fence for what feels like an eternity. I wish he would say something. I may technically be engaged to his brother, but it was only to earn the vaccine. My connection to Teo is being replaced by Marcus, which is scary in about a hundred different ways. Am I really one of those girls who needs to have a boy? I never thought I was that way. Before Teo, I was content with my books. Sure, I wanted more than anything to be loved like the heroines were loved in them, but I *was* okay by myself. Maybe I need Marcus right now to help me know what unselfish love is all about.

But I'm not about to bring all this up with Marcus. He'll laugh. So I decide to join him—study the fence and its interlocking gnarls of wire, the silver metal glinting from the sun. There has to be a break. Jonas opened it up. "Do you think it's controlled by another remote?" I ask.

But Marcus isn't listening to me, he's too busy crouching down so that he's eye level with the fence. He scans the close-knit wires, though it's impossible to follow them all. There might be fifty that intersect, just in this small section.

"Even without the electrocution," I say, examining the twisted gnarls of the wire, "it looks like it hurts."

Marc shifts, crouching lower so that he's nearly to his knees. "Do you see any changes in color?" He peers closer at the fence. "Any places where the wires don't look aligned?"

I crouch down next to him, scan the sharp barbs, and study the angles at which the wire flows. Up, right, down, left. They're a labyrinth without any real pattern. It's impossible to tell if there's a break because the wires bunch so closely together. The cement at the bottom of the fence makes me feel trapped, like we'll never break out.

The clicking sound we heard before runs through my head. The click must mean something, so I ask him, "Why do you think it clicked?"

Marcus rubs his hand over the new growth of his beard. "It sounded mechanical. Maybe Jonas pulled a trigger to open the gate."

It's a good hypothesis. Easier than finding another remote. I search for a button on the fence. But I don't see anything there, so I scratch my hands along the dirt for a clue.

"A tree?" I suggest, then spin to search a few close by. I run my fingers on the rough, knobby bark, prick my thumb on what looks like crocodile teeth—thin and jagged. Freaking trees. I move to the next.

Combing the ground close by, Marcus bends down to examine an exposed, splitting root. "If I made a button, I'd put it here," he says, pointing to where the bark has worn away. I step closer to inspect it, too. Bark, thinly veiling the flesh of the tree, is the only feature we find. There are supposed to be buttons. A diagram or two. I run my finger over the tree root and tug on the bits of bark to see if any of it will move, when I slice my finger on a thorn concealed by deadened leaves. *Holy mother—freak.* I look up to Marcus to make some excuse for why I've hurt myself again, but he's staring at the fence, so I suck on my finger to draw out the blood.

Marc's eyes fall to the ground. "Maybe he did make a remote for this."

There has to be. Otherwise, Teo risks people getting out.

"I'll search for it," I offer, looking at the homes through the trees. "Tonight, while everyone's at Izzy's house."

Marcus laughs right in my face. "Think Teo won't notice if you leave?"

That's a little rude. Besides, that's not what I'm thinking. I'll slip my hand inside Teo's coat. But I doubt Marcus will like that any better, so I throw the question back at him. "What do you suggest?"

"I'll search." He shakes his head at me. "Look around for a stash of insulin, too."

His eyes rove over my legs, then jump up to my face. "Just show him a little leg, and you'll have him captive for hours."

I slug him on the arm, which feels *really* nice.

"Just sayin'." He laughs, his eyes sparkling again. "That's how I'd react."

All I can do is groan. "I'd rather pull a fire alarm."

"Assuming Teo has them," he says, shoulders slumping.

"Where'd he get this little community from, anyway?" I'd like to lean against a tree to relax, but those trees will probably jab me in the back. "He couldn't possibly have paid for it with his teacher's salary." I shift my feet from left to right.

Marc's cobalt eyes darken like I've struck a chord. "No, that's not how he paid for this place."

Now I'm getting visions of drug money and the mafia, but that would be ridiculous, so I nudge him on. "Then how?"

Marcus turns his back on me and I watch that muscular back and those low-rider jeans, gulping before looking higher to where he's grabbing some random tree branch. "There was an inheritance," he says, not bothering to turn and look at me. Not that I'm minding. The view's just fine with me.

"What, from a grandparent?" My eyes fall to those jeans again where they're resting just a little too snugly on his hips, but he turns around, catches me looking, and I glance away. It's okay that he caught me, though, because he just told me he thinks I'm pretty.

Marcus rubs his eyes, his chin, his hair, as if rubbing the stress from his face. "My dad."

"That's an awful lot of money he must have had lying around."

Marcus laughs and it's so beautiful, so clear that it matches his face. "Oil rigs." He smirks, looking away from me. "That was the business my dad was in. It paid well."

Marcus stops short like he doesn't want to add anything to that, but I have to know more.

"Okay," I say, trying to slow my reeling mind, "you're saying Teo took that money—from your dad's financial dealings." He must have been raking in the cash.

Marcus kicks a rock. "It was supposed to stay in the bank for college. He used his part for his precious Dartmouth, but he told me he was 'investing' mine."

That can't be right. Teo would never take his brother's money—oh my—of course he would. "But how could your mom let him do that? That was your money for school."

"Welcome to the Richardson family." Marcus shrugs. "Mom's dead, so Teo pisses the money away."

"Wow." I don't know what to say, so I stare at the knobby trees. "Your brother really screwed things up."

Blowing the steam he's collected in his lungs, Marcus says, "At least Teo's saving us from the Living Rot." He looks like he wants to say something else, but he keeps his mouth shut. I can almost feel a tangible wall coming between us. Just like before, he pulls on the front of his hair, and I want him to stop.

"You're doing it again," I tell him. "You're thinking about something, and you don't want me to know what it is."

Marcus looks at me, eyes wide as silver spoons. It's like he can't believe I've watched him long enough to know such a thing. *You are wrong, Marcus.* I smile thinly.

"It's just—" Marc scuffs his feet on an exposed tree root "—we make Teo out to be the bad guy, but really, what's so different between us?"

It's like he's become a prop in a child's game. *All around the mulberry bush, the monkey chased the weasel. The monkey stopped to pull up his sock, Pop! goes the weasel.* And Marcus is the weasel right when I least expect it. He can't possibly compare himself to Teo. It's like comparing an iron maiden with a yo-yo.

But his face reads earnestly. His blue eyes are clear. So I ask what he must be wanting me to ask him. "What do you mean?"

He runs his hand over his stubble, moves on to the back of his hair. "Just what I told you. We're really the same."

He couldn't be more wrong. "You are everything good that your brother is not."

His blue eyes flash, a spark amazingly like his brother's, though blue. "Am I? Don't take it personally, Cheyenne, but you barely know me."

For one humiliating millisecond, my voice makes a strangling sound before I'm able to close it off. How can he say that? I know we haven't grown up together, that we went to two different schools, but I've seen him, wanted to get to know him. Every time, *he* was the one who backed off.

"Let's just say I've screwed up before," he mumbles between his teeth.

When I shake my head, Marcus says, much too loudly, "I killed someone. Do you get it? I killed someone, so we really are alike."

He can't be serious. I've experienced so much warmth from him. He doesn't cause pain. It's like I'm dreaming, not really awake.

I'm sure there's an explanation—a freak accident. He fed someone turnips and they were lethally allergic. Someone slipped on some ice in front of his house. A worker fell from his roof, and he hasn't been able to forgive himself since. But then Marcus is opening his mouth and I have to really focus to understand everything.

"It was late," he tells me, watching the gnarled roots on the ground. "You could say I was missing my mom, so I grabbed one of dad's liquor bottles to—I don't know—I guess to find a friend. But then it was suddenly empty, and I didn't feel so good, so I made my way to the fridge for my insulin, but I remember being so confused because all of it—it was gone."

Marc walks around to the other side of the tree, putting distance between us, and I don't want to push him to be near me, so I gingerly lower myself to the dry ground, hugging my knees.

"You know," Marcus says, voice so monotone it doesn't sound like him, "it was stupid for me to be drinking, being diabetic." He kicks a few leaves. "I think, whether I lived or died that night, I didn't really care. But I knew I had to get some insulin, so I hopped in the car."

No. He said he'd been drinking.

"I tried pulling out of the garage—it took me a few tries—when my dad came outside."

I'm not really sure I can hear what his dad had to say. All I see is a scowling man marching out to the garage.

"Dad was drunk, too," Marc's saying. "Kept telling me to get out of the car, but I didn't care. He never cared for me, not like Mom—she's the one who always got my insulin. Teo helped me after she died, but when he went to Dartmouth, I was on my own—kept screwing it up.

"So I decided to drive to the pharmacy myself, because it's not like Dad would. Everything's sort of a blur after that," Marc mumbles, "but a few things I remember just fine. I remember Dad jumped in the car, and I tried pushing him out, so he punched me and I floored the gas."

No, no.

"We fishtailed our way through our neighborhood. I was mad at him. I just wanted him to leave. I remember thinking, 'If I drive fast enough, the car will separate and I'll be free.'"

Marc.

"When we got to the Target pharmacy, I knew I was supposed to slow down, but my reflexes were off, and I turned several seconds after I should have. There was this group of people—a mom, an elderly lady, and I remember someone small, a little kid."

No.

"But I missed them—"

Oh, thank God!

"—and I remember congratulating myself, but then I yanked the steering wheel left and plowed straight into this stop sign cemented into the ground."

My blood runs cold.

"At first, I thought it was awesome—I mean, I nailed the car like that and I wasn't even hurt. Sure, the windshield was blown to bits, but it was really cool. But then I remembered my dad, looked over, and the stop sign was stuck in his head—" he sucks in a breath and my heart's pounding in my ears. What's he saying? That's not what he's saying. I wait for him to continue, but he doesn't offer a breath.

I try to make sense of what he's just said. He killed his dad? No, there must be more to this story, so I don't say anything, squeeze my legs harder into my chest.

"Afterwards, the state asked to see me," Marc's saying, and I'm backpedaling because it can't be true. His dad can't be dead because of him. "Teo took me to court," he continues, "and, well, you know how my brother can be with people. Instead of me getting locked up, he got me community service."

Nothing's making sense anymore. Good people don't make things happen like this. He was a victim. He was missing his mom. He took charge of his own insulin supply and—no. No, no, no. Everything's hurting. My shoulders and heart feel heavy. When Marc talks to me, it's like his words are echoing, not coming together like they should in order to make sense.

When he says "seventy hours," and "a new man," I'm left wondering how he could ever be that. Because killing your father turns you into nothing. Nothing but sorrow and pain and numb. So he must be telling it wrong. His dad *forced* him to drive that car while drunk, and Marcus really did succeed in pushing him out of their car before he left.

But then Marcus is laughing, which sounds much more like someone's just kneed him in the groin. He's telling me drunk drivers shouldn't get second chances, that some days he wonders why someone didn't serve him with lethal injection instead. He tells me he's the reason his father is dead.

The echoes come faster, like someone's stuck me in a tomb; I'm on a Ferris wheel, but the words are moving too fast. He's the reason, he's the reason his father is dead.

Eventually the echoes slow, die down. Marcus has stopped talking, stares at the tree root again.

With his low voice rasping, he finally says, "So really, Teo and me are the same."

I'm in that tomb, trying to make sense of all the sounds. I never knew my father, thought that was bad enough, but to be the reason why he's dead? I'm glad I'm already on the ground.

I let my legs break loose from my clutch; they're asleep, all tingly like sand's shaking around from inside. I don't know what to say; I feel like there should be words coming out of my mouth, but what he said is true. He killed someone. I've tried to understand, but there's no way I can imagine what that feels like, to know the car *you* drove ended up becoming the vehicle for someone's death. My lips eventually move. "You were a minor."

Marcus walks around the tree toward me, eyes locking on mine as soon as he comes around. "One more screw-up and I'd be in juvie," he says, eyes more dead than flat. It's all beginning to make sense. That one math meet, where he recited the *Pease porridge hot* rhyme, was so odd, so misplaced, it must have been around the same time as his dad's death.

His dad.

No wonder Marcus has a hard time facing reality and reverts to clowning around.

"But you're living your life differently." I try keeping my eyes on his, but it's hard because my voice sounds wobbly and not really like my own. But it's the truth—he hasn't pulled an extravagant stunt at the math meets since junior year.

Marcus crashes down on the ground, leaning against the knobby tree.

"Trying. Not really succeeding." He picks up a rock and chucks it at the fence, which zaps it before it drops. Okay. Maybe that wasn't a rock since it zapped. "It's been a hard year." Of course it has. He lost his dad.

"But, and I'm really sorry to say this, but your dad wasn't even a nice guy," I find myself saying, remembering a few comments he's made about his dad, and knowing Teo is who he is because of who raised him.

"Doesn't matter." Marcus grits his teeth, his face hardening like stone. Stone, because it's easier to grow hard than feel the guilt and hurt.

Sometimes, when I feel guilty about something, my stomach curls—I have a hard time falling asleep. To think of the nights Marcus has lain awake, fighting the way that his stomach must curl. Guilt is a heavy, hollowing thing. It's simultaneously the most intangible and most corporeal emotion. Impossible to express, yet so full of weight.

Unsteadily, I find my feet, make my way over to Marcus, and plunk myself right down beside him on the moss and grass. But he doesn't so much as look up, and I wait for his response, for him to say something, but he doesn't and I know that he can't. I would be feeling the same way if I'd been the one to take my dad's life.

So, gingerly, I reach over and take Marc's hand, and because there's not a single serious thing I could say, or *not* say, I do what I swore I would never do.

I squeeze his hand.

It's corny. I'm halfway wishing I hadn't done it, but it's not like I can wipe Marc's memory, so I have to own the move. My hand feels warm and sweaty—yet calm—inside of his.

Calm. Huh. Such a foreign emotion. I've spent the last year panicked, lovesick, and deluding myself.

Marcus stares at our hands, and I suddenly want to hide again in that tomb.

Slipping my hand from Marcus's, I scratch the back of my neck. Not because it itches, but because it gives my hand something to do.

Marcus clears his throat. "Did you just squeeze my hand?"

My face pounds like a fever, and I know that can't be good, because it only feels that way when it blotches candy-apple red. I hate how I wear my emotions on my sleeve.

But Marcus doesn't seem to mind that I'm blushing, because a tremor of a smile ripples on the side of his mouth. It's not a look of relief, or even acceptance, but it's something of an acknowledgement, and that just may be a start. The entire time I've known him, *he's* been the one to buoy me up. Perhaps I can be the anchor for a change.

I change topics, because I can feel the awkward silence pouring from us both, I say, "So, you still want to leave?"

His gaze shifts and his eyes harden, but a speck of light remains. "Oh, yeah."

But I must be sure that we're both on the same page. "You're completely on board with this," I repeat. I'd understand if he had issues leaving his brother. Okay, I don't think that will be a problem at all.

Marcus frowns, staring again at the fence. "Well, I'd feel a lot better if I could get my hands on that vaccine."

"Okay." I glance at the fence, too. "While you're searching for the remote, I'll look in Teo's coat." Crap. So much for not admitting that out loud.

"Are you *crazy*?" Marcus asks, jumping to his feet. "Don't even think about trying that, Cheyenne. You've seen how my brother reacts to things he doesn't expect."

Yes, I've seen it, but I'm hoping I'll be the exception for once. Teo does have a thing for me. But Marc's hard gaze is searching me, so I nod. "Yeah, okay." We'll see.

Finding my way back to my feet, I try to envision us all at Izzy's and how we'll know the right time to leave, but then the worst scenario of all strikes me. "What if we can't find the vaccine in time?"

Marcus shrugs, but that shrug is more like a war cry, because those blue eyes are so bright. "To hell with it," he says, smiling. "I'll get infected and take a giant bite out of my brother's head."

I hiccup inside, not sure what to think. I don't want Teo to see a grisly end. He's the one person on the planet who cherishes me. I rub the ring on my hand, remembering how he wrote, "For Persephone. My only." At the same time, I know Marcus is right. We do need to put Teo's life behind our own, because Teo's mood swings shouldn't determine who gets to live.

16

Seven couples crowd into Izzy's living room, shocked by the inside of her house. While the others certainly celebrate their couples' themes, this one tops all the rest; I've never seen a river inside a house.

"Look at that," one of the Doublemint boys says, "there's even a little boat."

The famous Lady of Shalott painting greets visitors in the hall. While her actual story isn't directly related to Tristan's and Isolde's, the painting is the perfect link between the two tales—a boat ride in the water is central to both stories, and both involve death.

I remember the story pretty well. Tristan was sent in a boat to pick up Isolde and transport her for her marriage to his uncle. That boat ride was the beginning of something great. Tristan and Isolde fell madly in love, but Tristan's uncle, King Mark, ensured their romance would never last. Of course, the story ended tragically rather than happily ever after.

But that doesn't mean that's what will happen with Tristan and Izzy, and with the preparations I'm sure she's made, she'll be okay. While all of the stories seem to be centered around death, Teo has shown we can earn the vaccine, first with Romeo and Juliet, then me. So really, the killing part isn't an eventuality, but a risk. And the bright look on Izzy's face tells me she's certain her preparations will pull her through. I believe it. With the miniature canal running through the room and the little wooden boat, Izzy's living room makes the perfect setting.

Remembering the sparring session Tristan and Izzy practiced this morning, I ask Izzy as she passes by me, "When's the sword fight?"

She pauses by me in my usual spot in front of the curving stairs. "Later!" Izzy whispers, handing me a milky-white drink. "We thought we'd mix and mingle with our love potions first!" She pops a piece of gum.

Love potions. Izzy is brilliant. Isolde made a love potion for Tristan. I never would have thought to do that. Sipping the drink, I feel the tangy liquid coat my tongue. Pineapple and coconut. It's good. But I need to know whether or not they found props for the sword fight or if they'll pantomime everything. "Did you find any swords?" I ask as I take another sip.

Izzy pops her gum again. "We have one, but for the other, we found something that should work." She brings her finger and thumb up to her mouth and pretends to zip her lips, and I have to laugh. She practically bounces as she walks across the room toward Eloise and Abe, who are munching on their snacks by the snack counter. She's got a handle on everything.

Scanning the room for Marcus, I find him whispering with Cleo on the far side of the room. This time, instead of chaise lounges or benches, Cleo has him cornered on a futon pushed up against the wall. *Hussy.* Almost as if he's connected to my every move, Marcus looks toward me and smiles, like he's remembering our time together in the woods. There's something warm and comforting in his eyes, but it's much too fleeting, because he quickly glances away.

I focus on my drink, pushing all thoughts of Marcus away. I need to plot how to get to Ramus's and Bee's bodies, and how to search Teo's coat. Marcus needs to find a moment to leave to search for insulin, the vaccine, and a remote. But for now, I'm trapped. Teo's chatting with Jonas by the front door. I'm stuck slurping up my drink, the ice tempering my throat. Maybe Jonas grabbed Teo to discuss a breach in the fence. That would be nice. Then, we could all slip through. Of course, if it was a breach, I bet it wouldn't even exist long enough for Teo to know. Jonas seemed like the type who took action before it was required. Even with a breach, we'd be in the same place we are now.

"You polished that off pretty quick," Marcus says, suddenly standing by my side. I glance up, somewhat startled to find him on "my" side of the room. I lean back casually, letting the wrought-iron rails of the staircase dig into my back, blushing as I remember our two "almost" kisses. But, despite what one would think, wrought iron rails aren't all that comfortable, so I lean forward.

Desperately hoping I don't look like an idiot, I try slurping another sip of my drink but end up only sucking up air. Nice. Why am I only smooth when Teo's around?

"Here, have mine." Marcus offers his glass.

"Oh, no," I laugh his chivalry away. "That would make me a glutton."

"I don't think that would necessarily be a bad thing," Marcus says, locking his eyes on mine, which makes the stupid way I'm standing suddenly feel wobbly, so I straighten my legs.

For some reason, I'm staring at Marc's eyes again. Not the color, but the shape—how they're open and honest, not needing to be clever or right.

Cleo, ever on the warpath, follows Marcus from across the room. I watch her rock-hard calves flex as she steps over the moat; there's not a hint of fat or anything. And I think it's time to bury myself alive, because I've just caught myself checking Cleo out.

"Why, Number Eight," she says, eyeing Marcus and me, "you just go from one Richardson brother to the other." Wow, Cleo's just full of laughs.

I give her a laugh of my own. "At least I don't sit on their laps." *Slut*. I have to bite my lip, because I really want to add that last part, but I don't want Marc to think less of me. For some reason Cleo is his friend, and while I'll never get it—except that maybe he's in love with her curves—I decide to let my little line stand by itself and stare Cleo down until she squirms.

But Cleo purrs right into Marc's ear, "Shall we tell her about the fence?"

Wait, Cleo's in on the fence project, too? This has to be her idea, not Marc's. She was, no doubt, searching the periphery with him, her caramel-colored skin camouflaging perfectly with the trees. Ugh. She'd better not be out there with him at night.

Marcus opens his mouth like he's about to answer Cleo, but Teo, dressed in his black suit as always, enters the room. Marcus and I missed our window for searching for the remote! True, Marcus distracted me anyway, but we would have made a little more progress if Cleo hadn't decided to skank her way in. Striding to where I stand by the staircase, black fury exudes from Teo's face. He doesn't acknowledge the party, much less the little body of water slicing down the center of Izzy's room. But he's supposed to be happy, celebrating, because there's a ring on my finger. We're engaged.

Glancing at my empty drink, Teo holds his hand out for his brother's. "May I?" he asks, then immediately plucks the love potion from Marcus's grip. Now that was downright rude.

"Persephone," Teo's voice is uncharacteristically low, "tell me. What has the couple done to demonstrate their faithfulness tonight?"

I take a deep breath to ground myself for my greatest tribute to Izzy's and Tristan's efforts. It needs to bolster his confidence, so I need to play nicely, but straight to the point. "You, Teo," I say, "are partaking of their faithfulness this very moment." Surely he'll see that once he tastes the drink.

Teo slowly drops his eyes to the drink, staring at the milky-white liquid for a moment. "And how is that?" he jovially asks, but he's being sarcastic, which is so very far from how he should react. He should be smiling. Chuckling. Remarking that he's never tasted a more delicious drink. He's supposed to be in a great mood. We're newly engaged. He should be bragging, showing off my new ring, and, of course, be oblivious to everything between Marcus and me.

"This is a love potion," Marcus says, and I'm so glad he's here to defend Izzy now. I even like the way he's standing. So confident—shoulders squared, and arms and chest maybe twice the size of Teo's. "Remember?" Marc asks. "Isolde made it for Tristan?"

Teo's teeth show in an asymmetrical smile. "Ah, yes, thank you for that, Marcus. And how is your evening tonight?" Teo's words weigh on me so heavily it's hard to move. I don't like how he's gripping the wrought iron of the stairwell above my head, like he's looming over everybody.

Marc shrugs, stuffing his hands in his pockets. "Cleo and I were just wondering how you bring in your food." And now I'm wondering if Marcus *wants* to get into trouble, because Teo hates it when he stuffs his hands in his pockets—he never said so, but even now he's narrowing his eyes at his brother. It's like Marc's trying to pick a fight with Teo, or maybe he's searching for a hint about how Jonas leaves the subdivision through the fence.

Teo's eyes flash as he looks away from Marc. "I see," he says slowly. "And is that your only question? Or would you like me to go over my budget, too?"

Marc pales, and I think I might be paling, too. Teo's sarcasm is coated pretty heavily. I imagine his budget isn't something he'd like to discuss publicly, what with the money he's spent from their dad's lucrative oil business and the cost it must take to run this place. I mean, I've never heard of a generator that could support an entire subdivision before.

"I just wanted to know..." Marcus falters, "to see if you needed any help."

Teo turns to me as if in private, arms gripping the wrought-iron rails above my head. "Do you hear that, Persephone? My brother has offered his services. What a treat."

My fingers twitch at the close proximity of the remote in his suit, which has to be there. I should defend Marcus, but that might only make his position worse. I could pretend that I don't hear Teo's sarcasm and agree that Marc could be helpful, but I doubt Teo will believe that.

"And you, Cleopatra," Teo gestures toward Cleo with his drink, "do you offer your services as well?" Teo's cold, hard eyes run over Cleo's body. I clench my fingers tighter around my goblet, because even though I'm not still gaga over Teo, she does *not* have to draw every guy's attention in the room.

"Everyone!" Teo shouts. "I think we should take a vote. There are whisperings that the mindless masses mean to harm us; this is not a time for frivolity or rudimentary devotion." Wait, so there's a breach in the fence?

Pivoting from where he stands, Teo skulks around the group. He paces in front of Izzy, who's made her way over to the futon where Marc and Cleo were sitting on the east side. "Who here believes our host and hostess pass?" Teo asks. "Has their love potion demonstrated their devotion to Elysian Fields? Do you, in fact, believe this to be a sufficient expression of their tale?"

Of course it is. It reflects the story perfectly. Besides, he's now down to his seven. That's what he wanted all along, so we should be okay.

Izzy chirps in. "But that's not everything we have planned!" And she's right. Teo will *adore* the sword fight. She gestures to Tristan, standing high up on the balcony, and when he reaches for a curtain rod resting against the wall, my chest caves. A curtain rod isn't quite what I would say makes an adequate prop for a sword fight. Now, Lance's Excalibur replica looks fine, but the curtain rod? Not good.

The boys square off when Teo says what I'm thinking. "You're fighting with *those*?" Though that's not quite how I would say it. But the fact that they've planned a sword fight makes me think they should be okay. Romeo and Juliet only planned one activity with the ball—no, wait, they planned the skit at the end, too. So maybe Teo expects three links to the story. And swords that better resemble, well, swords.

Sal, hovering by the windows, plucks his glasses from his nose. Polishing them on his shirt, he answers Teo. "If I'm correct, critics of Wagner's masterpiece accused him of composing an opera too seductive, too wanton for dignified taste. 'Tristan and Isolde,' the play, was considered crass." Sal is *so* not helping Tristan and Izzy right now. I could dig a hole and toss him in.

Teo steps delicately over the moat toward Sal. Sal replaces his glasses and wipes a sheen of sweat on his forehead with the back of his hand, but Teo merely smiles at Sal's apparent anxiety. "And what do you mean by this?" Teo asks. "How does this help you rule for or against their demonstration?"

"The love potion was only the beginning," Sal says, breathing raggedly. "It was not the climax of the tale." No, Sal. *No, no, no.* "Tristan and Isolde's relationship was not merely a dalliance." He waves a shaking hand. "They committed to one another." But Izzy's not merely dallying. She's made her own love potion and concocted this action-packed scene. King Mark and Tristan really did fight in the story. I'll bet Lance is planning on playing King Mark.

"But we—!" Izzy gestures madly over to Lance and Tristan, but neither boy dares to move. Teo drops his head sideways and swivels it back and forth, which could be both a very good or very bad thing. He's relaxed, which, for most of us, means he should be happy, but with Teo, oh with Teo, there's really no way to know. A smile in someone's direction could mean he's pleased or that they are the next one to die. He turns, examines the others in the room— how Eloise, Juliet, and Gwen all huddle closely together by the snack counter, and how Ana's frowning, her eyes darting back and forth between Sal and Teo. Teo lifts his gaze back up at Tristan. "What have you to say?"

Please, Tristan, say something convincing. Say something eloquent, something that will make Teo proud.

I take a few steps back so I can have a better view of Tristan high above us on the balcony. He moves to set the curtain rod back against the wall, but the rod slips, marking the wall.

"Sorry," he squeaks, setting the rod upright, and I'm having serious doubts about Tristan offering a sweeping speech. He clears his throat a few times, and actually takes the time to fasten his long hair into a ponytail with shaking hands. "We, uh, just wanted to do something that worked with the tale." He whips a pink streak he missed away from his eyes and tucks it behind his ear.

Teo turns his gaze back down to the couples with him on the first floor. "And you, Izzy?" he asks, facing Izzy on the other side of the moat. "Are you incapable of further commitment?"

Oh, so he's digging for a proposal now. Okay, Izzy should have this.

Chewing her gum wildly, Izzy sputters, "I don't know if I know exactly what you're saying. If you mean to ask why we haven't talked about *marrying,* well, I guess I have to say we're pretty young. I mean, we're only seventeen! And I like your little neighborhood, Teo, but it doesn't even have a gym—"

Izzy cuts herself off, visibly aghast that she's spoken this grievance out loud. I don't know if I should start looking out for Jonas with that stun gun, or help defend Izzy against Teo. Izzy's looking from Teo up to Tristan, then back again, her eyes darting madly between them, no doubt scrambling for what to do.

"I'm sure we can think of other ways to prove our worth." She's stalling. "I mean, you haven't said much in the way of what we should be doing during the day. I could help out with that."

Silence washes over the room as the little boat in the moat knocks gently on the side of a fake rock. I stare at the boat, wishing I could grab Izzy and whisk us away. Then we could create her version of Elysian Fields where every house is connected to its own personal gym.

When I find the courage to look up at Teo, I flinch to find his jaw slack and his eyes more yellow than black. Without warning, he lurches back over the moat, grabbing Izzy by the wrists. He flings her empty goblet into the moat, but it smashes into the rock, shattering.

Someone by the snack counter takes in a sharp breath, followed by someone shushing them. No one wants to face Teo's wrath.

Teo spins to face Tristan, but he's much too high on the balcony. Teo's eyes dart about the room before shouting, "Assistance, now!"

At that instant, Jonas darts from the front door. Two or three steps at a time, he sprints up the stairs, straight for where Tristan stands at the top. I watch, helpless, as Lance sees Jonas coming and lifts up his sword—the Excalibur replica—like he means to deter Jonas and his stun gun. But this can't be happening. It can't. Because I remember the last time Teo let Jonas loose on a couple. They didn't live.

"*No*," someone mumbles, but I'm too terrified to look who. Someone shouts, halfway mumbles, but I can't look, I can't move.

Jonas jukes effortlessly around Lance, who's lifting the Excalibur high above his head. In one swift movement, he connects his stun gun to Tristan's chest. Tristan jolts, his loose pink streak jerking madly about his face, and a strangled voice somewhere behind me whimpers. I'm hyperventilating, because this can't be happening again. I can't even predict it, because this is nothing like what happens in Tristan's and Isolde's tale. Shouldn't Teo see this?

Izzy shrieks and runs toward me by the stairs, but she should be running the other way. Abe takes a step forward, but Eloise pulls him back, whispering frantically to him. I want to scream, *Run, Izzy!* But what can I do? If I show my disgust, Teo might massacre everyone in the room. Cleo knows it, because every vein in her face looks like it's going to pop, but she stands there, because she knows retaliating can mean her death.

I look to Marcus, who's already running for the bottom of the stairs, when Jonas pulls out a dagger from a strap on his leg. Lunging forward, Jonas plunges it straight into Tristan's chest. Izzy and I shriek and Abe's hand balls into a fist, but he doesn't move, doesn't move, no doubt knowing if he does, he'll be killed next. My heart's in my throat as I watch blood spurt from Tristan's mouth, his pink and green streaks fluttering as he falls to the floor.

Lance spins wildly for the stairs, his blond hair trailing behind him in a wisp. But he plows right into Marcus, and both boys, thrown off-balance, tumble down the stairs— Marc rams headfirst into the wrought-iron railing, and Lance flies straight down to the floor.

But the boys are a distraction, just a distraction, so I snap my head up again, only to see Jonas pulling the dagger out of Tristan's crimson-colored chest.

This is a life! I yearn to shriek into a megaphone, to launch my body onto Teo and pound his head with my fists. These are *people* and he's killing them, simply choosing who should live. And Teo's friend, Jonas? I want that dagger to plunge into *his* chest. I want to sprint up those stairs, slice up his intestines, and force Teo to feed. Teo says he's saved us from the Living Rot? No, Teo can go to hell, because the Living Rot is right here.

I stalk toward Teo, forming the words I'm desperate to say. *You are done as our leader. You want to hurt someone? Hurt me!*

My footsteps are glacial—almost laughably slow. I see the distance between us—he, on the other side of the moat by the windows, and me, trudging from the side of the stairs. But I'm getting there. I'm going to convince Teo to make sense, when a whir of white flashes right by me, and it takes me maybe only half a second to realize it's Jonas, his maniacal, mud-brown eyes now fastened on Izzy.

"Run, Izzy!" Eloise cries just as Abe slaps his hand over her mouth, and Eloise falls into his arms with a sob.

Izzy's face pales as she sees Jonas coming toward her with his bloodied dagger. The muscles in her jaw feather slightly before she spins away from Jonas toward the food, and when he lunges for her, she leaps into the air and flips over the moat, then flips again, back onto the kitchen side. She spins for the windows, reaches the back door, and I think she's about to open it when she seems to change her mind. She waits for Jonas to come closer before jumping into the air, kicking her legs out into a split, and connecting with Jonas's chest. He staggers backward. Izzy sprints for the kitchen and begins flinging open drawers.

All this time, I can't believe none of us have moved. Ana's cowering in the corner, wringing her hands like she wants to do something, and I grapple with the skirt of my dress, trying to think how I can stop this. Marc's glancing around, I'm guessing for a weapon, but Sal's folding his arms with a nasty smirk on his face. He can't *really* approve of Teo's world. I hate him. The girls by the snack counter cling madly to their partners, Eloise stuffing her head into Abe's shirt. And I'm suddenly wishing I'd trained with Izzy in cheerleading so I could help her escape.

Izzy's found a meat grinder, a potato masher, and a spatula. She flings these at Jonas's face, but he ducks away and lifts the dagger high above his head, and my heart's pumping rivers of blood in my throat.

"STOP!" Marcus cries, gripping his brother by the shoulders, and the veins in my body constrict.

Jonas freezes for a moment, locks eyes with our leader, and Teo nods, causing Jonas to lower his knife. *Ohmygosh.* I thought Izzy was dead—I fight back the urge to throw my arms around her now, slurp up piña coladas with her, just because we can. She's okay. She's going to be okay.

I glance over to Marcus, shooting him the most grateful look I can. A flicker of a "you're welcome" flashes over his eyes. But a blur of movement causes me to turn my head. That movement is the last one I would expect, because it's Jonas lowering his weapon straight into Izzy's chest, her eyes bulging in surprise.

He's killing my friend. I stare at the crimson flowing from her chest, unable to believe the location of the knife. Marcus had yelled, and Teo had nodded for Jonas to stop. I turn to Teo to see how he will deal with Jonas—if it will be his turn to die now—only to find a delighted smirk traveling over his lips.

I could puncture those lips right now. Squeeze them so tightly that blood gushes out. I want Teo to die the same ways as *all* the others. Get mauled alive by a lion, then stabbed again and again with a sword. By me.

Quiet splinters across the room before a high voice starts chirping, "OMG." It's Gwen, hair sticking out in tufts, mumbling the acronym over and over again. "OMG," she says again before burying her face in Lance's neck.

"Honestly," Teo says, and almost as an afterthought he tells Jonas, "Won't you take care of that?" He gestures vaguely at Gwen. Before I know what's happening, Jonas steps to Gwen, places his alabaster fingers on her head, and snaps her twig-like neck. Silence fills the room again and we're all statues. No one moves.

"Much better," Teo sighs as her body thuds to the floor. "The acronyms were getting on my nerves." He looks around the room and locks eyes on Lance. "Of course, what good is one without the other?"

Lance starts to move across the moat, but Jonas is already there. He reaches for Lance's neck, the movement so quick, so unbelievably fast. Then he's on the floor, too.

Teo breathes in like the air about him has become smooth. "It will be much more peaceful now."

It's impossible to breathe. My throat keeps catching on my screams and pain. I can't look away from them on the floor, and it's the last place I want to look. I can't believe he did this. I can't. I can't. Cold fingers wrap around my wrist. I don't look up as Teo lifts my hand high, showing my gold ring. "You must *prove yourselves* if you wish to earn the vaccine." He squeezes my hand tighter and pulls me to his sinewy body. I'm forced to look at him, and bile burns my throat, tears burn my eyes as he presses his lips to mine.

There is nothing I can do to understand this night. Why would Teo go to such great lengths to build a universe of seven, only to dash it to pieces so quickly?

I don't care what is on the outside. I will risk it—do anything to escape. I don't know how I loved this man. I wish I could undo it all.

Teo. Oh, Teo. How could you murder my friends?

I hurry back to my house and curl up in bed, pulling my knees to my chest. Marcus, please come tonight. I know it's against the rules, but you managed it before. Please tell me you have an idea about opening the fence. I will do anything to sail from the Gulf, to beyond, with you.

But instead of fingers, raindrops knock at my back door. They pelt, shower, trickle in indifference to Teo's world. It's the sound that fills my ears as I drift to sleep.

That night, I dream of leaving Elysian Fields for the very first time. There's a radiant field of wheat just past the fence, but I never actually see myself cross over—the dream picks up from the other side. The field of wheat matches my flaxen hair, and not only is the color of my hair golden, but my clothes are, too. That's when I see the others, dressed precisely the same way: Marcus and Ana, and because it's a dream, Izzy and Bee. The others are there, too, laughing about the "love potion" and Bee's attempt to strangle the lion with her bare hands.

In the very middle of the field, when we're fully hidden by the wheat, vials of insulin drop from the sky. When I reach up to grab one for Marcus, Teo cries my name. But we're too far away. We run deeper into the field, drifting away from his voice, and he doesn't follow because he can't see.

17

I don't understand why Teo brought us here in the first place. Why would he build Elysian Fields, fix a budget, and continue to add to the dead? Did he start construction before the Living Rot broke out again? He must have. Too much had been built when we arrived for it to be a last-minute plan. But he couldn't have been the only one to have known about the return of the Living Rot. Surely, the news would have told us if it was back. Or maybe Teo swept us away before we could hear.

There's a knock at the door, and groggily I find my feet. Maybe that's breakfast, but Jonas has never knocked before, just left the basket. Crossing the length of my pristine hardwood floor, I ease open the front door. It's overcast today—I've never seen Texas so consistently gloomy in May, like God knows to weep—and with this darkened day, dense humidity moves about me.

On my porch sits the usual basket, but this time a note is attached, which makes my stomach clench. Notes remind me of Izzy. And now she's dead. *Dead.* One minute I was planning another drink of piña coladas, and the next, I was looking at the bright crimson flowing over her green dress. *She's gone.* And there's nothing I can do. I wish I could cheat time and help her plan a party that would impress Teo enough to let her live.

Gripping the note in my hand, I move to the kitchen table and open the folded note written in a foreign scrawl:

Dear female resident:

To better prove your devotion to us at Elysian Fields, please stand outside by your front poplar tree at 10:00 am for a one-on-one session with your partner. The men will be permitted to cross the street to your yard for precisely one hour.

May you prove your faithfulness like never before.

The Consortium of Elysian Fields

I spin around to look at the clock on the wall: 9:30 am. I only have half an hour. I'd been hoping to spend time with Marcus, though I knew it probably wouldn't happen. That time we spent together was exactly what I needed to clear my head. I sincerely hope he isn't seeing Cleo when he's searching the fence. Maybe my meeting with Teo will be over soon and I can meet up with Marcus again.

Thirty minutes. I had better take a shower and don the Persephone persona Teo likes. Prove my faithfulness like never before? I'm not sure what that means, but this is precisely the moment I need; if I'm lucky, I can swipe the remote I've seen him use from his coat.

*   *   *

At three seconds to ten, I brush through the door, my pink dress fluttering behind me. I bring a blanket for us to sit on, though it's really to hide the remote, should I get my hands on it, and urge my shaking legs to move toward the poplar tree where Teo patiently waits on the grass.

"Persephone." He reaches out for me as I approach, and I try not to scowl at those death-inducing hands. "Impressive foresight." He nods at the blanket in my hands. *Good, he simply thinks it's to sit on.* Together, we stretch out the blanket, a throw I found in a linen closet, and gingerly, I kneel down. I'm not ready to focus on Teo yet—it's almost impossible to look at him when I know I need to get the remote, so I look to the other couples on the road. Abe, one house away, sits next to Eloise and places a dandelion in her hair, and I try seeing around them to the next yard, then remember it's vacant because Izzy and Tristan are no longer there. The yard beyond them is empty, too.

Hollow, I turn back to Teo, not believing this is how I must live. Pretend to love a man who sops up his boredom with the lives of my friends. His head tilts up a few inches, the lids of his eyes soaking in the sun's rays, which is an odd sight, since I would never think of Teo sunbathing. He's almost glowing in the sunlight, and I have to force down a feeling of wonder at that bronzed skin. *Teo is poison*, I repeat to myself.

"Persephone," he says, and I haven't repeated that thought long enough. How am I going to get my fingers on that remote? "May I tell you a bit more about our home?"

I nod. *Yes, Teo, tell me—what possesses you to murder on a whim?* "Please."

A casual smile plays on Teo's soft, round lips. I don't understand how he can be so serene. It makes me wonder if he was born that way, or if he picked up his cruel nature from his dad. I could believe that.

Staring up into the sky, Teo starts explaining something, and I can't tear my eyes off his black coat. He must be sweltering. But it's okay with me. If I can just scoot close enough, I can slip my fingers inside his coat, retrieve the remote, and conceal it beneath the blanket.

"While studying at Dartmouth," Teo says, "I enjoyed a literature class or two."

I shift a leg toward him so it's easier to lean toward his coat.

"My favorite dealt with mythology," he continues. "Did you know, for instance, that Hades segmented the Underworld into three separate kingdoms? Asphodel, Tartarus, and Elysium, or as some call it, Elysian Fields."

I stiffen, my knee brushing the bottom tip of his coat. I thought the subdivision name was one he'd plucked from a community he'd liked. Like Chisholm Trails, or Marine Creek. This can't be good.

"A surprise to you?" Teo asks me.

Of course it is. But I limit my reply to, "Yes."

Teo clucks his tongue as he runs his fingers over the bark of the poplar tree. It reminds me of the other tree he touched in Elysian Fields—the mulberry behind Ramus's house. I start shaking, and it's stupid because it's maybe ninety degrees. Or maybe I could use this. Say I need a bit of comfort and ask to borrow his coat.

Teo must see my twitching fingers—how I keep pulling on the short fibers of the blanket—because he says, "It frightens you. My dear Persephone, there is nothing to cause fear. Elysian Fields, as written in legend, is for the heroic, the virtuous, those who deserve a place to rest."

So what, the others weren't worthy? Just because they didn't know what "proving themselves" means to him? But I collect my fingers on my lap and force them not to twitch. "I see," I say, not moving my eyes from the spot where my knee's touching the smooth fabric of his coat.

Teo drops his hand from the poplar tree and shifts his gaze to me; I look away.

"What the common man does not understand," Teo says, "is the nature of Hades. Most consider him gross, evil, but that is not true. Hades of the Underworld was a god like the others, but consigned to live in a different place."

I just need to grab him around the head and lock lips. That's the only way I'm going to get close enough to that remote, and distract him from feeling me take it if he does have it with him. But I can't make myself do it, I just can't.

"In fact," he's saying, "mythology teaches us that his role was not evil, but passive. Maintaining balance. And that is what I have promised myself to do here."

I can't help but look up to his smiling face. *What is balanced about killing kids?* I try to see down the houses to catch a glimpse of Marcus, but he's too far away. But I want to see Marcus, I need to see Marcus, because with these twitching fingers of mine, I need someone to make them lie still.

Teo's watching me—his eyes bore into the side of my face—probably noticing how I'm so far away, so I take a deep breath and force myself to look back at his sallow face. "And what about your number seven?" I force myself to say. "Now you are down to five." Surely he can see he's possessed.

Teo chuckles, a low rumbling laugh in his throat. Leaning forward, he loops a piece of my hair around his finger and says quietly, "Oh, Persephone. How pleased it makes me, knowing you and I think alike."

I stiffen in his grasp, tell my hand to move inside his coat for the remote, but he's watching me, and it's impossible in the position I'm in. With my luck, the remote's on the other side, anyway.

Teo's waiting for some sort of acknowledgement or something. I stretch my lips tight, not really remembering what he just said, so I offer a blanket statement. "You're right."

"There is a secret, my love," Teo says, crisscrossing his legs to lean in to whisper into my ear, "that you cannot tell." His familiar scent of Listerine and smoke washes over me, thrilling me for maybe a microsecond before I squash that pathetic part of me. He has a secret. The naïve part of me believes he's going to pull out his remote and offer that I help run things for a bit.

His ebony eyes smolder, and it's like I make him nervous, because he looks away from me to the tree. I never knew I had that effect on him. It's good, though; it means he still believes I don't see us being apart.

"Before," Teo says, "I was misguided. Believed there to be a perfection, a godliness regarding the number seven—"

"There's not?" Teo has never admitted an error in the past.

"Oh, no," he says, licking his lips. "There is a far greater majesty in another number." He breaks off a piece of bark. "Have you any idea what it is?"

I shake my head, staring at the bark in his hands. Now I very much doubt that he's pulling out his remote.

"Three," he says proudly, as if he's announcing the number of his sons, but I am distracted by three black ants marching, as focused and uncaring as Teo is. "I gave you the hint, you know, when I said Hades kept *three* sections in his kingdom below."

I want to curl up, cover my head. He's taking lives, dropping us like we're already dead. When he kills us, it's like he doesn't *feel* anything. That's what psychopaths are, right? People who do horrendous things and don't feel a thing.

Well, there you have it. My first love, kiss, and obsession is a psychopath. And I thought my mom's boyfriends were bad.

"And so, my dear Persephone, I need your help, much like Jonas once needed mine."

The air is a thick gulf of water pressing down on my head. "Jonas?" He seems like the last person to need Teo's help. His kung fu moves made it look like he can take care of himself.

Maybe I could say I'll help him if he lets me take charge of the remote. Flutter my eyelashes and remind him of that time we spent in his room.

But Teo spreads his lips in a patronizing smile. "One detail at a time, my love. Let us not say too much." He pats my head like I'm a child, and I wonder if people with psychopathic tendencies think everyone is below them.

"I suppose," Teo says, "it will take you some time to accept the fact that I do make mistakes." I choke a little, but I coolly swallow down my spit, because Teo would *not* understand me laughing right now.

Petting the blanket like it's made of satin, Teo goes on. "I was blinded by the number seven; I hope you can accept that. But will you forgive me? Help me determine the most faithful three?"

How can he think I would do that—list who he kills next? Panic tightens in my chest, and it's like Teo can see it, because his eyes narrow. I force myself to nod, my mind reeling. Maybe this is the way I can save the rest. If I can convince Teo to force those he doesn't want to leave, and if I can get them the vaccine, they might stand a chance. It would take a lot of persuading, but if I could help them escape Elysian Fields, maybe they could find a refuge from the Living Rot somewhere else.

But Teo's waiting for an answer, and I have to be as convincing as possible. If he discovers my plan to give everyone he's brought here a free ticket to the outside world, he won't be happy, so I force my voice to sound as unfeeling as possible. "You should kick them out."

Teo narrows his eyes, and they become two black slits in the daylight. "And why would you say that?"

Perspiration trickles down my back; this is when the convincing starts. I need to be logical, and see things his way. I need to save everyone. Not the way I failed Bee and Izzy, Gwen and the boys, too. I narrow my eyes like I saw him do and speak as callously as I can. "Didn't you say Elysian Fields in the myth was only for the pure? Those who don't deserve to live here should be ostracized from our society. To let them die in this place would mean an honorable death." *Yes.* They might evade the sickness. Get to the Gulf. Maybe I should convince him Marc should go, but I want Marcus to stay.

Narrowing his eyes again, Teo says, "I find it interesting that I asked you *who* you thought should leave and you offered *how* the disfavored should go. I shall remember this. You seem to be fixated on the thought."

All I can see are the others dropping—like Izzy and Bee. And Ramus. And Tristan. Lance and Gwen. Six deaths are on my hands. He's killing them and I'm letting it be. I can't allow this; I need to show him this plan is pointless—that he'll never be happy even if he gets down to three.

"And that concludes our date." Teo jumps to his feet just as my heart lands in my throat. I got so caught up in the fact that he's getting down to three couples that I didn't reach for the remote. I make myself follow, grasp for words that float around in my head. I could ask him to kiss me. I could throw my arms around him.

"It was a morning of bliss," Teo says as he brushes his lips across my face, my hair. I tense for a millisecond to reach inside his coat when he brushes his lips on my throat.

Warmth surges up and down my chest. *I like it. My neck actually likes it.* I deserve to be flogged and dragged down this hellish street.

Shaken, I thrust my hand in his coat, but just in time, Teo stoops down to grab the blanket. Setting it in my hands, he says, "Again, thank you, my love, but I fear ostracism is against my ideals. Better for our neighbors to face a death of haste than face the rage of Hades should they try to leave."

And then he's gone, and I've failed to get the remote.

Shaking and angry with myself, I watch the four remaining men stroll to the street after Teo. They do not dawdle, but stride purposefully to their homes. I try to see down the line, watch each of them as they leave, but Abe's happy gait distracts me. He kisses Eloise's letter again and again, but he doesn't dare turn to wave goodbye.

How will Teo pick which of the remaining couples should stay? Will two of them be the girls who haven't held the parties in their own homes, or are they destined to failure no matter what they prepare? Or maybe Teo will accept whatever these ladies do, now that he seems to be in a more contented mood.

I need to speak with Marcus; I need to know what he's learned about the fence, if it's possible for us to escape. Because the clock's ticking and there's no telling how long Teo will stay content like this.

18

Walking toward my red brick house and its pencil-thin trees, I notice my mailbox lid has fallen wide open, so I reach inside. My fingers touch a letter, and when I rip it open, it's in the same handwriting as the letter from before. This must be Jonas's writing, because now it states that he will host the next party.

Part of me is relieved—this gives the remaining couples more time to plan their soirées. But why would Jonas host a party? Maybe it has something to do with what Teo said about Jonas owing him.

Once inside my house, I'm torn as to what to do. It's early, not even lunchtime. Yesterday, I might have expected Izzy to pop in with a plan, but there is no Izzy. No one to pop aerials or gush over boys. If I could, I'd go to my room and pull the blankets over my head, but that is not how to "best" Teo. I need to research our escape. Marcus and Cleo may be rustling around in some trees, so I *need* to find them.

Whisking through Bee's house and out the back door, I fly past the backyards—narrowly missing a few of those anthills again—and once I find the spot where I saw Marcus yesterday, behind Cleo's house, I jump into the trees.

I round the short and extra-knobby one I found Marc standing near yesterday, but I come up empty. No Marcus.

What did I think he was doing? Sitting around here all day hoping to find me? There's no way I'm going to find him in the trees. I still can't believe I didn't grab the remote.

Picking my way through the spikey trees, I pray the people contaminated with the Living Rot didn't take Ramus and Bee. I can only imagine what they would do to them with their blood-dripping teeth.

Running now, I whip past branches and bark and leaves, everything a green and brown blur. A few thorns snag on my skirt like claws on a witch's bony fingertips, but I keep going, because I *must* see Ramus and Bee.

When I reach the fence, though, nothing catches my eye from the other side. The body bags—they're supposed to be there. I move down the fence line in case I'm not in the same spot, narrow my eyes to slits to peek through the wires. But beyond the fence I only see more woods and trees. Maybe a field after that, but it's hard to see.

I'm not seeing dark shadows. No body bags. My heart leaps to my throat; I'm too late.

As I'm batting away a low tree branch tickling the back of my leg, a low voice makes me stop.

"You sure know how to make that tree look good," Marcus says, tromping toward me.

It has to be the cheesiest pickup line I've ever heard, but he's here. Maybe he was looking for me. I'm lucky it wasn't Teo or Jonas who found me.

Five or six seconds too late, I say, "Just one of my many hidden talents." I don't have the heart to bring up Ramus and Bee.

My timing is awful, but Marcus is quick on the uptake. "Like walking quietly in the woods at night?" He ambles closer, the sun skittering through the leaves highlighting the blues in his eyes.

I scowl. "Whatever. I was wearing the wrong kind of shoes." *Wrong kind of shoes?*

"Ah, yes," he plants himself in front of me, "tennis shoes are terrible for walking in the woods."

I grunt, because there's nothing brilliant I can say to that, but a slow smile twitches Marc's upper lip. I'm not sure how, but we're suddenly inches apart, and I'm not entirely sure who closed the distance. We're nearly chest to chest, and—

Dear God, why's he so shiny? He's sopping wet.

"Marc?" I take a step back, because there's something wrong with him. I am hot, but not enough to get sweaty. The sweat coating his chest makes it look like he's just stepped out of the shower. His face is dripping wet. This has to be a diabetes thing.

Marcus doesn't move. His steaming hand holds onto the small of my back, and I don't want to spoil this moment, but I know that I should—something's very wrong. "Marc?" I look into his eyes. "Is your insulin working all right?"

He shrugs. Lots of shrugging from Marcus—I wonder if that's something he picked up from all those weekends hanging out with Ramus—that indifferent side. I should tell him about my conversation with Teo and how he's planning to get down to three couples, but Marc's talking again and there isn't time. In the slow, lazy way he has with telling me things, he says, "I may have exaggerated a little how much insulin I have left."

My stomach spirals straight down. "How much do you have left?" A day or two, probably.

He shrugs again, but he doesn't answer what I asked. Instead, he toys with one of those grenade-like seeds with his boot. Why's he avoiding answering me? It can't be because he didn't hear me, and I know it's not because he doesn't trust me. He doesn't have any left.

I feel my mouth working, but no sound comes out. "You ran out, didn't you?"

There's no way I'm bringing up the other couples now, because Marcus already has too much on his plate. He should be in a hospital, hooked up to an IV.

Marcus shrugs again. "I have a few hours left. I'm stretching it out." I'm about done with all this shrugging. He needs to take it easy, lie down. But he also shouldn't have lied to me. He should have told me exactly how much he had from the beginning.

"We need to find Teo, now!" I tug his hand. This is stupid, hanging out in the woods when he's about to crash. What if he has a seizure or falls over or something? I don't even know CPR. I can't dial 911 or anything—

But Marcus acts like he doesn't hear me. He smiles this goofy, close-lipped smirk. "You know," he says, "I'm going to be dead soon, anyway. I know you think of me as just a friend, but it would mean a lot to me if we could—" He stares at my lips. If he only *knew* how badly I want to kiss him. To know if his kisses could rival Teo's. I'm such a whack-job for even thinking about Teo right now, but some part of me responds to Teo for some reason, and I need to know if that part of me can respond to someone who *isn't* crazy.

But we can't kiss now. Not yet. Because he wants to kiss me like it's his final wish or something, and that is the last thing I will ever accept—Marcus, gone. The idea ties all sorts of knots and squeezes them inside my gut. I want to kiss Marcus. *So* much. But putting my lips to his now would make it seem like I agree with him giving up. We're *not* giving up. We need to get that insulin now.

Marcus must be reading my mind, because he kicks that rock he was toying with and says, "I know where it is." The rock hits another tree and bounces back, rolling before it stops.

I could wrap my hands around his chiseled, sweat-caked body and toss him from these woods—straight for the houses and that insulin. Why's he standing around? "Then show me!" I plead.

Eyes trained on the fence, Marc smiles, which looks more like a frown. "Ol 'bino left it in the car." But he needs his medicine now. That's why he's staring at the fence; he knows he needs to get out. He doesn't need to go back to the compound. He needs Teo's *car*. To think Teo's SUV could be parked a few meters past the fence. If we could just slip right through it, he'd be okay.

But how does he know this, exactly? Teo never mentioned this to me. "Did Jonas tell you or something?"

Marcus laughs like I'm insulting him now. "Yep, because we're best buds."

I'm so not above slapping him. "How do you know that's where the vials are?"

He rolls his eyes like I'm slow. "I heard Jonas and Teo talking about it, okay?"

I'm not real fond of his tone, but I guess it's okay since he's sick from having such high blood sugar—he must be carefully parsing out whatever insulin he has left. We need a plan to get the insulin, break through this fence, and I need the opportunity to get to know him more. Teo makes me feel melancholy—has always made me feel that way. But I should be with someone who makes me feel positive, happy, and I can see that Marcus would do that, but we need to save him first.

As he's crouching to study the cement along the ground, the back of Marc's shirt hitches up just enough that I catch a sliver of skin on his back, which isn't as tan as Teo's, but nice. Smooth-looking. And toned. Kneeling next to him, I stare at the mass of barbed wire blocking us from the outside and wilt a little when I remember again how Ramus's and Bee's body bags are gone. *Gone.* Here I've been checking Marcus out, and Ramus and Bee have been taken by *them.*

"What could make it click?" Marcus asks, shaking his head in frustration.

I still think it's the remote, and I think it has to be the one in Teo's coat. A universal remote kind of thing, only made for impending death. I just need to kiss Teo and slip it out. It's not an idea Marcus likes, but I really don't think we'll come up with something better, so I say, "We'll figure something out. If we can't get over the fence, we could lock Teo up."

Marcus's upper lip twitches like he's working hard not to be mad. Not that I blame him. Staying here has to be the last thing he wants. I don't want it, either, and of course that's a lousy idea since his insulin is on the other side.

Giving up on the magic button to open the fence, I sit on a flat rock on the forest floor. I don't want to go back yet; I'd rather spend more time with Marcus in these woods. Not that I should be wasting these precious moments with him—we should be opening the fence—but Jonas's party will be in an hour or two, and Teo will get suspicious if I cross to his side of the street. He wants to get down to *three* couples. I'd like to share this with Marcus, but that's the last thing he needs—something else to stress over, apart from the fence and insulin.

Sitting next to me on the forest floor, Marc raises one knee, rests his elbow on top, and braces his forehead like even sitting here costs him too much energy. I'd like to tell him to lie down. Go to sleep or something; use just a little bit of insulin. But that would be precisely the wrong thing to say; just to prove me wrong, he'd start running laps.

So I wait, studying his sopping wet shirt, which clings to his chest. My, aren't those nicely formed pecs. I wonder if he works out, if he's one of those guys with rock-hard abs, or just enough definition but not too much.

Bringing my knees to my chest, I have to ask him, "Are you doing okay?" Because the sweat running down his face only reiterates the fact that he shouldn't be out here, but in bed.

Marcus takes a deep breath, like he's filling up an inflatable tank, and when he releases it, it's like he's waited too long for it to deflate. "Know what gets me?"

I shake my head, having absolutely no clue what he's thinking.

"You're *exactly* the type of girl I wanted you to be."

It takes everything I have not to smile stupidly. For a millisecond my face starts twitching, but the *good* type of twitching, because though everything's going to hell, he's telling me he likes me. *Likes me.* I'm not sure why, but I'll take it.

"You're different." I hug my knees, trying to keep my voice from getting all fluttery. "I always thought you were playful. That's about—"

"—it," Marcus finishes lamely. He's not angry or vengeful or full of plans like his brother would be; he just sits there, beaten, staring at that fence.

"You never did tell me what happened the first time." I gesture to the bruise on Marcus's face, imagining it was Teo again.

His lips curl into a smile. "Oh, you don't need to ask."

"Teo?"

He shrugs. "I've always been the rabble-rouser. That's why I'm surprised my brother brought me here in the first place, but I suppose even my brother's wishes are affected by blood."

When he says blood, my mind immediately goes to the endless crimson oozing from Izzy's chest, but he means the bond between brothers, and that's why he's making a bitter face like something smells bad. But the only scent I pick up from Marcus is eucalyptus and the sawdust from the two pairs of seven homes, which makes my nose twitch. I'm about to sneeze—

I stop my nose on his sleeve. This only makes it worse, because now all I can smell are the sweet dampness wafting off his shirt and the paints Marcus lent to me, and all I want to do is forget about my other senses and breathe.

Marcus must be thinking I'm a little off base, what with the tip of my nose resting on his sleeve, so I close the distance to his shoulder and let my head drop onto the very top. It reminds me of sandstone covered in a cloak. He's sturdy but not immoveable, and the layer between us is thin but just enough.

"What would you do if I sat next to you in class?" Marcus asks, and it's the warmest type of sound because I can feel the calm vibrations of his voice. "You know, if we went to the same school?"

I feel a bit foolish for wanting to burrow inside his words and fall asleep. "Share my book," I suggest, because maybe Marcus left his book at home by mistake.

"I'd go for that." Gingerly, he plucks my hand from the backs of my knees and holds it like it's under the desk. It's damp but still nice. "Book sharing has perks."

"I'd offer you some Skittles," I smile, reaching into a pretend pocket and handing him an invisible bunch.

Marcus gathers the little circles in his free hand and drops two or three in his mouth. He groans, then slips one inside of my mouth. "At lunchtime," he says, "we would get Slurpees. And by seventh period I'd ask you out."

"For a movie?"

"To a dance."

"I'd rather go bowling."

Marcus cracks open a smile. "I'll bet."

I think about night's cool fingers wrapping us up, snatching us away from all the problems we can't fix. The electric fence melts, and we find his insulin in Teo's SUV. I don't know how we've stolen this moment, but it's just what I always thought it would be. Marc *does* make me feel happy, light. With Teo, I feel scared, heavy. That's not how love should be.

The sun's dipping low, blinking through the trees, and I know it's almost time for Jonas's party. We have to go back, yet it's good for us to go back. Every second we waste out here without Marc's insulin is one second closer to his death. I *need* Teo's remote; it has to open this fence.

"So, we'll get the remote?" I ask him, because now I can think of little else.

Marcus nods gravely, his eyes looking more sunken than blue. "Just be careful, Cheyenne. Because I'll do anything to have that chance with you."

I perk up an eyebrow, unsure what he means.

"To sit with you in class." He smiles sheepishly. "I'd do anything to share a book with you."

19

"Persephone," Teo says when I open my front door for him before we head to Jonas's house. He holds a small box out to me, and all I can do is stare at that black suit, thinking of his remote. I wish I could freeze time—snatch away the remote and leave.

I look down at the box in his hands. He's offering me a present. Did my visit with Marcus make me forget I'm supposed to give him one, too? But Teo gently sets the box in my hands and I step backward to let him in, forcing my eyes away from his coat. The box is made of metal, but with air holes throughout. An insect is inside.

"What's this?" I ask, trying to make sense of the bug. I've never received an insect as a present. Hopefully it's not a metaphor for a mating ritual.

But there's only one bug, and Teo smiles wanly. "It's a damselfly," he says. "You usually find them near water, but I found her in the woods behind my house last night." He reaches over and unlatches the lid. I think the bug will fly away, but there's a layer of sheer fabric keeping her trapped inside.

I study the insect, never having heard the name before, though it looks familiar. Wings held closely together top off her slender, cobalt body, and two round eyes stare up at me, almost like a puppy's eyes. I glance up briefly at Teo. "She's not a dragonfly?"

Teo studies the creature in my hands and shakes his head. "This little jewel is more slender than a dragonfly and holds her wings together, like she's always on the defensive. Dragonflies flaunt their wings."

I'm not sure why Teo brought the damselfly for me, but I can see that he's proud, that he wants me to acknowledge his gift. My most cunning reaction would be to wrap my arms around him and snake my hand inside his coat. But I'm holding the bug and he's turned to the side, which would make everything awkward. Besides, I don't know if I can make myself kiss him now. It would remind me of how I actually enjoyed kissing him in the rain. Knowing I have to at least *say* something, I try, "Thank you."

He reaches over and rests two fingers on the top of my hand, and while physically his touch is as light as a butterfly's, I feel like he has the ability to bolt me down. I shouldn't let him have this power over me. I should feel like I have the ability to step away.

"I give her to you," Teo says, eyes round and hopeful, "because she is a metaphor for our earlier talk."

So, she is a metaphor. Apparently I know Teo better than I thought. Anxious, I keep my eyes on the bug; her feelers attack a leaf. Maybe this has something to do with his three kingdoms in Elysian Fields.

"Do you remember how I explained what you are to me?" Teo asks, bracing an arm on the dresser that still stands by the door, covering an arch. "The strength of humility, counterbalancing my greed? All of that can be represented by this damselfly." He points at the bug in the cage. "A damselfly is really an underdeveloped dragonfly, but some consider her to be the superior of the two. See these eyes? How they are wide apart? Dragonflies' eyes are close together. The damselfly sees much more. I think she's the wiser of the two." He moves his arm away and stands up straight.

What he's saying makes sense, and I'm not sure what to make of it. For half a second I feel like royalty in a palace, where my potential suitors bring exotic gifts. I'm finding the gesture sweet and flattering, but I hate the idea of considering anything Teo does as good. Here he's offering me presents, when he should be offering insulin to his brother. I thank him again, as briefly yet as sincerely as I can under the circumstances, and take his arm to walk to Jonas's. Maybe I'll find the perfect opportunity to slip my hand inside his coat on the way.

The flat, sterile air is suffocating; the clouds stiffen, too nervous to rain. As we walk to Jonas's, it's like the clouds are connecting with us, with our fear.

Teo glances at my lilac dress, a silk gown barely kissing the tops of my knees with long, wispy sleeves. Knee-length means easy running, long sleeves mean a way to conceal the remote; everything hinges on finding the remote to the fence tonight.

"Purple is the color of royalty," Teo says, eyes roving from my neckline down over my chest. He's studied me like this before, but now it's like he's undressing me with his mind, which makes my stomach churn. "You have made an excellent choice with that dress," he adds as we walk down the street, my arm resting in his.

I nearly choke as I hold back a laugh. Little does he know just *how* great the choice is.

Teo's cold eyes rake over my face; he's waiting for a smile, a blush, something showing I'm grateful, so I force my mouth into a smile. "I'm glad you like it." He smiles a little, looking away.

We stroll, arm in arm, along the debris-free street, our strides almost matched. Before, this would have given me some form of satisfaction, knowing I can keep up with him, but now I wonder if maybe it's because my subconscious is catching on—that I *am* strong enough without him. I don't need to dawdle, wait for him to lead me now. I can be independent, which is both terrifying and freeing.

"So," Teo says, eyeing Abe and Eloise as they kiss while walking down the sidewalk, "have you managed to decide which three couples should remain?"

"Hmm?" What can I say to satisfy him *and* preserve the lives of the other couples? "Why don't we observe the couples—see how they behave tonight?"

Teo's grip around my waist tightens, his fingers gripping my hip hard, yet another reminder of that time we spent together in his room. "Have you managed to decide which three couples *should remain?*"

It feels like a hand has entered my chest cavity, wrapped its strong fingers around my heart, and squeezed. But I focus, force my heart to wait before pulsing out. What would Teo like to hear? That I have a plan and I'm on his team. So I drape a cold look of indifference on my face, mimicking the expression etched on his cheeks. "Of course, but I couldn't tell you now," I say, as if offering a game.

Pleasure twists on Teo's lips. "Is that right? You mean to treat me as if I am a toy?"

I lean in, forcing my head to lean into his arm, because I know I need to sell this, really sell this. Say the one thing that before I couldn't say. Bile simmers in my throat as I spit it out, "Only if it gives you pleasure, my love."

A low rumble bubbles in Teo's throat. "Yes, I would say that it does." Teo's response is both what I do and don't want. I'm glad that my acting has apparently improved, but I hate leading him on. I hate pretending this is who I am.

But this is what I must do until we can get everyone that vaccine and find a way to leave, and by then, Teo's hold on me will be *long* gone.

Steering me down the cement footpath leading straight for Jonas's porch, I feel Teo rest his chin on the top of my head before kissing my hair, which only makes me cringe. I don't know if poison has a scent, but if I were to describe how it smells, it would be cologne and conspiracy and Teo's smoky-musk scent.

Once we're on the porch, Marcus and Cleo stroll up right behind us, hand in hand. Clad in his gray knit shirt, Marcus studies his brother's arm around my waist, and I blush because I wish he didn't see. Rings of sweat cake Marc's shirt. *Oh, Marc. Have you run out of insulin?* Cleo bends in to whisper something in Marcus's ear, and whatever she says makes him laugh, so maybe he still has some left, but I have to believe the laugh is forced, because there are circles under his eyes. He shouldn't even be on his feet.

Jonas greets us at the door, lips pressed together in a flat smile, nodding without so much as a word. It's like he's an android or something. I can't imagine how he and Teo met. It makes me wonder if Elysian Fields was his idea or Teo's.

As we shuffle into the living room, Cleo brushes her chest against Marc's arm. "Oh, excuse me," she laughs, shaking the beads on her head, but I notice she doesn't move away. Marcus seems to freeze, and for a horrible minute I think he's trying to make the moment last, but then he chuckles before moving away. I love Marcus just about ten thousand different ways right now.

Teo steers me to a black leather couch and gently urges me to sit, while he stands like he's chivalrous or something.

Glancing around, I remember this room well—it's the living room where I first woke up in Elysian Fields. The gray walls and black furniture give the room a masculine, sleek feel, one that suits Teo, but not Jonas so much. I'm not sure what type of a place I picture Jonas in. Maybe some God-forsaken land underground where, instead of people, he could stun bats.

But since Teo no longer lives here, I suppose his plans have changed. The more I've learned about him, the more I can see he is incapable of staying the same. He wanted the number seven, now the number three. He furnished this house for himself, now he's stolen Ramus's. He claims to love me, but he watches Cleo, too.

Ana looks out the windows where she's sitting again by Sal, her face so far away, it makes me wonder if she pretends she's somewhere else. Sal frowns at the ground, in his own little world, too. I pray Teo will spare them.

Teo has been oddly quiet, and I glance at him, but his eyes are elsewhere—over by the stairs on Cleo's nearly translucent dress. The low lighting makes her skin seem to glow, and unveiled hunger simmers in Teo's gaze. Men can be so predictable sometimes.

"She is beautiful, isn't she?" Teo mutters, as if to himself. I don't know if he expects an answer, but I remain quiet, more than a little annoyed that I have to think about Cleo again. For two more minutes, I watch as Teo studies Cleo—her low neckline, the almost animalistic curl to her lips. She whips her beads frequently, all of her advances directed toward Marc, but Marc's running his fingers over his insulin pump, which is both the best and worst thing. Best, because that means he's ignoring Cleo, worst because it means we need to get him insulin, *now*.

"You are being rather dull," Teo says, without glancing away from Cleo and her Scotch tape dress.

I stare at her, too, envisioning the tape getting mangled in all the right places, and then getting stuck; I have all sorts of ideas for improving the way Cleo looks. But what was

Teo saying? That I'm being rather dull. So I give him the first cop out that comes to mind. "You know how I feel."

Teo tsks his tongue, and I know he expects more. "Why must you always be so transparent?" Which is hilarious, considering my Scotch tape idea. "Take Cleopatra, for instance," he adds. "She has a catty sensuality. You might try that."

I study Cleo over by those wrought-iron stairs, knowing that's where I usually am, wondering how I usually look. Obviously, I don't have the boobs, and my skin is like sheetrock next to hers, but Cleo's hands rove around Marc's waist and I can't help but think she's a little ridiculous. I like that I can keep my hands to myself. Most of the time, anyway. Of course, there have been mess-ups, like that time with Teo in his room, and that time in the rain, but I have learned from my mistakes.

The only thing I can think to say to Teo is that his taste is temporarily off, but that will make him mad, so I don't say anything. Plus, now Marc's joining Romeo and Juliet's card game in the center of the room. He pulls up an end table and sits, and it takes a bit of concentration not to cheer. He told me I was *exactly* the type of girl he thought I'd be, *and* he said I was pretty.

But Teo doesn't seem to like Marc's reaction to Cleo, because he hisses, "Fool," before striding across the room to Cleo, who's frowning at Marcus for leaving her alone.

Reaching inside his coat, Teo pulls out a handkerchief and offers it to Cleo with a smile, like he's pretending she's in tears for Marcus leaving her alone like that. A curl twists Cleo's lips as she takes the handkerchief and dabs at her batty eyes.

Teo actually throws his head back and laughs. This game between them makes it so much easier to hate Teo. But I have to be careful, because this could be the end of Teo and me. And I doubt he would be generous enough to reassign me to Marcus. We'd be his next disposables on a whim. I glance over to Marcus and decide he's too focused on the game to look up, but then he glances up at me. Just a clear-eyed look, but it might as well be a backrub, because I'm suddenly all warm and tingly, and I can't begin to imagine what a *real* backrub would feel like from him.

Teo calls my name and waves for me to join him and Cleo by the stairs. I glance over at the snacks, wishing I could make some excuse to join Abe and Eloise at the counter, but my heart plummets. Abe and Eloise look painfully lonely without Lance and Gwen.

Feeling as though someone's yanked out my organs, I make my way over to Teo with the fakest smile I've ever had. I don't even care that it's obviously fake.

"You tell us, Persephone," Teo tells me once I've joined him and Cleo by the stairs. "Do you believe it might be possible to save ourselves from such inadequacy?" He gestures to the corner by the windows, where Ana and Sal stand, and I scramble for something to veer the conversation away from them, because I *don't* want him singling out Ana again. *So, tell me about your treats? Oh, I guess Jonas is hosting; where exactly is he?*

"You could always have them *dance*," Cleo says, brushing her touchy-feely hand on Teo's arm.

The two bow their heads together and laugh, like making fun of people is foreplay, or something. I look away, feeling the blood rush to my cheeks, my gaze landing on Romeo and Juliet—no longer with Marc.

He's gone! Left to look for the remote? Maybe get the other one from Jonas? I hope that's not what he's doing, because Jonas would snap his neck. But Teo could realize at any second that Marc's gone, so I must do something—distract Teo so he doesn't notice, and also search his coat.

"Tell us, Hades," I say, leaning toward him like Cleo isn't there, purposely letting my eyes rove over his body like I'm checking him out. If I can get him close enough, I can slip my fingers inside his coat. He smiles, leaning back against the wrought-iron rails. "How did you and Jonas come to be friends?" I ask, taking a step closer, unable to tear my eyes off the front of his suit coat.

"*Yes, tell us, Hades,*" Cleo mimics my voice. Laughing again, she flips her beads.

But with the way I'm openly stepping toward Teo and letting my eyes simmer, it's like Teo's forgotten Cleo's here, and he turns his back on her. Wrapping an iron hand around my waist, Teo calls for Jonas. "Our Persephone would like to know how we met, my friend." I'd hoped for a moment I could lean in, but Teo's not paying attention to me, so I look around the room to find Teo's friend. I can't find him until Teo takes a few steps toward the center of the room and looks high above him, to the balcony.

Ah, Jonas. There he is. It's hard to tell from this distance, but he looks torn, tilting his head as if wanting to nod, but his lips frown almost like he wants the origin of their friendship to be kept a secret. I wonder why.

"It was your freshman year, was it not?" Teo says, clutching my waist. "You had been thrown in with some imbeciles who could not get past the way you look."

Anger flashes over Jonas's eyes, but he immediately smooths his gaze, simultaneously tapping the stun gun on his belt.

I glance over at Abe and Eloise, who step away from the snack counter, Abe wrapping his strong arms around Eloise. The couple lifts their heads high to study Jonas on the balcony.

"You rescued me," Jonas answers, and it's like he bows with his words. I can recognize that devotion flashing in Jonas's eyes, because it's a look I've often held in my own.

Teo drops his head sideways and swivels it to the side. "But it was a mutual arrangement," he says, gesturing up to his friend. "Jonas here is the most talented artist, devoted friend, and hardworking individual I have ever met. Tell them, Jonas," Teo glances at Romeo and Juliet in the chairs beside us, "how long it takes you to bake the muffins we all enjoy every morning."

Jonas looks down, clearly embarrassed, bits of pink dusting the tops of his ears. "Just a few minutes," he mumbles, his words wafting down the stairs.

Teo turns to Romeo and Juliet, his eyes wide. "He can whip them up in under four!"

Romeo opens his mouth and says, "Wow," and Juliet raises her eyebrows as if clearly impressed. Abe and Eloise step closer to all of us in the center of the room. Eloise keeps nodding her head, smiling broadly, and Abe's only maybe a step behind, smiling with closed lips.

"Needless to say," Teo looks once again up at Jonas, "I knew he belonged here. He is the cog that turns the wheel. We would be nowhere without my faithful friend. That's why I had him host tonight. To explain."

Eloise lifts her hand to her face and whispers something to Abe, and Cleo joins us in the center of the room to say something to Juliet. The chatter is barely above rumbling, but Teo claps his hands.

"And now," Teo says, "I believe it is time to see why my brother insists on snooping in Jonas's house."

My heart ricochets inside my chest. I want to run, become invisible, and retrieve Marcus from wherever he is in the house. But here I am, stranded in the middle of this room, completely useless against helping Marcus reappear.

He wants to know where Marcus is? I'll need to distract him, *and* get his remote.

"What can you mean?" I say, studying his face and letting my eyes wander down to his chest, but when I glance up, he isn't even watching me. That was a waste. So I wrap my arms around his lean body, try to remember what it was like kissing him in the rain, and I move my hands inside his suit jacket to hug him without the coat.

Teo's body freezes. Oh, God, please no. He's going to slap me now. Or maybe he doesn't know what I'm doing—merely has something against public displays of affection. He's going to say: *We do not touch each other like this in front of others.* In the past, I would have felt the same way.

Instead, he buries his face in my hair and breathes in deeply. "*Oh,*" he says, "you have no idea what you do to me."

I move my pinky up, trying to search the inside pocket of his coat, but the pocket is too high, so I brace his back with one hand so my other can sneak inside that pocket for the remote. He's kissing my hair, skimming his lips across my cheeks.

Plastic. My heart flails around the inside of my chest. Slamming my lips into his, I kiss him just like when we were in the rain. I move my mouth slowly, rubbing my hand down the stubble of his face.

Teo groans right when I snatch the remote in my fist. I open my mouth over his, and I kiss him like hunger's coursing through me. Even his face is quaking. But the kisses do not send ripples of pleasure down to my knees. I'm kissing him, but I'm not feeling anything. I pretend that I am, and hopefully Teo can't feel the difference.

"Where did you get this one, Hades?" Cleo sighs the loudest sigh I think I've ever heard.

We break apart, and I'm panting, mostly because there's a very good chance he'll discover the remote on me. Glancing away, I find Marcus strutting down the hall, openly, like he's *hoping* Teo will find him. But I have the remote! I need to pass it to him since I don't have a pocket in this skirt.

Turning to Marcus, Teo claps his younger brother on the back. "And where were you?"

I tuck the remote in my hand and up my sleeve.

Marcus mumbles something, grinning broadly, which makes Teo laugh. I have no clue what he said, but it looks like he's in the clear.

My next goal is to make it okay for us to go outside. A game, maybe? Like sardines, but something more.

Wrapping my hand around the crook of Teo's arm, I coat my voice in false confidence. "I have an idea for choosing those who deserve to go."

Marc's eyebrows perk up in curiosity, but I pretend to only see Teo; not that that's an easy thing to do, since avoiding Marcus's face is like avoiding cupcakes. I turn my arm so just Marc can see the tip of the remote.

"We should play a game," I explain, and Marcus immediately takes the remote from my hand as he passes behind me. From the corner of my eye, I see him tuck it into his jeans pocket, and I quickly gesture to the others scattered across the room—Sal and Ana in their corner, and Abe and Eloise and Romeo and Juliet clustered together in the middle of the floor. "Those who don't perform well…" I purposely don't finish the thought, allowing Teo to fill in the blank.

Teo tilts his head to the side as if considering my suggestion. "And what game were you thinking?"

Sardines, but I know the game is much too juvenile for Teo. It needs to be something he can respect, something that will increase his authority as our leader. Like an emperor of

Rome. I think of the Coliseum and the gladiators forced to fight within. Teo would love that.

But Marcus offers a game. "Truth or Dare."

I almost choke. Gladiators to this? Surely Teo will not be impressed.

But, to my amazement, Teo laughs. "Ah, the memories," he says, clapping Marcus on the back. And for the first time, maybe ever, the brothers huddle closely together, laughing.

"Our father would play this game with us," Teo says. "He had some—what would you say, Marcus? *Talents* for the game?"

Marcus, of all things, fist-bumps Teo. "Remember the squirrels?"

Teo laughs a laugh I've never heard—high-pitched and entirely unreserved. "Oedipus and Jocasta," he sighs. "The rodents never did like what Father did to their paws after my dare."

Marc chuckles, deep in his throat, but looks away.

"What did he do?" I ask, placing my arm awkwardly on the back of the couch.

Teo's eyes lock with mine, which immediately makes me suffocate. "Why, he chopped them off." And suddenly I don't like the idea of playing this game. No one should play.

But Teo claps his hands together as if this is the best idea he's ever heard. "Everyone! I would like to invite you all to play a game. Jonas, our dear host, I expect you will have no problem with this?"

Jonas, now arranging bowls over on the refreshment counter, bows grandly, like it's the most important job he's ever been asked to do.

Teo glances around the room eagerly, as if choosing between Oedipus or Jocasta. But he returns to me. "Persephone. Won't you please choose our first contestant?"

Mouth dry, I scan the room. My first choice is to change Teo's mind completely, but I've already distracted him twice, so that leaves picking someone, and there's only one person I don't like in this room: Sal. I hate the way he's always belittling Ana in front of everyone else. So I say, "Sal," shuddering because I'm not particularly sad.

Sal, in the back corner with Ana, meets my gaze. I'm pretty sure he can tell I don't mind singling him out.

"My dear neighbor, Salim." Teo smiles. "Truth," he licks his lips, "or Dare?"

Sal pushes his glasses up the bridge of his nose, then glares at Ana. He blames her for my choice. That's why it was so easy to pick him. Ana shoves a piece of celery from the window ledge into her pocket, as if she's worried she'll get in trouble for leaving the celery out.

Sal thrusts out his chin. "Truth." I pray to God that he doesn't do something that will get Ana in trouble along with him.

"Excellent, Salim," Teo says, grinning at Marcus, as if sharing a secret joke. Sal should have said dare, then.

Marc, quick on the uptake, shoots his brother a gleaming smile, as if Truth is what he hoped Sal would say, but I have a feeling that's not true.

Teo considers Sal's answer only for a moment as his eyes dart over to Ana in front of the windows. "Whom would you say is not committed to our community, here at Elysian Fields?" he asks.

My heart pummels my chest. *Not now. He can't make his choice yet.*

Sal removes his glasses and polishes them on his green polo before replacing them again. "I request a new partner, sir." He rubs his hands on his jeans. "Mine does not approve of your world. She wants to leave." *No! He's singling Ana out.*

Teo stiffens. Ana, sweet Ana's face blanches as white as the walls, a string of celery clinging to her upper lip. I wish we lived in a *Star Trek* episode and could ask the bridge to beam us up. But Teo seems to relish the calm, methodical approach today. Turning to Ana, he asks, "Is that true, Anarkali?"

Ana shakes her head furiously, making the shawl on her head slip. "No, not at all!" she says as I scramble for some way to help. "He just doesn't like me. We never get along." Which is true. Sal is a classic douche.

Lips turned downward, Teo looks at me, and I brace myself on the couch. "Do you remember, Persephone, what we did with the last couple who could not commit?"

I can't allow Teo to do the same thing to Ana and Sal. I need to stop him now. Ana is my friend—she gave me the list of names. Protected me. And now she's stuck with Sal.

Floundering for an answer, I grimace at the options. I tell the truth, and Teo drops the axe. I smudge the boundaries, and I risk a greater temper when I don't give him the answer he wants. So I reach for a third option, and it's a far reach, but I pray Teo will agree. "Teo, you should put us to a test." I weave my fingers into his; do everything I can to not look at Marcus's face, because even I don't like the look of Teo's and my hands together.

Teo's thumb rubs the back of my ring, and everything but my muscles flinch. "And what do you mean?" he asks.

"It's a test of reunion," I say, watching Romeo and Juliet shrink closer to each other, the both of them scrunched onto one chair. Juliet hides behind Romeo's plaid shirt, and Eloise and Abe have managed to squeeze together into the other chair. "Each couple will separate," I explain, glancing at Ana, who's taking slow, deep breaths. "The goal will be to find each other again."

Teo's eyebrow arches, but I'm happy with my suggestion; this is what Marcus and I need to get away. Only I'm taking Ana. She's as good as dead if she stays.

"Set a timer," I explain the game. "The men must go to the men's side of the street, the women to the women's— outside, of course. In five minutes, Hades or Jonas will sound the foghorn. The men will then find the women. The last two couples to return will lose."

Abe and Eloise rise from their seat, staring at me wide-eyed. Abe calms his companion, but she's quietly shrieking. Abe's heels pump up and down, like he's more than ready to look for her. He probably thinks he might win. I hope he does, because I don't have a way to bring everyone, and Eloise and Abe winning might give them a leg up. I hate that I can't save everyone right now, but this is my best-case scenario. Hopefully, by the time I am gone, it won't be long before they figure out how to get out, too. It's the only way we can all be free.

"No one is allowed to hide inside," Teo says, clarifying my game.

I nod, glancing at Marc. This is it—does he know what we must do? He's smiling—I have to trust that we're on the same page. "So, let us begin!" Teo claps, singing over the group. *This is it.* I don't have time to look for Marc, because the couples are splitting madly apart, flocking to the front door—geese scrambling for safety. I locate Ana just as she's about to squeeze through.

I run up behind her. "Follow me," I hiss as loudly as I dare into her ear.

Ana glances behind her, eyes springing open wide, but when she sees me run, she follows me through the back door.

Whisking right past her, I run past Juliet and Cleo's houses, dash along the side of Ana's house, veering for the woods. Ana's right behind me.

Her breathing's only slightly harder than my own—probably because of that sari she has to wear. I wish she could throw it off. "Are we going to escape?" she whimpers, desperate.

"Y...yes," I answer, turning again for the trees. "We have the remote!"

Ana half-giggles, half-squeals, and we dodge thorny branches—I actually manage to veer around them like Marc. Ana's not doing too badly until her scarf snags on a tree branch and she tosses it straight down to the ground.

When we reach the fence, Marcus is already there, shoving a log under the barbed wire.

"What are you doing?" I ask, feeling the blood drain from my face. My voice drops to a whimper, because this isn't playing out right. "Didn't you bring the remote?"

The log bounces uselessly to the ground. "It doesn't work!"

This isn't happening. The night feels much too hot, and the fence is impossible to get through. This isn't happening. We were supposed to escape.

I grab the black piece of plastic from the ground and start hitting buttons, but none of them do anything. Teo's going to be looking for us—if he isn't already. But this remote was supposed to work. Why isn't it working? I try hitting two buttons at once like one's shift. But none of the combinations do a thing. I stare at the useless piece of plastic in my hands and ask, "What are we going to do?"

Marcus looks at me, shoulders sagging.

I crouch down to the ground and rub my fingers over the cement's edge, searching for a button, because we *need* his insulin on the other side. But I find nothing but leaves and soil and rocks, and when my fingers brush up against Marcus's shoes, he moves away to pry a log beneath the fence. But the wires sit too close to the cement. I whip around, run to the trees, and begin searching their gnarled trunks for any type of button.

Ana's small voice—thin, like ice—is what finally makes me stop. "You don't even have the vaccine."

Her accusation makes my blood, every last vein, freeze. How could I—how? How could I have forgotten about the vaccine? I can't believe I was so thoughtless that I *forgot* the most important part. I stagger, having to support myself against a gnarled tree trunk. "Teo—he was going to—Sal—remember how he—Sal wanted you out."

Ana studies me, anger rippling off her face. "I don't care *what* Sal said," and she is so, so right. My cheeks are burning and my chest cavity is deflating, as I can do no better than stare at the weedy ground. When I glance up, Ana hisses, "I can't believe I followed you. We'd better turn back."

Everything inside me is hollow. I just exposed their lives. Teo could catch Ana and Marc, and I tried escaping without the vaccine.

Leaves and tree roots crunch as Ana leaves. This is the worst thing I've ever done in my life. My stomach curls, clenches, and I feel like I might throw up. I clutch at my stomach, find myself staring at but not really seeing the blotches of brown and yellow ground. How could I risk everyone's lives like this? A memory of Teo's taunting in class plays in the back of my mind. *Analyze the problem, Miss Laurent. Do not allow your emotions to rule your head.*

Bitter tears threaten to fall, so I fling the remote at the fence. I watch it spark as it hits the fence, and only then does it occur to me that I should've saved it to sneak it back into Teo's coat.

Marcus stares at the remote on the ground now, paces, but comes back to me. Gripping me by the arm, he forces me back through the dark trees. The trees huddle closer together, their leaves emerging as fingers with sharp, stinging nails. The crocodile teeth of the bark I saw earlier have taken root in the trees' smiles; their shadows jeer, mock me for not seeing things: *Brilliant, aren't you, Cheyenne? Endangering your friends. It's hard to see what Teo or his brother ever saw in you. You're nothing.*

One branch snatches a wad of my hair. I shriek—not loudly—but the fear does escape my lips. Marc helps me unwind my hair, speaking to me softly. "I didn't tell you the name for these trees: Hercules's club. They think they're all bad, but don't let them get to you. They're more bark than bite."

I know Marc is trying to make me feel better, but his sense of humor is so off. I've sabotaged everything by trying to leave without the vaccine *and* using a faulty remote. He shouldn't be helping me. He should be in a hospital, sleeping.

"We were supposed to escape." I squirm as he continues working my hair from the thorns and twigs. "I can't believe I—" I take a deep breath and try to fill in the blank, but can't because the fear is too real. Ana and Marc both risk getting caught because of me. The body bags flash in my mind again, and I have to force myself not to cry. A swift tug from Marcus pulls the leaves clean off the branch, though they cling to my hair. He combs at the leaves, trying to push them off, and I don't know what I've done for him to be so nice.

"It'll all work out," Marcus is telling me, then nudges me forward, encouraging me to sprint, so I scramble for the houses. I don't know how he can be so forgiving. He's the one missing his insulin. He's the one who should be panicking, throwing remotes.

We veer past thistles and another collection of those grenade-like seeds before we make it back to the clearing. I remember the game, how I should be looking for Teo and Marcus should be with Cleo. Ana and Sal should be together, too.

Sprinting away from us, Ana's sari flaps wide open, revealing her milk-white legs. She's a few meters from her house when—no, oh no, no—Jonas emerges from around her house along with the other couples, and Teo brings up the rear.

Black stubble masks a livid face. It's happened—no God, please. It's happened. He's found us. And there's no escape.

"Persephone, Ana, Marc," Teo's eyes simmer, "you are the last ones."

20

Teo clutches my hands, the ebony of his eyes merging with mine. Wedding vows—that's what it feels like we're about to exchange, but we're not. Raindrops sprinkle, tickle my face.

"Teo?" I ask, but he doesn't answer, merely stares at the hair sticking to my neck.

I look to the others, how the remaining women in their bright dresses decorate Sal's front yard like Christmas ornaments—Juliet in purple, Cleo in red, and Eloise in her black. Ana, though, is far below me in her orange sari. Teo's already forced her into his trap, a roofless, elevator-like prison of brick dug into the ground. It has something to do with the Salim and Anarkali tale, the one Sal and Ana are named after. The men stand there, too, but no one says a thing. Jonas aims his stun gun at Marcus, and my heels teeter at the edge of the prison of brick.

Strangling the throbbing pulse in my wrists, Teo addresses the crowd in a voice of steel and metal.

"There was once a slave girl named Anarkali," he says, "who fell in love with the wrong man. His name was Prince Salim, and it was said he loved her back." He's going to lock me down there with Ana next.

"But one day, Salim's father, the powerful Emperor Akbar, learned of his son's lowly choice. He ordered the girl to be thrown into a prison, then buried alive behind a wall of brick." Buried—alive?

"Salim was devastated. He would never see his love again. So he did what any love-besotted prince would do—"

I try backing away but the hole's right behind me. Shoving me hard, into the hole, he finishes, "He left her there to rot."

High above me, Teo reaches into his suit pocket, but comes up empty. He's looking for the remote I took from him. Fire lurches in his eyes, and he snaps his gaze to Jonas, who knows what to do. With one free hand, Jonas digs into his pocket and pulls out his remote, just like Teo's. *That's* probably the one that opens the fence.

Jonas clicks a button, causing a roof of brick to begin to close over us. They're leaving us here, but Teo is supposed to love me. We're supposed to be together.

All I can see are the frown lines on Teo's face, the coals burning inside the ebony. I expect him to scream at me, but the burning coals flicker out before there's nothing. Teo's eyes widen, and his jaw grows slack. He's hollow, empty. He knows he's losing me.

*   *   *

Darkness. No light. There aren't any cracks in the bricks, no cracks in the grassy ground beneath us. The walls are brick, like the newly closed roof. I don't even want to think what Teo will do to Marc. He won't kill his brother, will he? I can't see any way he'll give his brother insulin now.

I cover my face with my hands; how could I have done this? I risked Ana's and Marc's lives. I'm the reason so many are dead, the reason we're all in trouble. I'm the cause for all of this.

Falling to my knees, I reach out to touch Ana's hand, but she jerks it away. *I am so sorry, Ana. You are right to hate me.*

I consider clawing my way around the ground, but I know the rock-hard Texas clay. The brick walls, too, will never budge. We're trapped here, trapped. Ana and I will never get out.

$$*\qquad *\qquad *$$

"HELLO! HEY! HELLO!" Does Teo really mean to leave us inside? I kick a wall; it's like kicking the granite counters in Bee's house. "MARCUS! TEO! JONAS! HELLO!" I jump up and press the palm of my hand against the top of the tomb. The bricks are cold, unyielding. I crash back to the ground, careful to veer around Ana. She won't talk. I stomp, scuff my feet; I pound them into the ground.

I'm stuck in a hole and I don't know if we will ever get out.

If we're in front of Sal's house, that means we're next to Marc's—right by where that snake came out. I rock back and forth on my feet.

I rock.

I rock.

I rock.

$$*\qquad *\qquad *$$

Penitence is a black, erasing thing; it overcomes you, wipes you clean. Current time no longer exists, and I'm thrown back into my memories, facing what I do not wish to see. Flashes of yearning and not belonging overwhelm me. Colors of memories flash in my mind, unbidden. They're green and blue and orange and red—the colors of thirty helium-filled balloons, their strings clutched in my hands. A school day, early in the fall; class had let out, and I was struggling.

For some reason I had volunteered to help with a dance. Not just any dance, but Sadie Hawkins, where the girls asked the boys for a change. And who would I go with? Teo Richardson, as always. That would never happen, though, because Teo was off-limits, though at the time I felt the age difference shouldn't matter; there were, after all, six years between Mayor Tydal and Mom, exactly the same number as between Teo and me. And I'd just turned eighteen. But instead of allowing teenagers to act naturally, the school had us do "far-reaching" things, like stuff thirty helium-filled balloons inside the trunk of my much too small car.

I stood in that hot parking lot, torn as to how to get them in, when I saw Teo approaching from the other side. His car was only parked three spaces past mine, so he'd have to pass me to leave. This was one of my favorite strategies—park next to his car and linger as long as I could after school if I couldn't find the guts or opportunity to make it inside his classroom.

Teo was two or three cars off when he said, "It looks like we may need to revisit simple mathematics."

I groaned as he approached, my heart racing, floating. I had to stay calm. "*Why* did I offer to help with this dance?" I asked.

"Because you know the other students would be miserable without you."

Heat trickled up the back of my neck. These little comments sustained me through senior year. Some people lived on three square meals a day, others snacked away at vending machines, but my sustenance was comprised almost entirely of the kind things Teo might or might not say. Today looked like one of those very good days. Even the sun was gleaming.

"Here's what we shall do." Teo started taking balloons away from me. "We will pretend *I* am the one who volunteered and I asked you to get the other half."

He stood there just looking at me, with fifteen balloons in one hand, and my little girl barometer went crazy knowing I was more attracted to him right then than when he played his violin. His face was almost entirely devoid of shadows, almost light. The ebony in his eyes looked lighter than usual, and all of his facial muscles relaxed. He was smiling.

"That would be great," I managed, wishing I could take a picture of Teo. To have something to keep of him. With that expression he looked to be nearly my age.

Part of me was nervous that I wouldn't be able to fit the remaining balloons when Teo said, "Wait a moment," and strode away to put his balloons inside his car. He drove a full-size Infiniti—one with back seats. I watched as he methodically placed each and every balloon in the back seat. Once his hands were free, he turned and strode toward me. I know I am fulfilling every cliché in the book when I say my heart was thrashing, my stomach twisting, and the wind tousled the hair around my face, but they all did happen. There may have even been music playing.

Taking the balloon strings from my hand, Teo asked, "Shall we?"

I nodded as we placed each of the remaining balloons in the back of my car. Watching his cornflower tie flap sideways away from his white shirt, I appreciated how he matched what I wore, too—a cornflower plaid skirt. We may only have been wearing Khabela's school colors, but it was one more comparison that helped me feel like we were together. Teo looked young for his age, and thinking of the idea of us going together to a dance was captivating. If we went to another town where no one knew us, we could go somewhere neutral, like a club. They would think we were dating—college students, maybe.

Teo reached over and brushed the top of my hand. "Follow me over?" he asked as a car lumbered past.

I wished we didn't have to drive separately, but I could watch him through the windshield, and maybe he would glance at me through his rearview mirror. And that was better than nothing.

"When we get there," I asked, "will you help me again? I don't want them to blow away."

Teo's hand moved from the back of my hand to my face. The movement was quick, as if it hadn't taken place. But I felt it, relished its searing mark. When he dropped his hand again, he said quietly, "I would do anything for you."

He stepped away. To the other students and teachers in the parking lot, we must have looked like a teacher chatting with his student. There was now a full foot between us and I longed to close it, to know what it felt like to have his words seep into my skin again.

Teo's eyes were all over me. My eyes, my mouth, my chin. He looked down farther, and I knew I should have been blushing, but I liked the idea of Teo's eyes devouring me. We were two lone candles, burning in exactly the wrong place, for it was daytime, and we were at my high school and no one could see the flames.

"Hey Mr.—Teo." A student waved.

I felt like someone had grabbed my tongue, held it in place, and stuck it in cement. There was so much I wanted to say, to express how I felt. But Teo broke the connection and walked a few paces back.

"Follow me?" he asked.

I felt my eyes well up—which was ridiculous, because the way he said it, which no doubt had to be in my head, was like he was asking me to follow him *beyond* our helium balloon delivery. But that was impossible. There was no place for two candles like us to light the room.

21

There is no way to track time in isolation. Three hours. Seven. Twenty. Whether my eyes are open or closed, the darkness remains the same.

I try again to speak with Ana, but she won't respond. I explain why I had believed there was a remote for the fence in the first place, that I should be stuck in front of a firing squad for forgetting about the vaccine. I tell her about the pressure I felt to find a way out, the desperation to find more insulin. But she doesn't respond to anything, so I claw at the bricks with my hands and feet.

*   *   *

A sprinkle of light grows overhead. The bricks are moving! I start to reach for them, but recoil because maybe I'll get stunned for trying. My stomach rolls. We're moving up—the ground's rising below my feet. We inch upward, upward, and I know who will stand at the top. I crouch, unsure how fast the blow will come, one arm over my face, trembling.

When the ground stops rising, still no one hits me, but instead a soft breeze teases my hair. I ready myself for Teo's wrath, but it doesn't come, so I drop my arm.

I look up. Teo's looming over me. His lips are turned downward, and his eyes look like lightning. He's not happy I tried to escape. I wonder if this will make him ask Jonas to do away with me.

I contemplate standing, but I don't want to move without Ana; maybe I should wait for her to stand first. But she's sitting down, clutching her knees tightly to her chest, dirt caked on her face. She looks so defeated, crouched down low like that.

The other couples stand behind Teo, two by two, forming a circle like they never left. Cleo holds onto Marcus, though he staggers like he's about to pass out. Marcus needs to be in a hospital. I should be able to help him, to give him the insulin.

"You do realize you disappointed me," Teo says, his words running over me like a semi. He takes in my quivering eyes, trembling cheeks. My shaking becomes so uncontrollable that I look away to the yellowed grass.

"I gave you the vaccine, and how did you repay me? You—" he grabs my chin so that I'm forced to look at his face—"who have pledged to be with me?"

Yes, I pledged it, but only because he made me. I try dropping my gaze, but he's lifting my chin so high it makes it almost impossible not to see his face without closing my eyes completely. I now know why I didn't want to look up before. Not because he would hit me, but because I didn't want to see him scarred, emotionally damaged. And when I look into those ebony eyes, that's what I see—scarring. They're bright and sad and longing and torn. Like he very much wants to hit me.

Flexing his jaw, the muscles along Teo's stubble flicker. He looks sad. I hate how it hurts me to see him so miserable and questioning. He opens his mouth, but his words don't flow like they normally do. He clamps his jaw shut once before his mouth is open again, and the words are tumbling: "What happened to 'my only'?"

I don't want to answer—I've spent so much time thinking we'd be together that it's much too difficult to express why we should be apart. Liquid simmers in my eyes, but I look away and blink them back. I won't cry for him again.

Teo releases my chin, and when my eyes drop, I find that his hands are twitching. But I'm the one who's always had the twitching hands. I've always been the one grappling for something. I look out at the street, and it feels wrong that the brick-made homes look exactly like they did in the beginning. The bricks should be falling apart, everything should be unraveling.

"Do you realize I have given you the ultimate gift?" Teo whispers so intensely, it feels like he shouts. "A world fulfilling all your fantasies, and you pretend to like it just so you can leave?" I have to blink again, because even now I feel bad that I'm hurting him, but it's the way it has to be. Teo is perfectly silent now. It's like he's reached his pinnacle, and the only direction for him is down, loud to quiet, like the decrescendos he played on his violin. It's as if he can see the change in me. With one footstep, he moves toward me. His words are quiet. "I was going to save you."

He needs me to love him, and I have always loved him. But he doesn't know, because I never told him. I need to tell him so he can eventually understand why I need to leave. Fighting back the tears, I cry, "I have always loved you." And it's true. From the first moment he said my name, I knew. "You have always saved me."

He saved me from the isolation at school, listened to me talk about literature, and urged me to try new paths in math. And the CD. And the balloons. Teo was my everything.

The distance between us now makes me realize we are so far from that—we're simply going through the motions. I feel it, and I know Teo must, too. But he's not ready to. He can't let go, perhaps will never let go.

Someone sobs loudly; Juliet is crying into Romeo's shirt. Here Teo and I are talking, but something's off. Someone's missing. Next to Romeo and Juliet stands Sal, toying with that block of wood again, and on the other side Cleo is holding Marcus up. Where are Abe and Eloise? They should be with us now. Eloise should be wrapped up in Abe's strong arms—

Four different spots inside my chest feel like they're going to burst. Teo didn't hurt them—he couldn't have hurt them—but my mouth is hanging open. "Where are Eloise and Abe?"

Teo smiles crookedly. "You missed an amusing night."

I do not like the idea of the word "amusing" coming from Teo at this time.

"Abelard and Eloise put up a nice little front," he tells me. "Inside, the only noise that could be heard was Gregorian chants—all the guests were required to meditate in prayer. I was given the spot of honor." Teo's eyes open up out of awe and respect.

But something's wrong. "Teo, where are they?"

"Aren't you curious about their tale?" He closes his eyes, revealing purpling eyelids like he hasn't gotten any sleep. "Literature," he says. "Now that is a topic I could relish all night."

There's a goodness to Teo—the stories are what drew us together—but he needs to get to the point, to tell me where Abe and Eloise are.

Teo pats my hand again, like I'm a child—and he *so* needs to learn that I'm not. "Abelard was a monk, Eloise his student. They began an imprudent relationship, and when Eloise became pregnant, her rash uncle castrated the poor monk and sent Eloise away. She became a nun."

I flinch. How could Teo relive a tale like this? Castration. Please, God, don't tell me Teo did that to Abe.

"Of course, I am not barbaric," Teo says as if reading my thoughts. "In the end, when they did not please me, I simply cut out their tongues."

The blood rushes from my cheeks. I'm so dizzy and cold. *He didn't.* How could he? He is *nothing* good. I have to fight back the violent urge to wrench myself away from him, scream at his battered face. *He cut out their tongues. We should do that to him.* I look over at the other couples, where Juliet sobs more loudly into Romeo's shirt. Marcus's ghost-white face is twitching, and lasers seem to be sprouting from Cleo's eyes. Ana, next to me, shakes silently.

Teo is poison and darkness. How could I ever love him now? There's no innate goodness in him, no flickering light. He is worse than death.

"But they're okay," I say, because my mouth is opening. Not that I expect them to be okay, but I can't accept that they're not.

Teo's rolling his eyes. "This isn't a hospital, Persephone. People who choose to get their tongues cut out without seeking medical attention typically do not live."

The muscles constrict in my throat. Someone should rip out *his* tongue. Watch him choke on his own blood. When I speak again, my voice is not my own. "How could you do this?"

"What do you mean?" he asks.

I throw my hands in the air. "How could you bring us to this place?"

Teo's deathly eyes lock on me like he can see right through me. "Why, you asked me to."

It's like someone's ripped my head off my body and I'm staring at us talking from far above. He can't honestly believe what he's saying. Or maybe he gets off on lying. What does he mean?

"The good news is," Teo says as he eyes the other couples in the group, "we only need to dismiss one more couple. Romeo and Juliet or Sal and Ana do not need to live." My stomach squeezes. "But let us not get too far ahead of ourselves." He smiles, actually opens his mouth and shows his teeth, which are white and mouthwatering, yet yellowing closer to his cheeks. "We have a much better stage."

Teo turns for the street and waves his hand forward, beckoning. "To the roof!" he cries, but what roof? Why would we want to go there? He's walking away from Sal's yard and down the street, I'm guessing toward Ramus's old house, but I don't want to follow him now.

I look around at the other couples, how Cleo's clenching her jaw, when Jonas steps out, stun gun flashing. "Listen to him," he says, scowling.

I could scream that I'm done. Done following his bidding, done being his Persephone. But Marcus staggers after Teo, and Cleo has to catch up so that he doesn't fall over when he walks. Romeo and Juliet and Sal and Ana are coming, too, so I follow them, because I don't have a choice.

22

"Unbearable moment, isn't it?" Teo studies the smattering of yellows and reds smudging across the evening sky, with dark cavities under his eyes. Teo has always breathed shadows and darkness, but there's been a hint of something else, too, and that something is missing. Teo is losing his footing. I have always been his anchor, and for the first time he is floating without me. I'm glad he's floating without me.

He knows it, can detect it. Why else would I try to leave? I glance at the other couples on the rooftop, and my stupid mind conjures up Abe and Eloise, sitting in the very center, kissing each other's ears, but they're not there because Teo cut out their tongues and let them bleed to death. Instead, there stands Jonas rapping his stun gun in his hands, smiling at me, inches from the trap door we crawled up. *Oh*, to rap that stun gun on him.

Marc and Cleo sit to the left, Marc's entire body trembling. We shouldn't be sitting on this rooftop waiting for Teo to speak—we should be demanding that he hand over that insulin—but Jonas would stun us immediately. We have to *do* something.

Romeo and Juliet, on the other side of Jonas, huddle closely together, like making themselves small might make it harder for Teo and Jonas to see them. I remember that trick. I did it often at Khabela last year, but that's not who I am anymore.

Ana and Sal sit together near the back, but for the first time it looks like they're actually getting along. Ana's whispering something to Sal and he actually nods back somewhat civilly. For Ana, I feel relieved.

Teo prowls around the roof, circling his couples like he's trying to hang on to control, but that's long past now. Murderers aren't allowed to have friends. "Let me tell you a story," he says, frowning. "Something you need to know. Something everyone here needs to find out."

Marcus locks his jaw, and Romeo pulls Juliet tight against his chest, but all I can do is stare at that stun gun in Jonas's hands. One wrong move and he'll zap us, and there is nothing to keep us from falling off this roof.

"There was once an instructor," Teo walks inside the perimeter of the group, up the slight incline of the roof, "who was the most stifled man in all the land. He sought to impart wisdom, but his students' brains were forever stuck in boxes. They took their notes, blandly accepted classes, never stretching." These would be my classmates. I hadn't any idea he felt like that.

"But then a new girl arrived," Teo turns his hollow face to me, "and she was different from the others."

Different. Different could be good or bad.

"She rarely spoke, hid behind her unblemished hair, but it was plain to see she adored math."

He didn't need to spell that out. Something like a chuckle murmurs from Cleo's throat, and I hate that she's seeing this side of me. I hate that everyone can see.

"The girl's mind had a flexibility," Teo continues as he rests a hand on Romeo's shoulder. "She tried things the other students did not, but she questioned herself, and it was apparent she was searching."

For friends, but only the type of friends who play nicely.

"Knowing she needed guidance," Teo says, "the math teacher soon fell for the girl; her fragility combined with his pride was far too tempting. So he courted her, wooed the girl—the best he could within the confines of their society—and when the timing was right, he took her."

To think I was glad to be taken. I need to be shot. Trampled to death by a wildebeest stampede.

"But that is not the only person he took," Teo moves away from Romeo and walks to the center of the group, stopping right next to Jonas, "for the man knew the woman needed friends." He gazes at the neighborhood right below him. "Neighbors, to share what they would have. But not just any neighbors—ones whose brains didn't quite fit in boxes." So this is why he chose Marc's classmates from Griffin, the artsy school.

Veering around a pipe jutting from the top of the roof, Teo turns to Sal and Ana at the back. "So the man watched the students at his brother's school, noticed many of them broken. One boy," he nods toward Sal, "not only carved wood, but he also *knew* math. No one appreciated his dual gifts. Another," he spins to face Juliet on the right, "was in a one-dimensional relationship, and didn't know how to get out. A ravishing model," he glances at Cleo on the left, "had unrealistic dreams."

As if recounting the tale at arm's length isn't doing quite what he wants, Teo shifts, connecting with us directly. "All of you, *all of you* needed to be fixed. And the world you would live in would be infinitely better than what you had known."

But did he not think for a moment we might not want to be *fixed*? Or at least think we might want to work out our own problems, if that's what they are?

Teo moves next to me by the edge of the roof, glancing at the homes lining his segmented street. He studies each one, one after another, after another. Pausing at the last one, he turns to watch Romeo fidgeting with Juliet's engagement ring.

"In the beginning," Teo says, "we enjoyed our little world. Such talent, unrestrained fervor, was precisely what I had foreseen. And you proved yourselves, started earning the vaccine." Yes, Teo adored Romeo's and Juliet's party, and then he adored my painting.

"But then?" Teo spins to face me. "Our most prized jewel tried to run away." His eyes pour into mine, and mine simmer as I refuse to look away.

"What did you hope to accomplish, Miss Laurent?" His voice rises so that it's pitched high. "Use the vaccine as a shield against the disease?" He lifts his dark face to the ribboned sky, laughing like that's the most idiotic thing he's ever heard. He almost looks beautiful the way his eyes shine, the way his lean body opens up with his legs planted wide. But then he turns those black eyes on me like daggers, as he spits, "Well, the joke's on you. There *is* no disease. Do you honestly believe a generator could power all of this?" He gestures at the houses on his street. "It's simply attached to the regular power grid. It was easy enough to buy the right people off."

I flinch, teetering dangerously close to the edge. No disease? He's lying. I take a full step forward, unable to make sense of what he said. I got the vaccine, saw the footage, everything. But he's laughing and my head's pounding, and when I turn every which way to see the others, I find Ana's wide eyes; she's just as lost as me.

Teo must see my mind reeling, but I must be too slow for him because his fingers are twitching. "It isn't *real*," he hisses. Tendrils of fire dance in his eyes, and it's like they're applauding, laughing, taunting. *And you thought yourself clever. Just see what you have missed!*

The vaccine…there's no need? So if we'd found a breach in the fence, we could have just left? Right in front of me is Ana, shaking, with a quivering lip; Romeo looks like he's taken a bullet to his chest the way his eyes blink open wide, and Juliet's patting his hand, leaning in closer to whisper something in his ear. But Marcus is shaking his head. That's when I remember what he said before: *What I don't get is why my brother "rewards" us with a vaccine when we live in a society that's supposedly impenetrable.* Marcus, you were so right.

Which makes me realize something. "You said our parents told us to stay away," I tell Teo. It wasn't just Teo, either. Abe said he spoke directly with his grandmother.

Teo grows stone cold. He's staring at me, mouth hanging open. *Crap.* He was speaking and I've run over whatever he had to say. But there's nothing I can do, no way to change what I've done, so I take in a ragged breath. "You said our parents told everyone to stay away, but there is no Living Rot, no resurfacing." How could he ever have gotten them to lie like that? They wouldn't have wanted us to stay away.

Teo's mouth works like he's trying to speak, but it's taking him a bit of effort to tuck his astonishment away. Pursing his lips, he says, "It was easy enough to convince them to cooperate when otherwise, the assurance of their children's lives might grow unsteady."

He threatened them. What did he say to Mayor Tydal, to my mother? Mayor Tydal might not technically be in the picture anymore, but Teo had a way of being thorough. Did he tell them that, if they tried to find us, he would simply snap our necks the way he did to Lance and Gwen? That must be how he got the actors to portray the Living Rot on the footage he showed us, the people panicking near Griffin. It was all a set-up.

Cleo, on the opposite side of the roof, is actually snarling, and Marcus is gripping her hand, not out of support or the illusion that they are a pair, but because Marcus, of all people, is holding her back. Sal grips Ana by the arm and pulls her up, and the two stand there, tense, like they might actually do something.

When I look around the group, every single person is seething. They agreed to play along, but only because he told them the Living Rot was back. They didn't want to leave their parents, but took comfort in the fact that that's what their parents had wanted—for their kids to be safe. Now, it's like the final piece for rebellion is finally falling into place. Before, we were terrified he'd kill us, but he threatened our parents? That is so very far from okay.

"You lied to them," I say. Why did I ever love such a man? He was alluring, yes, but I should have known. His kindness is a memory. Like with the balloons. Now it doesn't matter. Now I can see Teo for the monster he is. He's nauseating.

"As I was saying." Teo smiles falsely, shrugging his jacket off. "Is it just me, or is it hot up here?" He sets it gently down like it's more important than a person or pet. "I believe our world is getting rather dull." He turns to me, rolling up his sleeves. "And since we have this issue of needing to get down to three, perhaps Persephone can help me."

I stare at his suit jacket, mere inches from me, remembering how I thought swiping the remote from his coat was our ticket out of here. He needs to understand his vision is waning. That he must tell us how to leave.

Picking his way across the somewhat steep roof, Teo takes his place next to Ana and Sal, who're standing so closely their elbows are touching.

Teo leans into the pair, smirking at Ana's taped skirts. "I do believe it is far past time for this couple to leave." He sighs dramatically.

"Or these two," he says, hopping over to Romeo and Juliet on the right. "They have not done anything noteworthy lately." He smiles like he's feeling more pleased than hurt. Juliet's ringed finger twitches, like she'd like to scratch the eyeballs out of his face.

Throwing his head back, Teo laughs maniacally, like some sort of villain in a play. He's stepping away from all of us, no longer wanting us on his stage. He is alone except for Jonas now, and his grip on his couples is disintegrating.

If it weren't for Jonas, we'd attack Teo on the roof. Cleo's already broken away from Marc's grip, and Sal and Romeo flank Marcus at the back. Teo, seemingly oblivious, asks, "Persephone, who do you wish to leave?"

Cleo reaches for that pipe that's jutting out from the top of the roof when Marcus growls, "Why don't *you* pick?"

And it's like Marc's question makes everyone teeter; Teo hasn't fully lost his hold on everybody. Even Cleo pauses from wrenching that pipe from the roof, like she wants to know the answer herself. *Yes*, she must be thinking, *who would Teo pick?*

But he doesn't need to pick anybody. We could all live— he could see.

Holding up a finger, Teo pauses. "Matters would really be much simpler if one couple just—"

And without finishing his sentence, Teo shoves Romeo off the roof. He means to push Juliet, too, but she scrambles out of Teo's reach.

I scream. So does Juliet. Marcus is shouting, his face deathly white, and at first I'm not sure why he's the loudest, but then I remember Romeo is his friend.

Stomach in my mouth, I peer over the edge to find one of Romeo's legs bent back behind him, almost touching his back. I dry heave, throw my hand over my mouth. Romeo's crooked body is like a clay form on the ground. An arm twists around at a sickening angle, and nothing moves; not even his fingers twitch.

Juliet throws a punch toward Teo, but he grabs her around the front, bringing her trembling body into his.

"Do not force things," Teo tells us through Juliet's hair. I can't believe I wanted to protect him before. "I will push her off," he says. He glances over the edge. "I have done it before." He is sick, *sick*.

"Cleo," Teo says, spotting her gripping the pipe she's wrenched from the roof, "drop the weapon, please."

But Cleo has no intention of dropping it, and I don't think she should—except that Jonas is lifting his stun gun now. But she doesn't see him. She takes a few steps closer and growls, "The only one with unrealistic dreams is you." And when she lifts the pipe higher, like she means to strike him across the face, Jonas jabs his stun gun into her back, and she drops in a heap on the shingled roof. I worry she'll roll off the side, but that bit of roof is flatter than the rest, so she should be safe.

"Please, Teo," Juliet's saying over and over, her nutcracker smile long gone, "we did like you said. We passed, remember?"

Teo studies the top of Juliet's black hair below his face. It's like I can hear his thoughts in my head: *To push, or not to push? That is the question.* That's the type of question the sick bastard would ask after studying the same books as me.

He can't do this; Teo can't dismiss her life. Before, I never said anything, because I was certain he'd ask Jonas to slay everyone in the room, lash out at anyone next. But I can stop this murder—I can save Juliet. "You have to stop this!" I cry to Teo, clutching his arm. "This isn't right." Teo's eyes soften, and I watch as his grip loosens around Juliet.

Jaw slack, he turns to me. "What has happened to you?" His eyes are open so wide, it's like he doesn't know who I am.

I open my mouth—I mean to tell him maybe I was broken before, but I'm smoothing all the cracks, when a blur of white crosses my line of sight. I know that movement. It's Jonas, moving straight for Juliet. I reach out to stop him, but with one hand he knocks her away from Teo, his stun gun swinging loose in the other. She teeters, millimeters from the edge, screeching. I grapple for her hand, but her hands are flying about her too quickly, like she's trying to grab onto something, but she's too scared to see.

Jonas splays out his fingers to push her off, when two things simultaneously happen next: Cleo, apparently awake again, yanks that stun gun straight out of his hands, and Jonas's fingers connect with Juliet's face and shove her off the roof.

I'm shrieking. My mouth is open and screams are ripping out, but mostly what I'm seeing doesn't make sense. She's a paper doll, fluttering in the wind. But that isn't quite right because she's real, and there's an awful noise when her body hits the ground. Like hundreds of bones crunching.

When I look down, Juliet's neck is bent backward like someone's snapped her head right off—it's too much. Too much. I lean over and retch. The fluids rush from my mouth, narrowly missing Teo's black shoes, but they keep coming, and Teo pulls my hair out of my face like he's here for me, like he's helping. Fire ants swim in my veins. I could reach up and spew right in his face.

My stomach settles, and I manage to stand up straight when blue lights flash—Cleo's connecting the stun gun to Jonas's chest. But he just stands there, smiling this apathetic grin, because those shocks didn't do a thing. He must be wearing a bulletproof vest or something similar that can block it. Jonas leaps away from Cleo, sprints for the trap door, and jumps straight down into Ramus's house to get away. Cleo's eyes glint like she wants to follow, but she grits her teeth and glances back at Marcus, who's just sitting there, like clay.

Teo, standing right beside me, is staring at Juliet's form on the ground. He's frowning, like he's sad. Shaking his head slowly, he says, "I was going to let her live." But he was willing to push her off just before I made him stop. It's like her death is now a minor inconvenience to him, like the simple idea of letting her live would have been something nice.

I glance over to Sal and Ana, whose gazes are fixed on that trap door. I don't imagine we have much time since Jonas has probably run off to find other weapons—another stun gun or perhaps a sword. Sal and Ana must be thinking the same thing, because they're rising to their feet and moving for that trap door. Geese scrambling for a foothold.

Sighing deeply, Teo turns to that clay form of Marcus perched on the roof. I wish I could transport him to a hospital in Austin this very moment. Get the insulin he needs flowing into him through an IV.

Teo's eyes droop downward, taking in Marc's sight. "Cleo?" he asks, glancing at the girl who now wields the stun gun. "Be a doll and patch Marcus up?"

Wait—he's giving Marc his insulin now? But how's she going to get through the fence? Cleo stares at Teo when he gestures at his suit coat. "There's a vial of insulin in there."

There's—what? I grabbed a faulty remote, and he had a vial of insulin right there all along. I could gouge my own eyes out; I've made a horrific mess of helping us escape. My only solace is that Marcus will have his insulin now.

Cleo's eyes spring open as she leaps for the coat, and a twinge of jealousy crawls through me when I see that she's the one that gets to help him out. But it doesn't matter. It doesn't matter. Because Marcus is getting his insulin now.

Teo's ebony eyes lock on me, flickering. I shudder beneath his gaze as he whispers, "Let us, you and I, go for a walk, Persephone."

23

Without waiting for a response, Teo tugs me through the trapdoor and steers me through Ramus's beige-colored house out onto the street. The stars blink at us, shining. We march around Bee's house, toward the gnarled trees. I'm not sure why, but I think he's taking me to the fence. I'm not sure what that means for me now. The Living Rot is fake, so he's letting me out?

I'd like to ask about the others, see if they're coming, too. Or maybe his plan is to push only me out. If that's the case, maybe I can run for help. Hop in the SUV and drive straight through the fence. That should make it open up.

But Marc's getting his insulin, and now I need to set things with Teo right. I need him to know there's no way in hell things can be the way he wants them to be.

Dropping my hand like it's scalding him or something, Teo moves two or three steps away from me as we hit the woods. Turning toward me, his voice hitches when he says, "You do not appreciate what I have built."

Is that what the French rebels said to the nobles after building the guillotine? I could laugh right now out loud, or cry. I could pull on the stubble of his head, but he's waiting, and I need to sound collected, so I say it as simply as I can, "You say we're broken when we're not."

Teo barks a pained, hollow laugh, and it's unbelievable to me that the pain somehow rips through me, too. "And that is your reproof?" he asks.

I square my shoulders, because he *needs* to see what I mean. Killing is killing. There's no way around that. "Yes," I say.

Teo moves inside the clutches of the trees, and I follow him, but not because I must. He doesn't have that power over me anymore. He needs to know I can't be with him now. I won't go along with his lies. Everything about his world is wrong. Elysian Fields is a prison of hate. "How could you think I ever wanted this?" I have to ask.

The muscles flicker along his jaw, echoing a slight movement of the leaves. "Perhaps you choose not to know," he says. *Choose not to know*—I'm over the cryptic answers. I hate how he always holds the answers very close, just like he did in class. *Anyone remember my favorite function?* he'd ask, and I'd pull my hair out trying to guess.

His eyes wander over my face, and I don't want to look at him, but I do—the sideburns running down his olive cheeks, the yellowing cavities around his eyes. I loved him once, and he's waiting for some sort of feedback from me. I don't want to touch him, but there's something I must do. So I step to him and take his hand. "Close your eyes," I say, and it surprises me, but he listens. "What do you see?"

Teo's long lashes kiss the bottoms of his eyes. "I see us together, you and I."

"Do you?" Because I don't.

His eyes snap open, obviously shocked by my tone. His voice is low, pained, as he says, "Of course I do."

I think of the years between us, how I'm eighteen and he's twenty-four. How if the school board knew of our relationship, he would be banned from my school. But he is not the only one to be blamed. He is not the only one who felt that way. Teo is disillusioned and selfish and dark, but he is not the only one who's been all of these things.

Teo turns away from me, his hands and shoulders shaking. In a low moan, he cries, "You are not listening to me!"

But he has to feel how our connection is gone. We can't be together now. I won't allow it.

Turning his face to me again, Teo's eyes flicker with fire, only this time it's like the fire's about to go out. "You visited me…" he prompts, and I'm not so sure I know what he means.

He licks his lips, darting his eyes to the ground cover and the knobby tree roots. Closing his eyes, he moans, "Remember our last day together? Before we came here?"

And I can see his classroom door open up. I know what he's talking about, because it's the moment I can never forget.

In my mind, I see that day perfectly. How I lingered outside Teo's classroom when all the students had left. The windows were always open—he seemed to welcome anyone and everything. Especially the breeze. Teo's classroom was made up of sunspots, a few stray insects, the natural heat. So when I trickled inside his classroom, I felt like another one of the elements looking for rest. That's what I told myself, anyway. The truth was, the draw to him was infinitely stronger, like a hummingbird's attraction to red. But Teo was more than a color. He was much more than a person or a place.

I remember making my way into his classroom, thinking about how he let us call him by his first name. Around the other teachers and our parents, he instructed us to refer to him by his proper title. "They get sensitive about things like that," he had said. Naïve, we all agreed.

When I saw him gathering textbooks, I swooped in to help, eager to please. Neither of us said anything, but I knew his every movement, could detect his every step. We were tethered together, he and I, and I wondered if he might be as conscious of the connection as me.

When we finished with the textbooks and moved on to straightening the chairs, he asked, "Are you enjoying my class?"

I was relieved I could answer with a yes.

"And what of your future?" he asked, suddenly turning toward me as I reached for a stray graphing calculator.

Bashful, I handed it to him. Our fingers touched; currents of electricity jolted through our skin. We didn't move.

"College," I managed to say. He was so close I thought I could hear the heartbeats beneath his skin.

"And what do you know of the arts?" I could detect the Listerine on his breath, count the individual whiskers of five o'clock shadow.

"I'm taking AP English." I was barely aware of the words falling from my mouth; I was too busy studying his swelling lips. They formed the vowels and consonants seamlessly. It was always so obvious my math teacher was schooled in the arts.

What happened after that is the moment I relived every night for six days when I went to bed, for Teo kissed me just then, precisely as I'd always hoped. He held me, so adult-like, unlike the lustfulness of boys my own age. He tipped up my chin, read my trembling face, and said, "I do believe you are the most beautiful creation I have ever seen."

Some say words shouldn't mean so much—our actions take precedence over them. But the words Teo Richardson said that day reached inside of me. The impossibilities welled up inside of me—I knew of the restrictions regarding teachers and students. But it didn't make sense, was somehow the wrong law. So I trembled and shattered, felt my ribcage contract. I couldn't breathe. All the air bubbles were trapped, so I forced them all out, exhaled, and said, "I wish you and I could be."

And that's when I felt my ribcage expand, that impractical hope starting to take root. Before, I had trembled and shattered, but then I regrew because Teo held my face, told me he would make it happen, and I *knew*. I knew he would do something about my wish. I knew it wasn't a futile dream lamely spent. Teo was the type of man who accomplished things. That's why I loved him. That's why I said it.

Teo's looking at me now. I breathe on my fingers, the tips oddly cold despite the Texas heat. I have a new kind of frostbite where my flesh hardens from the inside, and I remember the question I asked him before: *How could you think I ever wanted this?*

Teo cups my face, breathes the fresh Listerine into my face, and says what I already know. "You told me you did."

They are gone, all gone because of a futile wish I should never have made. What possessed me to make a wish like that? *I wish you and I could be.*

But this isn't what I had in mind. This is never what I wanted. Though I loved Teo, I can't look past what he's done. What I've done. And I don't want it to happen. I do everything I can to harden my face. Water gathers in my eyes, but I won't cry over him again. I won't. I won't. So I force them back.

"It makes you sad." Teo's jaw quivers, and fear splits open his eyes like he knows he's losing me. He grips my hand tightly, almost so tight that it hurts, but his eyes droop down when he says, "We belong together, you and I." Like it will change something.

"But you're killing people!" I cry.

Teo's eyes brighten before he looks away. I'm not entirely sure why his eyes look so bright until the light of the moon shows me—there's water spilling down his cheeks. He's weeping for me.

The water behind my own eyes trembles, begs to overflow, which is so soft of me, but I've never seen Teo cry. It's like his tears are contagious or something. But I've shed more than enough tears for him—he *cut out* Abe's and Eloise's tongues, shoved Romeo and Juliet off the roof. He doesn't deserve a single tear shed, so again I blink them back.

With shaking hands, Teo reaches into his pants pocket, and I can't think what he's moving to retrieve. He already gave me the ring, and then that bug, but when he pulls his hand out of his pocket, I find a book—red and black—my copy of *Jane Eyre*. The one with the torn cover, the one I gave to him when the secretary tried confiscating my books. I'd forgotten about it.

Handing it to me, he says, voice pained, "I couldn't fix it. Somehow, it was better off ripped."

I stare at the torn book in my hands. The entire book is now damaged and bent. When I look up again, Teo's walking away, stumbling farther and farther into the trees.

"Teo?" I run toward him, clutching the book to my chest, ducking in and around the crocodile teeth, the scratching branches, the stinging leaves. I need to understand his plan now. Maybe he's going to let us out.

"Teo!" I cry again, but he's too far ahead. So I run faster as tree branches rip at my skirt and snag my hair.

Teo doesn't answer; he merely continues on. Tree after tree. Droning on like someone has reprogrammed him, and I don't understand why he isn't turning around for me.

When he reaches the fence line, he stops, and I'm only a breath behind him, so I touch his arm. "Will you let us out now?" Why else would he move for the fence?

But he doesn't turn. I study his eyes, his hair, slightly longer than a week before, and realize I have never seen a face so devoid of emotion in my life.

"Teo?" I reach for his face, but something stops me. I'm not sure what it is until I see the expression on his face. Gradually turning his head, his dark eyes bore into mine. And when he smiles at me faintly, I cry out, because I know what he's about to do. He's leaning toward the barbed wires, and I'm reaching my hands out to make him stop, but I'm slow. Much too slow. He's falling, face first, into the electric fence.

Teo's body jolts; his head takes the brunt of the shock. I move to cover my eyes, but there's this part of me that wants to look. His entire body is vibrating so madly, it's like he's not human, but a plastic toy shaken violently in a toddler's fist. And the smell—burnt flesh. Like someone's barbecuing. And then there's this *click*, precisely the sound Jonas made before. A portion of the fence opens up and swings wide like a normal door, and I see why. Teo's head hit the bottom wire, which clicks again when he slumps to the ground. He's dead. He's really dead. He's opened the fence for me. I don't know if he meant to open the fence for me. And I don't care.

I drop my book at my feet.

24

When the others join me, the night air is cool and still, the stars twinkling above us so brightly that I know dawn will be here soon. There's no Jonas. I'm not sure where he is. When Cleo prowls up, gripping his stun gun in her hands, I grab her bronzed arm.

"Where's Jonas?" I ask, because he could leap out at us at any moment—snap our necks, stab us with swords.

Cleo taps the stun gun against her leg, and that animalistic curl I've always loathed stretches across her lips. "I may have stunned him once or twice."

Marcus staggers up from behind her. "Try ten," he says, rolling his bloodshot eyes.

But I thought Jonas got away. Jumped through that trap door on Teo's roof. He must have come back, jumped out at them again. But they couldn't have been fast enough. Jonas moves so quickly, it's like he's some kung fu master.

"He sort of tried stabbing Cleo with one of his swords when she was fixing me up," Marcus says, searching my face. He taps his insulin pump, and I can see what he means. He has his insulin now—thank you, God—so Cleo must have stunned Jonas just in time.

"So you left him there?" My voice goes up like I'm pitying Jonas now, but that's not how I'm feeling—I just don't like the idea that he could get at us.

Marcus shakes his head. "Nope." He digs in his pocket and pulls out the remote I'd thrown at the fence when we were trying to escape—the one that wouldn't work. I hadn't noticed him pick it up. Why is he showing me this?

Cleo's upper lip curls. "We tossed him in that cage—"

"You know," Marc's eyes narrow, "where Ramus and Bee—"

The cage. They tossed him in that cage with the red curtain—with the lion—and used that remote. Cleo's and Marc's stone-cold faces stare back at me, not laughing. Eyes not so much as glinting. I think I might like Cleo a little now. She fixed up Marcus and deposited our last enemy in that cage. And Jonas isn't waiting to pounce on us. I'm trembling, and there's no reason to be trembling.

Marc and Cleo face each other, communicating somehow. Marc's eyes narrow like he wants to know something, and Cleo's eyes dart backward. A little hole of jealousy burns inside of me. In the time that I've worked to separate myself from Teo, Cleo and Marcus have struck up some awful romance where they can communicate without words. A twig snaps, and I look up to find Sal joining us, carrying a backpack. Ana scrambles up from behind him, bits of mud splattered on her face. I wish I could run to her, hug her—cheer that she's safe. But I guess that wouldn't be appropriate since I nearly got her killed. Not that I blame her. I wouldn't want to be my friend, either, after all that I've done. But her eyes light up when she sees me standing next to Marc and Cleo, so I flash her a smile. Maybe we *can* be friends.

I look for the others after Ana, keep staring at the trees interlocking in the dark woods, but no more come. No one else is alive in Elysian Fields. So much death. I *asked* for this place.

I glance up at Marcus, a rock lodged inside my gut because so many have died. "Let's say goodbye," I say, though I'm not entirely sure how. Maybe we can go home, bring our parents back here, and all search for the bodies of their sons and daughters who have passed. We need to do that.

A flash of movement catches my eye; Marcus is walking away from me. Where's he going? He trudges past a couple of trees before stooping down and picking up a large, rectangular piece of sheetrock so big it covers his chest and neck. Maybe it's a dartboard or something. Walking toward me, a smile twitches his upper lip, like this piece of sheetrock makes him really happy. It must have something to do with what he and Cleo were talking about.

"What's that?" I ask in time to see Cleo moving away from me. Her heavily made-up eyes brighten and her lips twitch up. She's smiling at me? I'm not really sure what to do with that. I never imagined a civil look between us after everything that has happened, so I just gape at her as she moves toward the fence.

Marcus grins at me, his exhausted eyes brightening enough to match his smile. "I didn't have a lot of options for canvases," he says. "Cleo actually gave me the idea when you were working on yours." He turns the sheetrock around and shows me so I can see.

It's a painting, bright colors singing from the white background. At the top, Romeo tips an invisible hat for Juliet—she's dancing, and he's holding a pair of spoons. Beneath them are Tristan and Izzy, holding hands and clinking their love potions one more time. It's hard not to blink; tears keep gathering in my eyes. Ramus and Bee stand at the bottom, their faces like moonbeams as they face their greatest threat, the lion. Abe and Eloise, fumbling with Eloise's skirts, are laughing, and Lance and Gwen hold a drum and bird. The rest of us are there, too, but I can't look away from those we've lost.

Where I would have chosen muted hues, Marcus has splashed the scene with primary colors, a mood utterly unlike what we have experienced here at Elysian Fields. Genuine smiles spill across everyone's lips, and I notice he's curved our street into a circle.

After studying the piece for much too little time, I glance up at Marcus, realizing he's watching me. "Your painting," I falter, unsure how to phrase it. "You definitely didn't do gothic."

Marcus smiles sadly. "Nah, that's your gift." My heart leaps like I'm jumping.

I glance over to the others by the open fence to see what they're doing when Cleo snatches a pair of keys from Sal's backpack. I'm not entirely sure how Sal got them, but I'm guessing he found them in Teo's suit jacket, just like Marc and Cleo found Marc's insulin where I should have looked.

"Where do you think Hades would park his car?" Cleo asks, jingling the keys in her hand. But she's not waiting for an answer. She walks right through the open fence, and Sal and Ana follow her out, Ana's orange sari glinting as the sun peeks over the horizon.

My eyes automatically find Marc's—those blue eyes, clear like an infant's. Clutching his painting in one hand, he strides to me and offers a damp hand to step through the open fence together. I clutch his hand tightly within my own, and as we step to the other side, my connection to his brother completely unravels.

I'm free.

"We're pretty sure we know where Teo keeps the SUV," Marc's saying. "Izzy told us before—said the drugs Teo used for bringing us here didn't work too well on her. Something about endorphins."

That sounds precisely like Izzy. She deserves to be with us, but I stare down at Marc's beautiful depiction and realize she is, in a way. I just wish it were real.

Holding the painting out to me as we stand on the other side, Marcus says, "I made it for you."

But I can't take it from him. It doesn't feel right. His talent belongs somewhere else, like a museum. Or a gallery. I begin to shake my head, when Marc grabs my chin. "Don't be stupid."

His insistence only makes me want to refuse harder, but the typhoon in his eyes keeps me quiet. The bluest of blue. How long was I trapped inside the ebony, believing them to be for me?

"You're thinking about him," Marcus says, wrinkles burrowing below his hairline. "You okay?"

I nod and Marcus reaches out and grabs my arm, but his bloodshot eyes and clammy hands tell me, once again, that I should be the one helping him.

We grapple for each other.

Clutching my hand, Marcus says, "You know, I've never been romantic. I know how chicks dig that deep, foreboding crap. But I have something on my brother."

"Oh?" I love the feel of his calloused hands.

"I have skills," he says, nodding toward his painting, "and so do you. Now, I may not be the 'reading poetry under the moonlight' type, but I do like art. We should combine our talents. Paint a heaven and hell piece. I paint heaven—"

"—and I paint hell." I smile slightly. But something nags inside of me. "Do you think that says something about me? That everything I paint turns out dark?"

"Well, yeah," Marc says, and I flinch at his response. But Marcus holds my hand harder, like granite holding sandstone in place. "You paint the dark because you understand it, Cheyenne. You know what it feels like, but it's actually foreign to you. Because you are good."

I could be saying the same to him—he was the one doubting himself in the first place, but he doesn't know why Elysian Fields exists. I think about my last moments with Teo, how he helped me see how I was the catalyst for all that had come. I went to him and asked him to make us happen, and he answered my request. And then, when I didn't appreciate all that he'd done, he took his own life.

These thoughts all come together and make me wobble even more. I try to ignore the regret, but I can't get away from the truth—that I'm the reason for so much sorrow, so much pain.

Marcus is quiet for a while, which makes me grateful, because he must detect what I can't say. When Cleo waves for us to join them, Marcus holds up one finger to them before turning to me, his voice never more even than now.

"I'll never be able to know exactly what you had with him," he says, "but I'm guessing even now he's messing with your head." I wish I could tell Marcus it's not simply messing with me—it's the truth—when he says, "Regardless of what you're feeling, Cheyenne, *he* killed our friends."

It would have taken him a very long time to build these homes. What he said to me may have been true—I did ask for us to be together—but now I can see Teo was merely waiting for an invitation from me.

And I know that it's the truth, but it feels twisted somehow. It'll be a long while before everything makes sense. But I know Marcus will be there to help me, holding a torch in the darkness.

Ana laughs, and Sal and Cleo cheer. Sal tosses his backpack high in the air—they've found the SUV. Cleo starts throwing branches off the top, but I can't seem to move past the thistles close to my feet. It's like they are this minimal barrier, blocking me from the rest of the group. Teo's world is behind us, the unknown ahead, and it's a little frightening right now.

Marc's hand slips into mine, and he squeezes it. I smile, because it's the thing I never expected to like. My hand feels like it's tingling. Marc looks at me, his eyes wild and blue, and for a second it's like he's hesitant to move, too. I start to say something—I have no idea what—but that's when he closes the distance, and his lips are on top of mine. He's blueberries and warm lemon meringue pie, and I want to taste it all. A jackhammer slams beneath his shirt, and he's not alone. My chest, my neck, my back are exploding. Teo's *not* the only one who can do that to me.

When Marcus pulls away from me, I know we're together now, and there will be *lots* of kissing. I know he gets me, and it's okay if the bad stuff seeps through because we are both here and neither of us are broken.

"I'm into you," I say, whispering into the damp warmth of Marc's neck.

"I'm into *you*," Marcus repeats, and the burn from his flesh is the glow and ember of bonfires radiating on the beach.

I try to put together something to say, but my words bounce off the insides of my cheeks. Marcus doesn't seem to mind, though. His lips are kissing my jaw, trailing to the other side, and connecting again with my own lips. My lips and my jaw are crackling. I dig my fingers in his hair, and when his arms pull me closer, my heart pounds inside my chest like a manic ping-pong ball, and the fire surging through my veins feels like I've been sprinting. I run my hands down his back; when he runs his fingers down my jaw, my face glows like that torch I envisioned before is lighting my insides.

"Come on!" Cleo yells from the SUV. Marcus pulls away, that lazy smile I've come to love creeping across his face. He kisses my hand and leads me toward the car, the skin on my hand sizzling.

Cleo's in the front seat, Sal beside her, and Marcus and I slide in back next to Ana. The car hums with life as Cleo turns the key, and we lurch forward. I can't believe she tossed Jonas in with that lion. Part of me wishes I got to stay behind and listen to the roars avenging Ramus and Bee. Staring at the ornate beading I've hated so long, I decide maybe I should ask her real name, once we're farther from this place. I'll learn all their names—Ana's and Sal's. Everybody's.

Marcus brushes his chapped lips on my cheek, making the blood rush to my face. Dawn breaks, a light pink shade at the tips of the sky. Flecks of gold, splashes of purple and green flowers seem to whisk past us, though I know we really whisk past them. It's all beautiful, and for once, I see the world as it truly is and how it could be.

I can think. I can move. I can breathe. My eyes are naked; I am awake.

WHAT IF THE NAZIS
HAD WON THE WAR?

The personification of Aryan purity, Ellyssa has spent her whole life under her creator's strict training and guidance; her purpose is to eradicate inferior beings. She was genetically engineered to be the perfect soldier: strong, intelligent, unemotional, and telepathic...

Only Ellyssa isn't perfect.

SPENCER HILL PRESS • spencerhillpress.com

Jenna Oliver doesn't have time to get involved with one boy, let alone two.
All Jenna wants is to escape her evaporating small town and her alcoholic mother. She's determined she'll go to college and find a life that is wholly hers—one that isn't tainted by her family's past. But when the McAlister twins move to town and Jenna gets involved with both of them, she learns the life she planned may not be the one she gets.

Ian McAlister doesn't want to start over; he wants to remember.
Ian can't recall a single thing from the last three months—and he seems to be losing more memories every day. His family knows the truth, but no one will tell him what really happened before he lost his memory. When he meets Jenna, Ian believes that he can be normal again because she makes not remembering something he can handle.

The secret Ian can't remember is the one Luke McAlister can't forget.
Luke has always lived in the shadow of his twin brother until Jenna stumbles into his life. She sees past who he's supposed to be, and her kiss brings back the spark that life stole. Even though Luke feels like his brother deserves her more, Luke can't resist Jenna—which is the trigger that makes Ian's memory return.

**Jenna, Ian, and Luke are about to learn there are only
so many secrets you can keep before the truth comes to reclaim you.**

SPENCER HILL CONTEMPORARY • spencerhillcontemporary.com

ACKNOWLEDGEMENTS

Thank you, my inner demon, for pushing me to write this book. Cheyenne's loves and fears are so much a part of me, it wasn't acting, writing this. More importantly, thank you Grayman (my own personal superhero and husband) for existing and showing me the light I am not. You are my best friend, the guy who holds me together, my rock.

Brian, Aidan, Lincoln. You are my precious babies, and I love you all. You give my life the meaning I needed to pursue this. I am so blessed to have you all in my life.

My babysitters, too numerous to list, are etched into my heart, but Irene, Lenee, Kathy, Margaret, Bonnie, and Cherine, thanks for loving my children like your own and for being so stoked about seeing this book in print.

My sister, Cammie, my shrink. The one who gets the books, music, and shows I love. The one who *always* listens and I miss THIS much. Thank you for believing in me, and teaching me how to reverence art. My fierce sister, Chris. Thank you for encouraging me to pursue my passion (something I haven't heard enough in my life, something you do *so* well on your own) and for always challenging me to leave the house. The rest of my family's support: Travis, Kerri, Lance, Carl, Barbara, Kim, Will, Mom, Dad, Ben, Paul, Ashlee, and Gramps. My fun uncles and aunts, nieces and nephews. Cousins, too. Thanks for your excitement.

My brilliant, fun, and ingenious editor, Danielle Ellison, you are the one God sent. I prayed for you, the stars aligned, and you sent me a revise and resubmit. Thanks for pounding the hell out of *The Dollhouse Asylum* and helping me rework it from the ground up. Your name should be next to mine on the cover of this book.

My second editor, Rich. Spencer Hill calls you "The Closer" for a reason. You are crazy good with details. Thanks for pointing out diabetics keep their insulin not in dressers, but in the refrigerator (nice one, Mary) and for giving me some praise one night when I really needed it. I've loved working with you.

The others on my Spencer Hill Press team: Lindsay, Kate, Kendra, Patricia, Rachel, Jazmin, Laura, Jill Marie, Christin, Kathryn, Cindy, Anna, and Rebecca. Thank you for your encouragement, excitement, and expertise. My writing couldn't have been in better hands.

Jeremy West, you created the best cover a girl could ever hope for. I LOVE IT, and so does the rest of the world. Jeffrey and Jeremy, thank you for revealing my book on This Week in YA. It never gets old watching you introduce my book on your show.

Derrick, for brainstorming with Danielle and identifying the most amazing title for my book.

Kat Salazar, thank you for picking my story out of the slush. You gave me more than I can say. Thanks for believing in my writing and selling my book.

My writing friends (most of whom are on Twitter) thanks for buoying me up. Nicole, thanks for being my *first* writing friend, and thank you to my sweet and unfortunate first readers: Tamara, Laura, David, Ann, Cammie, Summer, Cherine, Jerry, and Justin. Thanks for not telling me to give it up while I could because my story was a big pile of murlush. My cultlings (Cult Dollhouse Asylum), I adore you guys so much! And thank you to my church friends.

My book trailer team! Mark, Bailee, Mikaela, Stephanie, Dustin, and my extras: Joey, Mari, Maddie, Britt, Chance, and Adam. Your hours of commitment mean so much, and filming this was the most fun I've ever had on a group project.

Dave Wolverton, thank you for helping me see which parts in this story I needed to trash, and for walking me through a basic outline of this book. Your workshop gave me the bones of the story that I needed to find Kat.

My Heavenly Father. Thank you for knowing the desires in my heart; for pushing me, and for always giving me more than I ever thought.

And thank you, dear reader, for opening your mind and heart. May you find the light amidst the dark.

ABOUT THE AUTHOR

Mary Gray has a fascination with all things creepy. That's why all her favorite stories usually involve panic attacks and hyperventilating. In real life, she prefers to type away on her computer, ogle over her favorite TV shows, and savor fiction. When she's not immersed in other worlds, she and her husband get their exercise by chasing after their three children. *The Dollhouse Asylum* is her first novel.